THE LAKE

Rachel McLean writes thrillers that make your pulse race and your brain tick. Originally a self-publishing sensation, she has sold millions of copies digitally, with massive success in the UK, and a growing reach internationally. She is the author of the Dorset Crime novels and the spin-off McBride & Tanner series and Cumbria Crime series. In 2021, she won the Kindle Storyteller Award with *The Corfe Castle Murders* and her books regularly hit No1 in the Bookstat ebook chart on launch.

Joel Hames is a Lancashire-based writer of crime fiction, and the editor of million-selling books across multiple genres. Joel's own works include the Dead North series featuring lawyer Sam Williams, and the psychological thriller *The Lies I Tell*. Most recently, he has been working with titan of crime fiction Rachel McLean on the hugely successful Cumbria Crime series.

ALSO BY RACHEL MCLEAN AND JOEL HAMES

Cumbria Crime series

The Harbour
The Mine
The Cairn
The Barn
The Lake
The Wood
...and more to come

RACHEL McLEAN & JOEL HAMES

CUMBRIA CRIME BOOK 5

THE LAKE

Copyright © 2025 by Rachel McLean and Joel Hames

All rights reserved.

No part of this book may be reproduced in any form or by any electronic or mechanical means, including information storage and retrieval systems, without written permission from the author, except for the use of brief quotations in a book review.

This is a work of fiction. Names, characters, businesses, places, events and incidents are either the products of the author's imagination or used in a fictitious manner. Any resemblance to actual persons, living or dead, or actual events is purely coincidental.

Ackroyd Publishing

ackroydpublishing.com

Printed and bound in the UK by CPI Group (Uk) Ltd, Croydon CR0 4YY

CHAPTER ONE

TERRI GLANCED AT HER WATCH. Midday.

They'd only been there half an hour, and she was bored.

She stood on the rocky shore of Ennerdale Water, kicking at the stones, watching her girlfriend crouch down, pick things up, turn them over, then put them down again.

Erica had assured her there would be treasure here. Pots. Bottles. Ashtrays. *Old* stuff. Terri wasn't interested in old stuff, but Erica had a way of making boring things fun, so she'd agreed to come along and help search the area for antiques.

So far, they'd found rocks. Rocks, stones, bits of ice, lumps of dog shit that had been here so long they probably *were* antiques. The fells rose around the lake, dark and foreboding in the weak light, the trees bare, patches of snow scattered here and there, the lake itself the same dull, lifeless grey as the thick bank of clouds above it. They were on the rocky shore of a tiny bay that Erica had described as a beautiful, secluded beach, and Terri had thought that sounded romantic. Maybe, in the right weather, it was.

But not today. It was January, and Terri was freezing on top of being bored. There'd been a pub here, once, Erica had said. The Anglers' Hotel. They'd demolished it back in the sixties so they could raise the level of the lake, and then they'd decided not to raise the level of the lake after all, but it was too late by then, so this lovely old place that had been there for centuries was now just rock, rubble, and weeds.

And Victorian ashtrays, or whatever it was Erica was desperate to find.

Terri hugged herself, shivered, and kicked at a small sheet of ice by her feet, watching as the cracks formed and the little shards began to sink. Shame the pub wasn't there anymore. A pint by the fireplace, snuggled up with Erica – that would be just the ticket.

She glanced toward the lake, then back at Erica, who was standing up now, her hands on her hips, staring at something on the shoreline.

Maybe she'd found something. A Victorian bottle, something the Victorians probably didn't care about or they wouldn't have dumped it here. If Erica had found something, they could pick it up and go home, maybe find a pub with a fireplace on the way back, and Terri could pretend she'd enjoyed the trip.

"What have you found?" she called.

Erica didn't move. Terri walked toward her, stepping around the bits of ice. She'd worn the wrong shoes, and she could already feel the damp seeping into her socks. Erica was still staring at whatever had grabbed her attention.

"What is it?" Terri asked. "Found an ashtray or something?"

Erica turned. Her face was pale, her eyes wide, her mouth open in a horrified O.

CHAPTER ONE

Whatever Erica had seen, it wasn't an ashtray.

"What?" Terri repeated, then trotted up to her girlfriend. She stood beside her and followed Erica's gaze to the shoreline, where thicker sheets of ice bobbed in the wind, grinding against each other like miniature icebergs.

"There." Erica pointed to a spot ahead and to the left.

There was something there. Something long and thin, and grey – or was it blue? Yes. Blue. And beside it, another one. It was...

"Oh my God," Terri whispered. She reached out and wrapped her arms around Erica. "Oh my God."

A piece of ice shifted and revealed the point at which the two long things met.

Legs. Two legs in blue jeans, a hip, and yes, something above that, too.

Erica was shaking. Terri wanted to pull her away, back up the path to the car, and home, with the heating on, under the covers, and forget about it all.

She couldn't do that.

She removed one arm from her girlfriend's waist, reached into her pocket, pulled out her phone, and dialled.

"Police," she said, swallowing. "Police, please. Ennerdale. Where the Anglers' Hotel used to be. There's a dead body in the lake."

CHAPTER TWO

DI Zoe Finch sat on a metal chair in front of a metal table in a small, private room whose whitewashed walls were broken only by four cameras. Both chair and table were bolted to the floor, and Carrie Wright, the woman sitting opposite her, was handcuffed.

It had taken nearly three hours to get to HMP Low Newton, where Carrie Wright, formerly Sergeant Carrie Wright of Cumbria Police, was on remand awaiting trial on drugs and misconduct charges. Three hours, on top of the week it had taken to squeeze permission from the authorities to go and visit the woman.

And Zoe still wasn't sure why she was there. Carrie had asked to see her, but hadn't explained why.

This had better not be a waste of time.

"Why did you want to see me?" Zoe asked, once the formalities were out of the way.

Carrie had insisted the meeting be completely private, no guards in the room, which raised Zoe's hopes a little. If she didn't have something worth saying, she wouldn't be worried

CHAPTER TWO

about who heard it. The cameras were on, but muted. The guards were outside, ready to charge in if needed. And in a break with standard procedure, Carrie was cuffed.

"I wanted to say thank you."

Zoe frowned. "Thank you?"

"When Huz was killed. I know you told them to keep an eye on me. Otherwise..."

Zoe knew what she meant.

Back in October, Carrie's operation, which involved busting low-level dealers, stealing their supply, and getting students to distribute it out of the county, had been targeted by one of those dealers. Huz, a CSI who'd also been involved, had been murdered. Carrie had been in custody at the time, being questioned by the Professional Standards Division, and giving so little away they'd been tempted to let her go and keep an eye on her movements. Zoe had realised the killer might come after Carrie, and warned PSD to hang on to her.

"It's taken me nearly three hours to get here, Carrie," Zoe said. "Have you got anything to tell me?"

"You know about the operation."

"I know you were busting dealers and getting Huz to arrange the distribution, yes. I don't know how you knew which dealers to bust, though. I don't know who else was involved. And your record was clean, Carrie. You were a good copper. I can't see any major debts. You're not an addict. So why did you do it?"

Carrie shrugged. "Blackmail."

Huz had been blackmailed, too. Zoe sat forward, waiting.

"I... I slept with this guy." Carrie blushed. "Not my husband. And someone... They said they'd tell him. They had footage."

"Where from? How?"

"I tried to get out, DI Finch. I told them I didn't care. That was when they said they'd kill him."

"Kill who?"

"Peter."

Peter was Carrie's husband. PSD had been all over him, all over the house, picked the couple's lives apart. Peter Wright was clean.

"And you believed them?"

Another shrug. "I wasn't taking the risk, was I?"

The fact that she was making good money out of the operation probably helped.

"They," said Zoe. "You said 'they.' 'They said they'd kill him.' Who's 'they,' Carrie?"

Carrie shook her head and Zoe sighed. Carrie Wright had been a pawn in someone else's game, someone who knew exactly when the dealers she was targeting would have received their supply. Someone with contacts both in organised crime, and within the police. But if Carrie knew who they were, she wasn't saying.

Zoe gritted her teeth. "Tell me about Harry Oldman."

Carrie's eyes widened. They'd asked her about Oldman when she'd first been arrested, but she'd had other things on her mind at the time.

"DS Oldman?" she said.

Zoe nodded.

"He was... He's retired, isn't he?"

"Yes," Zoe said. "But someone's been using his old login details to access sensitive information. Information that was then used to blackmail members of the public. Was that you?"

"Not me, DI Finch," said Carrie, and there was an

CHAPTER TWO

earnestness, a pleading quality to her voice, that made Zoe inclined to believe her.

Zoe stood up.

"You're leaving?"

"You don't seem to have much to tell me."

Carrie opened her mouth, then shut it again. She shook her head, slowly. "Can you come back again next week?" she asked.

"Three hours, Carrie."

"I might— I need to know I can trust you, DI Finch."

Zoe nodded, walked to the door, and tapped once. It opened, and she took a step outside. Then she turned and looked Carrie Wright in the eye.

There was that look again. Her husband had left her, she'd lost her job, and she'd be spending years in prison. Carrie Wright was desperate. Alone, and desperate.

"I'll think about it, Carrie. But don't waste my time. I'm not your therapy cop."

Zoe turned again and walked away, through the security checks, guards, and other inmates being marched through the corridors. All those eyes, watching her. This visit hadn't exactly been top secret. If anyone was interested in whether Carrie Wright was receiving visitors, they'd know by now.

They hadn't let her take her phone in with her, and when she finally retrieved it, she saw a series of missed calls from Tom Willis. No voicemail. She called him back as she was climbing into her car.

"Boss," he said.

"What's up, Tom?"

"Body, boss. They've found a dead body. I'm heading there now."

Zoe paused, her finger about to tap the Hub on her satnav.

"Where?" she asked.

"Ennerdale Water. I'll send you the location."

Ennerdale. She'd investigated a murder not far from there, back in May. This couldn't be linked, could it?

"Thanks, Tom," she said. "See if you can get hold of CSI and the pathologist. I'm a few hours away still, but I'll see you there."

CHAPTER THREE

Elterwater had the usual bittersweet flavour for DS Aaron Keyes.

There was no doubt it was a beautiful area. He had some wonderful memories from his childhood there, and his parents still lived nearby. But there had been problems, growing up here, black, then, as he got older, black and gay, and finally, black, gay, and a cop.

Since he'd left, all that had changed, and the place welcomed all-comers, as long as they had enough money. All-comers and, if Sinead Conway of Conway Developments got her way, a new theme park smack in the middle of the old quarry. Not everyone's cup of tea, but the world moved on, and if you didn't move with it, it just rolled right over you.

No one knew that better than Aaron. He'd been off work for weeks, recovering from PTSD and a host of associated conditions, and then he'd been on 'light duties,' which was even more boring than it sounded. On the fringes, watching the real work happen, while he carried out tasks that didn't really need to be done.

He smiled to himself as he parked his Volvo outside the old police station. As of tomorrow, all that was over. Back to full hours. Full responsibilities. He was still seeing Dr Filey, but now it was once a fortnight instead of four times a week.

If anyone who'd been forced to stand by a window in just his underwear and a pair of handcuffs while a murderer held a knife to his throat could be described as 'better,' Aaron was better. Enough to pay a visit to his old police station.

Detective Sergeant Isaac Bateman opened the main door to the station and stared at him in a horrified mixture of surprise and disgust. "Look what the cat dragged in."

"Good to see you too," replied Aaron.

Bateman was tall and well-built, with thick, dark hair and a bulbous nose protruding from a face that was permanently red. They'd been at school together. They hadn't got on back then either.

Bateman shook his head, turned, and walked away.

Aaron followed him to a small open-plan office – three desks, one unoccupied. It wasn't difficult to figure out which desk was Bateman's: crisp packets, pictures of the rugby team, and a mug emblazoned with the words 'I'D LIKE TO TAKE DOWN YOUR PARTICULARS' in block capitals. There was an orange scarf slung over one of the other chairs and a pile of papers on the desk in front of it. Whoever Bateman's colleague was, Aaron pitied them.

"Why are you here, Keyesie?" Bateman asked. "Come to laugh at the country cops, is it?"

Keyesie. He'd hated that at the time, the pretence that he was one of the lads, football and fighting and girls. Isaac Bateman knew that.

Don't rise to it.

CHAPTER THREE

Aaron pursed his lips. "I thought it would be nice to drop in and say hello."

"Hello," said a voice from behind him. Aaron turned to see DI Jasmine Woolley.

Bugger.

"DI Woolley," he said. He watched her frown, as if she couldn't remember who he was, then her face cleared.

"It's DS Keyes, isn't it? One of Zoe Finch's lot, from what I recall. All well, over in the big city?"

Whitehaven was no more big city than Bateman and Woolley were country cops, but it looked like those were the roles they'd decided on.

"All fine," he replied. He smiled at her, and knew from the look in her eyes how obviously fake that smile was.

"Well, I don't mean to be rude, but we're a little busy here."

Aaron glanced over to Bateman, who was leaning against the wall, picking at his teeth. He certainly didn't look busy. He grinned at Aaron.

"Of course," Aaron said. "Take care."

"Do give DI Finch my best, won't you?" said DI Woolley. "Oh, and Ralph, if you see him."

Aaron nodded. "Of course." He turned to walk away, then stopped and turned back. "Ralph?" he asked.

"DI Streeting," replied DI Woolley. "He and I are old friends."

He made a note of that, thanked her, and returned to his Volvo.

Jasmine Woolley had never been the friendliest person, but unfriendly senior officers were nothing new. Friends of Ralph Streeting were more unusual, though, and worth keeping an eye on, because Aaron and DI Finch were convinced that Streeting, the man responsible for the Organised Crime unit, was in the pocket of the very people he was supposed to be locking up.

Aaron had just slid into the driver's seat when his phone rang.

"What is it, Tom?" he asked.

"Body, Sarge. Ennerdale. I know you're not supposed to be full-time yet, but the boss is over in Durham, so I thought you'd better know. I'm heading over with Nina, so..."

"So I need to be back at base. Got it. I'm heading that way anyway. Keep me updated."

CHAPTER FOUR

Zoe's drive back from Durham to Cumbria had been punctuated by brief flurries of snow, and the sky was already darkening when the dull gleam of Ennerdale Water showed ahead.

But at least she didn't have to park and walk. Last time she'd been in this area, the body had been caught on a rockface close to the top of a fell.

Turning off the ancient potholed road by a farm, she followed an even more potholed track down towards the shore. The satnav was useless here, but she didn't need it; she could see the blue lights ahead.

There wasn't anything that you could call a car park, but there was a stretch of flattish ground covered in stones and weeds, and room for Zoe to pull up between the mortuary ambulance and a white CSI van. Tom's car was parked a little further down, and she'd already driven past Nina's Fiesta. From there, it was a two-minute walk to the lake shore, where she could see a forensic tent and a small group of people standing outside it.

Tom separated himself from them and came to meet her.

"What have we got?" she asked. "And where exactly are we?"

"Dead male," he replied, pointing towards the tent. "Two women found him under the ice. No ID on him. Dr Robertson's in there now. And Keisha."

"Keisha?"

"Huz's replacement. She's... You'll see, boss. She's different."

Zoe nodded.

"As for this place," Tom continued, gesturing broadly around, "it's the site of an old pub. Anglers' Hotel. Pulled down in the sixties."

"Has the body been there that long?"

"No, boss. Modern Belstaff jacket on him. Expensive one, too."

"And the women who found him?"

"Two local women." He pulled out his phone and checked his notes. "Erica Martin, Terri Swann. They were out here looking for old pottery and bottles and stuff. It's a thing, boss. People do it. Harriett took them back to the station, but we've got statements. I don't think there's any reason to doubt them."

Zoe nodded. PC Harriett Barnes had been here, then. She glanced back towards the tent, and wasn't surprised to recognise the enormous figure standing guard outside it. Roddy Chen, Harriett's partner.

Zoe was convinced Harriett was an undercover PSD officer, but she couldn't say anything to Carl; he wouldn't tell her, even if it was true. She'd mentioned her suspicion to Tom, but only because Tom had dated the woman briefly.

CHAPTER FOUR

That had been months ago, and the two of them hadn't discussed it since.

"Where's Nina?" Zoe asked. "I saw her car."

"Gone to knock on doors," Tom replied.

"There are doors to knock on?" Other than the farm, which was more than a quarter of a mile away, she hadn't seen any signs of life.

Tom pointed out over the lake, and Zoe thought she saw a faint light across a small bay.

"Susan Masters' place," he said. "She might have seen something."

Susan Masters had been a witness – and almost a victim – to a murder the team had worked on six months earlier. She'd attempted to blackmail the killer and lied to the police. Zoe had saved her life, but it was anyone's guess whether she'd be willing to talk this time round.

Zoe walked over to the tent and exchanged nods with Roddy Chen and an equally silent figure in white, who she assumed was the pathologist's assistant, before pulling on a forensic suit and stepping inside.

"Ah, DI Finch. Good to see you."

Doctor Chris Robertson, the pathologist for the West Cumbria area, lifted himself from where he was crouched over a prone figure lying on plastic sheeting. He still made a habit of attending crime scenes, long after most of his colleagues had given up the practice. Beside him was another figure, stick-thin, her face concealed by her mask.

"You too, Chris. I'm Zoe Finch," Zoe said, addressing the woman.

"Keisha Middleton. I'm on Stella Berry's team."

Zoe nodded. The woman sounded young, but Stella

wouldn't have taken on anyone who didn't know what they were doing.

"What have you got?" she asked.

"Male, in his thirties," Chris Robertson told her. "Looks like he might have been here a while."

"What does that mean? Months? Years?"

He shook his head. "Days. Want to take a look?"

Zoe bent down beside him. In the stark white lighting, the face was pale and misshapen, but at least it was there. The last body she'd seen that had spent any time underwater had been that of Victor Parlick, and there'd barely been enough to identify him as human.

"How did he die?" she asked.

The pathologist laughed. "Like to get to the point, don't you? Well, this one looks fairly obvious." He pointed to the man's neck. What she'd taken for a blade of grass was a long cut. "This poor fellow's had his throat cut. Sharp blade. I'll be able to give you more at the post-mortem, but that's it for now."

Zoe thanked him and turned to the CSI.

"Keisha. Have you found anything of interest?"

"Not in the area," the woman replied. "Not yet, at least. The light isn't great. Maybe tomorrow..."

Zoe nodded. She'd get a search team out here. See if more eyes could spot anything.

"What about ID?"

"Nothing, really. We've got a phone, but it's dead." Keisha lifted a clear evidence bag containing a basic smartphone.

"Can you bring it back to life?"

"If anyone can, I can," replied Keisha. "Technical data recovery is sort of my thing."

Zoe raised an eyebrow. "No idea how he got here? No car keys, nothing like that? No wallet?"

"Nothing. Sorry."

"Not your fault. We'll see if the search team can spot anything in daylight."

Zoe turned back to the pathologist. "Can you get prints off him?"

"Not yet," replied Chris. "Look."

He lifted an arm in his gloved hand and turned the dead man's right palm towards her.

She frowned. "What am I looking at?"

"The skin," he explained. "It's been soaked. That's why I think our chap's been here for days rather than just a few hours. It's too soft to get a print off it. But you can still see the ridges, just about."

Zoe stepped closer. Squinting, she could make out whorls and arches, less clear than usual, but definitely there.

"Let me get him back to the West Cumberland," Chris said. "In the right conditions, I'm sure we'll be able to lift prints."

Zoe thanked him and headed out. A dead man, with a dead phone, and nothing else to identify him. But Keisha seemed confident, and so did Chris.

She hoped they were right.

CHAPTER FIVE

"It's you, is it?" said Susan Masters.

"It's me," agreed Nina.

"I saw the lights across the water." Susan pointed, and Nina turned. She could see the bright white beam of the forensic lights, and the blue from the emergency vehicles. "What's going on?"

It was dark now, and the snow had started again. It was cold.

"Can I come in, Mrs Masters?"

Susan squinted at her before she nodded and stepped aside. "Go on, then. Don't let all the warm air out."

Nina glanced around the room as Susan shut the door behind her. She hadn't been there since she'd helped Susan's son, Marcus, after he'd been attacked by Dean Somerville. Nothing seemed to have changed.

"Marcus still living here?" she asked.

Susan shook her head, her expression grim.

"No. He... He didn't fancy it anymore."

Susan Masters hadn't just lied to the police. She'd lied to

her son as well. She'd pretended to be disabled. Marcus had been heartbroken by the deception. No benefit in probing further, not if she wanted Susan's cooperation.

"Can we sit down?"

Susan squinted at her again, before leading her through to the kitchen, a room Nina remembered well. She'd watched as Marcus's head had been bandaged here. Susan pointed to a chair. Nina sat, but Susan remained standing, watching her.

"What's this about, then? I've pleaded guilty. You know that, don't you? There's nothing else to say. I'm just waiting for the sentence."

"I understand, Mrs Masters. This is nothing to do with you, or anything you've been involved in."

"What is it, then?"

"You've seen the lights. There's been an incident."

As briefly as she could, Nina explained what had been found, and where. She didn't add the more personal details: the way she'd taken a step back, at the sight of the lake, the sheets of ice, the precariousness of it all even more alarming than the dead body. The way she'd spotted Susan's house and realised that even if the woman hadn't seen anything, at least the trip would get Nina away from the shore for an hour or two.

"Who is he, then, this dead man?"

"I'm afraid I can't tell you any more at the moment, Mrs Masters."

The woman wrinkled her nose. "So what do you want, then? If you won't even tell me who's been killed, what do you expect me to tell you?"

This was the moment. Susan Masters might decide to be helpful.

Nina wasn't holding out much hope. But...

"I was just wondering if you'd seen anything. Anything out of the ordinary, in that direction."

There was a brief silence before Susan barked a single word.

"When?"

Nina thought back to what the pathologist had said. "Any time in the last week or so."

"Hmmm." Susan turned.

Nina waited. Susan Masters was facing away from her, towards the living room, but she could see the woman's face reflected in the huge picture window that looked back out over the bay. Her mouth was a thin line, her eyes narrow as she stared at the police lights.

"Yes," she said, at last. "Few nights ago."

Nina felt her pulse quicken. She'd assumed this would be a waste of time, and had only come because she'd known someone was going to have to speak to Susan Masters eventually, and that was as good an excuse as any to get away.

"What did you see?" she asked.

"Heard, more like." Susan turned back to her. "I'm having a coffee. You want one?"

As she prepared the coffee – beans, cafetière, all that magic the boss seemed obsessed with too – Susan continued.

"Friday night. One in the morning. I don't sleep so well these days, not now I'm alone in the house."

She paused, as if waiting for a question. When Nina didn't ask one, she continued.

"I heard an engine idling on the road up there."

"Which road?" Nina asked.

"The one to the farm above the Anglers'. I couldn't sleep, so I got up and had a look outside. I saw lights up there."

"What sort of lights, Mrs Masters?"

"A car. And then a smaller light. Moving down to the water's edge. I wasn't sure about that, though. My eyes aren't so good these days. And then... Well, then I got bored. It's not normal, people wandering round there at night, but it's not like I can do anything about it. I went back to bed. Here's your coffee."

Nina sipped at the drink. It was bitter, and Susan had refused to add sugar. *Strange woman*.

"I'm awaiting sentencing," she said.

Nina nodded. She'd said that already. Why was she saying it again?

There was another silence.

"Thanks for the coffee," Nina said.

Susan nodded. "Tell your boss. DI Finch. Tell her I helped."

Nina smiled. "Of course. And we're very grateful for your assistance."

Susan Masters was bargaining, then. Hoping for a lighter sentence. She wouldn't get one, and as Nina ran through what she'd heard over the last fifteen minutes, she couldn't help wondering if the woman might have been making the whole thing up.

CHAPTER SIX

"OK, team. What have we got?"

It was good to be back in the Hub, and even better that everyone was there. Zoe tried to remember the last time they'd all been in the team room together, her, Aaron, Nina, and Tom.

She felt her skin go cold. It had been back when they'd been hunting down Tony Harris, while Tony Harris was busy hunting down everyone else. Killing the student, Neil Colvin. Killing Huz. If he'd got his way, killing Aaron.

"Not a lot, boss." Aaron stood by the big screen. "Location, body, the women who found it."

He tapped on his phone and the image on the screen cycled: a map of the area, a series of photos of the crime scene, then of the body, then of the two women, Erica and Terri.

"Where are they?" asked Zoe.

"Sent them home, boss," Tom told her. "They were still here when I got back. They really don't know anything. They were just having a day out."

CHAPTER SIX

"Digging through the ice for hundred-year-old crap?"

Tom nodded, and Zoe sighed. People had weird habits everywhere, but up here they seemed to have the weirdest habits of all.

"Anything on the door-to-door, Nina?"

"Uniform's still there, scouting out the farms. But I spoke to Susan Masters. She thinks she saw something. Friday night. Car up at the farmhouse above the shore. Then a light heading down to the lake."

"Fair enough. It's Tuesday now. We don't have a time of death, but the pathologist thinks we're looking at days, not weeks. So Friday fits. She see anything else?"

"It was one in the morning, boss. She went to sleep."

Nina was frowning.

"What is it?" Zoe asked.

"It's just... She wanted me to tell you she'd helped. Made a point of telling me she'd pleaded guilty and was waiting for the sentence. She seems to think you can put in a good word with the judge."

Zoe grunted. "She'll be waiting a long time if she expects anything like that. I hope you didn't say anything that might have led her to believe she'd be getting a favour."

"No, boss. But it's all a bit convenient, isn't it? I couldn't help thinking she might have made the whole thing up."

Zoe considered.

"It's possible. But the fact is, her house does have a view of the crime scene. If anyone saw anything, she's probably the most likely. I don't know if you'd call that convenient. Now, what about cameras? Anything useful on the roads?"

Aaron shook his head. "Nothing there. No public CCTV, no ANPR, nothing."

She watched his face. He wasn't really supposed to be back yet. Not for another day.

But she'd been observing him for weeks now. The whole time he'd been on light duties, she'd been alert to the slightest change in his moods. And he'd been fine.

Right now, he simply seemed disappointed. Nothing more than that.

He'd told her he was better. Dr Filey believed he was better. She couldn't spend her life worrying about Aaron's mental health.

She turned back to Tom. "The farms?"

"Sorry, boss. They've got dummy cameras up at the nearest two, said they didn't have much worth taking. After that, well, you're back on the main roads, and the farms are set back, so they don't have a view of passing traffic."

"OK." She tried not to frown as she looked at her team. Aaron was still standing. The DCs were at their desks, waiting for her to say something useful.

"OK," she said again. "Keisha's trying to recover data from the phone. Chris is confident he can get prints. Between the two of them, I hope we'll have an ID and some more background soon."

Tom was nodding. Nina didn't look so sure. Aaron was a blank.

"And ID is the priority. It's late. In the morning, I want everyone working on finding out who this man is. Tom, if you can push Chris, that'll help."

Tom nodded.

"Nina, I want you to liaise with Keisha. Think you can do that?"

Nina smiled. "Better me than any of the rest of you."

"Why?"

"Keisha's a bit gobby," Nina explained. "Doesn't know when to shut up. I'll be sure to put her in her place."

"I don't care how you do it, Nina. We need that data. Aaron, we need more Uniforms out there. I've already spoken to Inspector Keane, and he's given me a handful of bodies. Think you can manage them?"

"No problem, boss. I'll manage it from here and head to the scene if they need more direction."

She wound up the briefing, and Tom and Nina were in their coats and out of the room within seconds.

She couldn't spend her life worrying about Aaron's mental health, but she had to ask.

"How are you getting on, Aaron?"

"Good, boss." He was looking away from her, as if avoiding her eye.

"Look at me, Aaron. Are you OK?"

He turned to her. He was smiling. Almost laughing.

"Really, boss. I'm still having the sessions. Doing them online, now. It's going well. And yes, before you ask, me and Serge are getting on fine and Annabel's OK, and yes, I still get flashbacks, but not so often, and I know they're not real. It's getting better, boss. It really is."

"As long as you're sure. If things get too much, we can—"

"Boss," he said, "I know I shouldn't interrupt you, but if you're about to suggest I go back to two days a week or take some more leave, I might display what Dr Filey calls 'irrational emotional displacement behaviour manifesting in anger.'"

"What?"

"I'm fine, boss. I really am."

Had Aaron just made a joke?
"Good," she said, turning around to cover her surprise. "I'll see you tomorrow."

CHAPTER SEVEN

Zoe could smell it as soon as she walked into the house, and all the tension of the day seemed to fall away at once.

"Is that chicken jalfrezi?" she called out, kicking off her shoes and walking through to the kitchen. "What happened to your health kick?"

Carl enveloped her in a hug, before returning his attention to the various cartons on the table.

"I kicked it," he said. "Life's too short not to have the occasional takeaway."

They'd been in the new house for just over a week, and even though they were discovering the usual quirks and irritations that come with every home, Zoe was still thrilled with the place. It was in the centre of Whitehaven, or close enough, and it might not have been Birmingham, but at night she could hear the sounds of people enjoying themselves, enjoying life.

"I'm starving," she said, sitting down and opening one of the cartons.

"Oh." Carl looked disappointed. "I thought maybe we could keep this warm, eat it later."

"What did you have in mind?"

He glanced behind him, out of the window into the tiny garden. She followed his gaze and shook her head.

"It's freezing, Carl. It's snowing!"

He smiled. "Perfect weather for a hot tub."

Zoe leaned down, sniffed at the carton. It smelled delicious. But Carl was right. It could wait.

An hour later, they were back in the kitchen, wrapped in towels, with the heating on full blast, eating. Yoda, who'd stared disapprovingly out of the window at them as they soaked in the hot tub, seemed keen to be out.

"I don't think so," Zoe told the cat. "I think you're getting a bit of a reputation."

In the nine days they'd been there, Yoda had escaped twice, and both times she'd managed to get into a fight with another cat. It was inevitable, in a new place. Of course, it didn't help that there was a fish and chip shop three doors away. The fish happened to be excellent, but that didn't matter. Yoda would have fought over scraps of any quality.

"So how was your day?" Carl asked.

Zoe told him about her meeting with Carrie. Out in the garden, even with the hot tub running, they might have been overheard.

"Will you see her again?"

Zoe shrugged. "Probably. Odds are it's just a waste of time, but if she wants to see me, I can't risk losing that sort of intel."

Carl nodded. "I can't complain, I suppose. It's your time getting wasted. Anything else happen?"

"New case." She swallowed some curry and rice. "Dead

body, over by Ennerdale. No ID. No clues at all, to be honest."

"That's the way they usually start with you, though, isn't it?"

Zoe opened her mouth to object, then closed it again. An unidentified victim was hardly a rarity. And they always found what they were looking for in the end. They spent a few minutes eating, the silence broken only by the impatient mewing of the cat.

"Have you got anywhere with Elena?" Carl asked, as he began to pack away the containers. He'd wash them and take them back to the restaurant to be used again – the health kick might have ended before it had really begun, but it looked like the environmental kick was a bit more permanent.

"Not really," Zoe replied. "Still at Nina's. Still can't remember the details. Just that smell."

Elena Marin had been trafficked from Romania to the UK, used as a slave, and worse. Her friend had been murdered, but Elena had managed to get away and come to Zoe for help. She'd even stayed with Zoe and Carl for a few weeks, hidden away in Nicholas' room while he was at university, while Myron Carter, Ralph Streeting, and the rest of them thought she'd gone to Liverpool.

After a while, she'd moved over to Nina's instead. She'd been there for months, still hiding, learning to adjust, becoming as close to normal as she could be after the trauma she'd been through.

The idea was that she'd remember something. Enough to help Zoe find the rest of the women, because there were more of them still trapped. So far she'd remembered a warehouse where she'd been held after arriving in England.

And the smell of ammonia.

Zoe was sure that meant something. She just didn't know what.

They had photos taken with a telephoto lens by an artist, Olivia Bagsby, who was still in hiding herself. The photos had been taken at the port, and clearly showed Myron Carter shouting at Streeting, and pointing at a man whose back was to the camera. In a later shot, the man had turned and was identifiable as Victor Parlick.

Victor Parlick had wound up dead not long after. Zoe was convinced that the photographs showed Carter instructing Streeting to kill him, but being convinced wasn't the same as convincing the CPS, or a jury.

A second set of photos showed a group of women being marched past Streeting. Carter wasn't in that set, and again, even though it was obvious these women were the victims of a smuggling operation, the photos alone weren't enough to bring anyone in for questioning. Not without the women themselves.

If only Elena could remember something. If only they could find those women.

Zoe stood and moved over to the sink to help Carl with the washing up. She leaned against his back, felt the warmth of his body through the towel, closed her eyes for a moment and just breathed.

If any of that happened, they'd be a step closer to breaking Myron Carter. Maybe then she could relax.

CHAPTER EIGHT

THE BUZZ of people working around him was something Aaron had finally begun to appreciate again. It had taken a while, coping with the tapping on keyboards, swallowing, breathing. People just getting on with their lives as if lives weren't the most ridiculously fragile things in the world, as if swallowing and breathing weren't luxuries.

He no longer flinched when Tom sighed or Nina muttered in quiet exasperation. But this half hour, before anyone else got in, was still his favourite part of the working day.

The team room was in darkness when he arrived, the lights flickering on as he stepped inside. He sat at his desk and checked the call logs from overnight, but there'd been nothing interesting, at Ennerdale or anywhere else.

He pulled up the list of PCs at the scene. Barnes. Chen. Martinez. Collins. Cummings. Four good names and one bad, but surely even Cummings couldn't screw up a crime scene. Could he?

He picked a name, not entirely at random, and called.

"PC Harriett Barnes, Cumbria Police."

"Harriett, it's Aaron Keyes. Just checking in. Anything interesting overnight?"

"We took over an hour ago," she told him. "I turned up ten minutes early so I could run through everything with C Shift, but I needn't have bothered, Sarge. They haven't seen a thing."

"You've spread out a bit, right?"

"Not yet, Sarge. When it gets light, we will. But at the moment it's... Oh, hang on. I've got a call coming in from Rob Collins. Can I...?"

"Call me back, Harriett."

He turned back to his screen and flicked through the night's crimes, looking for anything that might provide an obvious link with their body, but there was nothing there, and his mind returned to Harriett Barnes. She'd arrived early, because she wasn't willing to rely on the call logs and wanted to hear about developments first hand. And then she'd challenged his suggestion to spread things out, and she'd been right to. They weren't there to guard the scene – there weren't enough police in the whole of Cumbria to do that. They were there to search, and they couldn't light up the whole lake. Best to concentrate resources in a small area until it was brighter.

The boss arrived two minutes later, Tom and Nina a few minutes after that, and Harriett Barnes still hadn't called back. If it had been someone else, he might have chased her down. But Harriett knew what she was doing.

"Right," the boss began. "I take it there's been no developments overnight?"

Aaron shook his head. Tom and Nina followed suit.

"Fine. You know what to do. Find out who the—"

CHAPTER EIGHT

Aaron's phone rang, and DI Finch stopped and looked at him.

"Harriett Barnes," he told her. "She's at the scene."

"Go on, then."

He hit the green button, and then the speaker.

"Harriett," he said. "You're on speaker. Whole team's here. Rob Collins have anything interesting to say?"

"There's a car, Sarge. At the Bowness Knot car park. It may have been abandoned."

Bowness Knot. It was where they'd rounded up the many, many witnesses at the Great Borne Fell Race. And less than two miles from where the dead man had been pulled from the ice.

"What makes you think that?" he asked.

"There's a ticket, but it expired four days ago. It's dead here, Sarge. No other cars."

"Could be a camper, Harriett."

"They've paid for parking, but not come back, which suggests whatever plans they had haven't worked out. Anyone camping in this weather would have let someone know, and if they'd got hurt or lost, Mountain Rescue would have dealt with it by now. I've just been in touch. They've had no calls here lately."

"What sort of car?"

"Peugeot 306. 2014." She read out the registration. "I've run the plates, Sarge. It's registered to a Josh McKenzie."

Aaron glanced around the room, meeting two blank looks and a frown from Tom.

"Ring any bells, Tom?" he asked.

"Not sure, Sarge."

The boss picked up Aaron's phone and took over.

"Harriett? It's DI Finch. Tell Rob to get into the car."

"Get into the car, Ma'am?"

"Break in. Yes. If this isn't connected to a murder investigation, then it's probably someone lost in the hills. And four days ago ties in with Susan Masters' lights. We could be looking at someone who planned on staying till Saturday but got themselves killed Friday night."

There was a tap on the door, and all four of them turned to see Detective Superintendent Kendrick standing there, smiling the smile that had briefly earned her the nickname 'The Crocodile.'

"Any chance of an update, Zoe?" she said.

DI Finch passed the phone back to Aaron with a shrug.

CHAPTER NINE

Nina turned to the sarge as the DI left with the super.

"Reckon the boss is in trouble, Sarge?"

He shook his head. "You know the super, Nina. That's just the way she talks. Now, while we wait to hear back from the scene, let's see what else we can find out. Nina, have you spoken to Keisha Middleton?"

Nina wrinkled her nose. "Not got hold of her yet, Sarge."

She'd called Keisha three times already, once at the lab and twice on her mobile. The mobile hadn't been answered; when the lab assistant had realised Nina was after Keisha Middleton, he'd gently suggested she try later, probably two or three hours later, ideally some time in the afternoon.

Nina had nothing but respect for people who kept their own hours, but right now, it was interfering with Nina's work. She dialled the mobile number again, and while she waited, ran the name Josh McKenzie through the PNC.

The results came up while the phone was still ringing, and she was letting out a low whistle when the ringing was replaced by something that was half word, half groan.

"Yeeer," said the voice, presumably Keisha.

"Keisha?"

"Yeeer."

"It's Nina Kapoor. DC Kapoor. Remember?"

"Yeah." More distinct now. "What time is it?"

"Nearly nine. Have you got anywhere with the phone?"

"Fuck's sake, Nina, give me a chance. It's not even daytime yet."

Nina glanced out of the window. Beside her, she heard a grunt from Tom, who'd been tapping away on his keyboard and nodding to himself.

"Do me a favour," she said, her attention more on her screen than her call. "Get cracking." She ended the call before Keisha could object, turned, and addressed the room in general.

"Josh McKenzie. If it's the same man, he's got a record. Cannabis and a couple of scraps. Fined for possession, community orders for drunk and disorderly."

"It's not that uncommon a name," the sarge pointed out.

Tom had turned halfway towards her, still tapping on his keyboard.

She nodded. "But those offences were both round here, in the last couple of years. If we can get prints, we can confirm the car and the ID at the same time. There's more up in Scotland, though. Five years ago."

She checked her screen.

"Looks like there were proceedings against him in Glasgow. DV, Sarge."

"What did he get?"

She tapped her keyboard. "He didn't. Charges were dropped. I don't know—"

"Josh McKenzie," said Tom, turning fully around.

CHAPTER NINE

"That's the man," Nina said. "Haven't you been listening?"

"No, I mean, I thought I recognised the name. Just been going through the team notes on the Laurence Eversholt case."

Nina suppressed a shudder. Laurence Eversholt was the man who'd died on the fell overlooking Ennerdale Water. There were already too many connections between the current case and that one.

"Remember the hotel?" Tom asked.

"I bet you do," Nina replied. As part of the investigation, Tom had spent some time at the Bassenthwaite Manor Hotel. *Lucky bastard.*

Tom ignored her. "I spoke to the receptionist, Kate," he continued. "She had that footage of Laurence and his fella, the doctor. We assumed it was blackmail, but the doctor insisted no one had come after them, so we never really dug into it."

"Yes," prompted DS Keyes, looking impatient.

"Right. Sorry, Sarge. Well, Kate's boyfriend was a chef. Name of Josh McKenzie. Barman described him as a wrong 'un. We thought at the time—"

"You're right," said the sarge. "I was looking into the blackmail stuff, but it turned out not to be relevant. OK. Follow up on the prints, Tom. Nina, keep pushing Keisha. I'll see what we can do about phone and banking records. And let's see what—"

The sarge was interrupted by his phone ringing. He listened for a moment before turning back to Nina and Tom.

"That was PC Collins. They got into the car. There's a bag with a few days' clothes, and a couple of sandwiches with use-by dates earlier in the week."

Nina drew in a breath. "That's—"

He shook his head. "All this tells us is that our dead man was expecting to be back in the car before now. We'll have to wait for the prints to be sure who he is. Although chances are, it's the same man."

"Why?" asked Tom.

"Because Rob tells me there's a set of chef's whites on the back seat."

CHAPTER TEN

Fiona gestured for Zoe to sit, but instead of taking her own seat, went to stand at the window. For a moment she stared in silence, looking out past the smears where, for the second year running, she'd failed to get rid of the multi-coloured Christmas frosting sprayed on the glass, past the car park and the A5086 towards the fells.

She turned, twisted her mouth into a half-smile, and said, "What's going on, Zoe?"

Zoe glanced over the super's shoulder, out of the window, where the snow had started again, the tiny specks of white dancing in the wind in small flurries.

"I... We're trying to establish an ID, Fiona," she said. "We've got a likely name, Josh McKenzie, but we need to firm that up. And then—"

"I'm not talking about your new case, Zoe. I'm talking about everything else. The investigation. The accountant. The money."

Ah that.

"Zhang was very helpful," Zoe said. "We're starting to build a picture, and I think..."

Fiona shook her head.

"I'm sorry, Zoe. I really am. But I'm going to need to see some results before long."

"I don't—"

"Let me speak for a moment. You came to me and asked for access to a forensic accountant. You explained why, and that all made sense. Payments made by a murderer who was running brothels staffed by illegal migrants."

"Victims of trafficking and modern slavery," Zoe corrected.

"Quite. Don't worry. I'm on your side. Their side. But if I've got this right, this man paid for these women through a series of offshore companies, and your forensic accountant was supposed to link these to local organised crime."

"Yes."

"And did he manage it?"

"Sort of."

The super shook her head. "You see, Zoe, this is what I mean about results. I understand the need for discretion. I've helped you without demanding much by way of updates. You've even got Alistair Freeburn running around after you, leaking God knows what confidential information. But you can't say vague things like 'sort of' forever. I will be needing results."

Zoe stared at Fiona.

What could she say? She wasn't ready to point the finger at Ralph Streeting. She had photos of women, with Ralph Streeting in the background, but they weren't good enough without the women themselves. She had enough to link the payments to one of Carter's companies, but not to Carter.

"Ryan Tobin," she said.

"Who?"

"A former suspect. He used to work for the company in question. He's the key. He's not the most cooperative person out there, but I think if I can get him to trust me, he'll be willing to provide us with the information we need to complement Zhang's findings."

"Right." Fiona walked to the window, stared out of it for a moment, then turned back to Zoe. "And how do you propose doing that? Don't tell me. It'll be another favour. Something else I'll have to keep to myself. And what I'm afraid of, Zoe, is that you'll spend months on whatever it is, and either you won't get anything out of this Ryan Tobin, or you will, and it'll be yet another case of *almost* or *sort of*."

Zoe hadn't seen Fiona like this. She waited, and eventually, Fiona returned to her desk and sat down.

"I can't promise anything," Zoe said. "But if it's going to make things difficult, I can stop asking you for favours."

Fiona sighed, glanced down at her desk, then looked back up.

"You don't have to stop asking for favours, Zoe. Your record here is impeccable. You've earned the right. It's just... If you could try to be a little less vague, I'd very much appreciate it."

"Understood."

Zoe stood and walked to the door. She turned back to see Fiona looking at her desk again, her mouth set in a thin line, her eyes blank. She frowned.

"Is everything OK, Fiona?"

The super looked up sharply, her expression confused, as if she'd forgotten Zoe was even there.

"Yes," she said, throwing on an unconvincing smile. "I'm fine, Zoe. I'm absolutely fine."

CHAPTER ELEVEN

ZOE WISHED she had a few minutes in her office. She'd have called her old boss, Lesley, or her former colleague, Mo. She'd have tried to call Carl and been greeted by his voicemail. She'd have dedicated a little time to figuring out what was wrong with the super.

But she didn't have a little time.

When she entered the team room, Tom was putting down his phone and grinning. Nina was frowning at her screen, and Aaron was filling in an online request for phone records.

She grabbed the chair from the empty desk – the desk that had, briefly, been Kay's – and sat down. "What have you got?"

Tom spoke first.

"Dr Robertson's managed to pull prints off the victim, boss. He's running the PM in an hour, but he's sending the prints through now. I should be able to run..." His phone gave a beep, and he glanced at it. "They're here, boss. I'll get them run now."

"Excellent. Nina?"

"Nothing from Keisha, boss. But assuming the dead guy *is* Josh McKenzie, then odds are it's the same guy who's got a minor record in Cumbria and a more worrying one up in Scotland."

"Go on."

"Possession, drunk and disorderly here. The Glasgow stuff was five years ago. Domestic violence, charges dropped before it could get to court."

"Any idea why?"

A shrug. "That's all I could find on the PNC."

Tom walked to the middle of the room. "It's him, boss. Prints confirm it. And there's something else."

He looked at Aaron, who nodded encouragingly.

"Josh McKenzie was a chef at the Bassenthwaite Manor Hotel."

Zoe's thoughts turned back to half a year ago, or more, as hot then as it was freezing now. Tom was checking out the smart hotel. Nina was sulking because she'd wanted to go instead. Laurence Eversholt had been staying there, having a secret affair with Harry Patel, the Workington GP. There had been footage of the two of them meeting, and the assumption had been that someone was trying to blackmail them. Nothing had come of it in the end, because Laurence Eversholt hadn't been blackmailed, and his death had nothing to do with Harry Patel or the Bassenthwaite Manor Hotel.

"The boyfriend," she said, remembering Tom's notes in the team mailbox.

He nodded. "The woman at reception, Kate. She gave me the footage. Her boyfriend, apparently, was a chef called Josh McKenzie. Described as a wrong 'un by

CHAPTER ELEVEN

the barman who thought he knew everyone else's business."

"So we come back to the idea of blackmail," she said, waving Tom back to his chair.

Might as well say it out loud.

"And Carrie Wright says she was blackmailed into her role. Huz said something similar."

"Exactly." Tom nodded, pleased she'd reached the same conclusion. Aaron was looking anxious.

"We're going to have to tell PSD, aren't we?" he said.

Tom's face fell. They all knew what that meant. What it had meant when they'd first tried to bring in Huz.

Once PSD got involved, they tended to take things over. Not officially, of course. PSD couldn't run a murder enquiry. But that didn't always stop them trying.

Zoe nodded. "Yes, we are. But at the moment, there's no reason to believe Josh's death has anything to do with the police or anything else PSD might be interested in. There's just a possible connection with the blackmail. Carrie Wright was caught with a man who wasn't her husband. It would be good to know where, exactly. I'll speak to Branthwaite, see if I can set up another meeting."

Nina was fidgeting in her chair. "Do you have to tell Branthwaite everything, boss?"

Zoe turned, ready to berate the DC for the very suggestion, and then stopped.

Did she?

There was an imbalance in the way they worked with PSD. With Carl, his boss DCI Branthwaite, his colleague DS Denise Gaskill. Information flowed one way, from Zoe's team to Carl's. When PSD knew things that could help CID, you had to force it out of them.

But PSD was there for a reason. And if Zoe didn't tell them everything, she might as well be working against them.

"Yes," she said with a sigh. "We do, I'm afraid. I'll call Branthwaite. Aaron, I want you at the hospital for the PM."

"Got it, boss."

"Tom, I want you at Bassenthwaite Manor. See what you can find out, but don't stir things up too much. Speak to his boss, his colleagues. Speak to his girlfriend, Kate. I want to know what this Josh was like, but I don't want anyone except Kate aware that we know about the blackmail angle."

"Got it."

"Nina, I need you to chase Keisha."

Nina nodded. "OK, boss." Her lip curled.

"That shouldn't take up too much of your time. So you can go with Tom. It's a big hotel. A lot of ground to cover. It'll probably need two of you anyway."

Nina grinned. "Thanks, boss."

CHAPTER TWELVE

"Ah, DS Keyes. Always a pleasure," said Dr Robertson as Aaron donned an apron and mask and followed him into the post-mortem suite.

He'd assumed that he'd never get used to this place. Assumed the memories of all the corpses, the strip lighting in the corridors, the smell of it all, would combine to set off some built-in reaction, something he'd have to swallow back and ignore.

But it hadn't worked out like that. He was looking down at a dead man lying naked on a table, so pale in the bright overhead lights he almost shone, and he felt nothing.

He'd have to discuss that with Dr Filey later. In the meantime, the pathologist was talking.

"You've met my assistant, Joseph?"

"Josephine," corrected the woman, her voice terse.

Aaron shook his head. *Joseph* was a step up from *my lad*.

"Now then." Dr Robertson reached up and switched on his microphone. "Let's begin." He pointed down at the body.

"The victim's clothing is with Stella at the lab. Expensive jacket, that."

Aaron had read the notes. Belstaff. Retailing for over a thousand pounds. A hotel chef might earn a decent wage, but that seemed a stretch.

"Let's start with what killed him," continued the pathologist. "This isn't a difficult one."

Dr Robertson traced a gloved finger over the wound in Josh McKenzie's throat.

"We have here a moderately deep laceration. The carotid hasn't been severed, but the jugular vein's gone. The wound has clear, sharp edges and there's very little tissue bridging. We're looking at a knife, and a sharp one."

"A chef's knife?"

The pathologist looked up. "Have you found the weapon?"

Aaron shook his head. "The deceased was a chef, so..."

"Could be," Dr Robertson said. "Would probably be sharp enough. He'd have died, either from blood loss or blood in the airways, within about ten minutes. There's your cause of death. No surprises so far."

Aaron bent over the body. Once you got past the wound and the pallor, it was in excellent condition.

"We've got a possible timeframe," he said. "Friday night, into Saturday morning, so nearly five days ago. But this—" He gestured at the corpse. "It looks so well preserved. Wouldn't it be more decomposed by now?"

"If we assume the man spent all his time in the water in the area where he was found, it was shallow, without much of a current. That part of Ennerdale Water is currently around four degrees, or at least it was last night." The pathologist looked up and grinned. "I had Joanna here measure it at the scene."

Dr Robertson's assistant made a small sound, as if she was about to say something. Aaron gave a tiny shake of his head, and she fell silent. If she hadn't learned the secret to working with Chris Robertson by now, she would soon enough. *Don't rise to it.*

The pathologist continued.

"The cold slows decomposition considerably, not to mention keeping the fish away. We do have some maceration of the skin, but less than you'd get in warmer conditions. Much longer and you'd have adipocere formation, but there's no sign of that yet. All of which is to say that yes, Friday night is perfectly plausible."

"Thanks. I assume you can't narrow the time of death any further?" Aaron asked.

"Unlikely. There are some new techniques that use mass spectrometry to analyse muscle protein, and I can send that off with the rest of the samples, but I wouldn't get your hopes up. We're looking at somewhere between two and eight days, so your window falls right in the middle. Now, let's just confirm a few things."

Aaron watched as the doctor pulled back the skin, the familiar Y-shaped incision exposing tissue and internal organs.

"The airways are relatively clear of water, a little blood, but not a huge amount, and the lungs aren't abnormally dilated. This man didn't drown, DS Keyes. He died from loss of blood, and then he was pushed into the lake."

The pathologist worked his way through the rest of the organs. There were samples to take, toxicology tests to run, but there was nothing to contradict the initial conclusion.

Josh McKenzie had been slashed across the throat, and when he'd bled out, he'd been pushed into Ennerdale Water, to lie among sheets of ice until he was found.

By all accounts, Josh McKenzie hadn't been the nicest of people, but that didn't matter. He'd had a painful death, a cold and lonely death, and no one, not even Josh McKenzie, deserved that.

CHAPTER THIRTEEN

Branthwaite answered after three rings, barking his name. "Branthwaite."

"DCI Branthwaite? It's Zoe Finch."

"One moment, if you don't mind."

She heard voices, slightly muffled; Branthwaite and another male. Was that Carl?

"I thought if you'd wanted to chat to your fella, you'd have called him. Now, what can I do for you, Zoe?"

Zoe couldn't help liking Branthwaite. Carl spoke highly of him, and in her dealings with the man, he'd been as cooperative as she expected from PSD. More so, if anything. He'd screwed up, letting Huz out just in time for him to get murdered, and chewing Nina out for second-guessing him over it. But that had been an honest mistake, and he'd apologised for it, in person, marching into the team room later that week like a one-man army and dumping a bunch of flowers on Nina's desk, while she'd stood there, open-mouthed.

But he had a job to do, and in Zoe's experience, his job tended to make hers harder.

"I'd like to see Carrie Wright again," she said.

"She told you anything useful?" he asked.

"Not yet, Sir. But we've got a murder victim here who might be connected to a blackmail ring. Carrie told us she was blackmailed, that's why she got into the whole thing in the first place."

"You believe her?"

"I do, yes. Huz said something similar. And Carrie won't give us any names."

"You and DI Whaley seem fixated on the notion that there *are* other names. Without good evidence to support that fixation, I must say."

She didn't contradict him.

"OK. If we had to wait for good evidence every time we followed anything up, we'd never follow up on anything. You can see her. I'll put in a word. When do you want to go?"

"Today. If I can."

"I'll make some calls, see if I can expedite it. You'll hear directly from the prison service. But I'm trusting you, Zoe. I don't know anything about your murder victim, and I don't think I want to, but if this looks like it should be a PSD case, I expect you to let me know."

Zoe thanked him and ended the call. She walked to the team room and spent a few minutes there, flicking through the details on the big screen. Nina and Tom were at the hotel and Aaron was at the PM, but sometimes it helped, seeing everything up there at scale.

There were photos from McKenzie's arrests, and a little detail on the Cumbrian convictions, but nothing that didn't apply to a thousand other petty criminals in the area. For the case in Scotland, the one that had been abandoned, there was close to nothing at all.

CHAPTER THIRTEEN

She searched local press, but apart from the report into the initial arrest, there was nothing there either. PNC didn't have anything. The station that had made the arrest had an open access arrangement with police forces across the UK, so she typed in her credentials and pulled up what little they had there.

McKenzie's wife – ex-wife, now – had decided not to give evidence.

Decided.

Always a loaded word, that. In any case, but particularly when it came to domestic violence. Why had Shona McKenzie – Shona Murray, as she was now called – *decided* not to give evidence?

If this had happened in Zoe's station, she'd simply call the arresting officer and find out. But the names had been redacted, and besides, there was no obligation for anyone up there to talk to her. An English DI sniffing around a Glasgow case from the wrong side of the border, possibly looking to blame people for things, wouldn't go down well.

But someone else, someone closer, might be able to make more headway. Returning to her office, she picked up her phone and dialled.

"Zoe!"

The sound of DS Mo Uddin's voice alone was enough to bring a smile to her face.

"Mo. How are you?"

"Oh, you know. Busy. Still holding out against going native."

"They've not got you in a kilt yet?"

"You've seen my legs, Zoe. No one wants that. Oh, I saw Nicholas last week, did he tell you?"

"He did," she lied. She'd barely spoken to Nicholas

lately. She'd called almost every day, but he was always going somewhere or doing something, promising to call her back, and forgetting to.

Nicholas was twenty-one years old, though. There was nothing unusual about it.

She asked after Catriona and the girls, and when they'd caught up, explained what she was looking for.

"So your offender's wound up dead, and you want me to find out why the ex dropped the charges?" he summarised when she'd finished.

"Exactly."

"Leave it with me," he told her. "I'll see what I can do."

CHAPTER FOURTEEN

"Bloody hell," Nina said, as they made their way along the mile-long driveway towards the grey stone mansion, her head swivelling from left to right and back again. To the left was the deer park, a wooded area dotted with snow-covered clearings. To the right was the nine-hole golf course.

"Watch the bloody road!" shouted Tom, and Nina grabbed the wheel and corrected before she met the low stone wall on the left.

"I had it under control," she muttered, slowing for the gravel car park. She could see the building in detail now, the narrow windows and what looked like turrets on top. To the right of the building, something glinted in the weak sunshine. She stopped the car and wound down her window to take a better look.

"Don't tell me they've got their own bloody lake, too," she said.

"Boating lake," Tom told her. "And there's—"

"There's a bloody fountain in the middle of it." She opened the door, stepping past a man in a dark uniform with a poorly groomed beard, who was staring at her car as if he'd never seen anything like it before.

"It's a Ford Fiesta," she told him. "Classic of its type."

He turned from the car to Nina, confusion on his face.

"How come the fountain's working when the lake's frozen over?" she asked. Tom was still climbing out of the car, hanging behind a little, as if he didn't really want to be associated with it.

"It's... It's not frozen in the middle." The man's accent was pure Cumbria, and it didn't seem to go with the uniform, or the boating lake, any more than the beard did.

"Right," she replied. Hopefully, she wouldn't have to go near it. One frozen lake in an investigation was bad luck. Two was something else. "If it's a boating lake, where are the boats?"

The man pointed towards a low wooden structure beside the lake. "Boathouse," he said. "Erm, Madam, may I ask if..."

"It's OK," said Tom. "DC Willis, Cumbria CID. I believe we've met before. That there is DC Kapoor. She's with me. Try to ignore the car."

The man turned towards Tom, then took a step back.

"Oh," he said, looking from Tom to Nina, then back again.

"Stuart, isn't it?" Tom said.

"That's right," said the man. "Stuart Sullivan." His gaze continued to flick between the two of them, then came to rest on Nina's Fiesta again. There were scratches all along one side, and marks from where the gulls' droppings had set into something with the staying power of superglue and the hardness of diamond. He stared for a moment, then shook his head and returned his attention to Nina.

"I'm sorry," he said. "What can I do for you?"

CHAPTER FOURTEEN

"We'd like to speak to the manager, please," she said.

The man nodded and set off towards the hotel, Nina and Tom following.

"It's still Peter Raymond, is it?" asked Tom as they walked.

Stuart Sullivan nodded. "Aye. Still 'im."

The accent had broadened, now it was clear they weren't guests. And there was something in Stuart Sullivan's tone of voice that suggested he wasn't fond of his manager.

Inside, the reception desk was empty.

"Sorry," said Stuart. "Bit short-staffed at the moment. Mind waiting 'ere, while I go find 'im for ya?"

"Fine," said Nina.

"Kate not about?" asked Tom.

"Nope," replied Sullivan, and walked away down a short, brown-carpeted corridor and around a corner.

While Tom headed for a plush armchair set by a low table piled with newspapers, Nina paced around the reception. It was a good-sized area; the carpet replaced here with something that might have been marble tiling but was probably vinyl designed to look like marble. There was a dark wooden desk, wide enough for two people to stand at, with a wall behind it made from matching wood. As they waited, a door Nina hadn't noticed in the wall opened. A woman walked through it and stopped behind the desk.

No one at the hotel knew why Nina and Tom were there yet. The longer they could keep it that way, the better.

"Can I help you?" the woman asked. She had short dark hair, and her cheeks were flushed and her breathing shallow.

"It's OK," said Tom. "We're just—"

"Right, then," said a loud voice from behind them.

Nina turned, astonished to see Keisha Middleton

approaching. Out of the mask and hair-covering and forensic suit, the woman was striking. Beautiful, even, her hair falling in artfully highlighted waves to her shoulders, her large brown eyes enhanced by dark, carefully applied eyeliner.

Nina stared at her. Keisha was supposed to be at the lab, recovering data from Josh McKenzie's phone. What was she doing here?

"Keisha?" she said.

"You know it," Keisha replied, her lips curling into a grin. Behind the reception desk, the woman was frowning in confusion. "Right," Keisha said again. "Where's the dead guy's room, then?"

CHAPTER FIFTEEN

"I must protest in the strongest possible terms," Peter Raymond said, as Tom and Nina sat in the armchairs opposite the manager's desk.

Raymond hadn't changed much in the eight months since Tom had last seen him; the same neatly pressed suit, the stubble carefully manicured to complement his tan. He'd arrived just as Nina was telling Keisha to keep her mouth shut, and the receptionist, Sarah, was descending into a state of panic. With unerringly unfortunate timing, a pair of elderly guests had walked in just behind Keisha, unnoticed by anyone else, and caught every word she'd said.

Keisha was waiting in reception now, probably complaining about it. The guests had been ushered away to the bar and offered free drinks to calm their nerves. And Raymond had gone on the offensive as soon as they were settled in his office.

"We really are sorry," Tom began, "but—"

"I mean," Raymond blustered, "what is all this nonsense?

We've got your CSI people running about the place panicking staff and guests, and meanwhile, my sous chef, who's absolutely indispensable to the operation of this hotel, seems to have disappeared."

Tom glanced at Nina. She gave a tiny nod.

"Would that be Josh McKenzie?" he asked.

"Yes," Raymond said, "why? What do you know about it?"

"When did Mr McKenzie disappear, precisely?"

Raymond's eyes narrowed. "Why?"

"It would be helpful if you could let us know, Mr Raymond," said Nina. She was smiling, but Tom could see the effort it was taking.

"Well, I'm not exactly sure," Raymond replied. "A few days ago. A week, perhaps."

"I'm sorry, did you say a week?" asked Tom.

"Possibly. It might have been less. As I just said, I don't know exactly. Why?"

"You say he's indispensable to the operation of the hotel, and he's been missing for up to a week?"

"Well," began Raymond, "perhaps—"

"And you didn't think to inform the police that Josh was missing?"

"Missing? He's just walked out, hasn't he? He's a grown man, DC... What was it? Wilson?"

"Willis, Mr Raymond."

"Well, he's a grown man. And in this business, people do rather come and go, unfortunately. It's one of the aspects of the industry you have to manage."

Tom glanced to the side again. Another little nod from Nina. Not that he needed it.

"I'm sorry to have to inform you that Josh McKenzie is

dead."

"Dead?"

"Dead," repeated Tom. "Now, we'll need to look into his role here. We'll need to examine his room and his work environment, and we'll need to speak to the rest of the staff. The more information we can find out about him, the better."

"Is this... Is it a suspicious death?" Raymond asked.

"We wouldn't be here if it wasn't. So I trust you'll be cooperative, Mr Raymond."

It wasn't a question. Raymond nodded.

"Good. The first thing I'd like, then, are details of Josh's previous employment."

"Very well."

Raymond went to a wooden filing cabinet against the far wall. He spent a minute or two rummaging through it, before turning to them empty-handed.

"I am sorry. I can tell you Josh had been working here for nearly two years. We picked him up from the King George's Dining Rooms. You know it?"

The King George's Dining Rooms was one of those insanely expensive little restaurants out in the middle of nowhere. It had Michelin stars, Tom thought, or was in line for them. Not the kind of place a lowly detective constable would experience first hand.

But the fact that he'd worked there implied McKenzie had known what he was doing.

"Do you have a copy of the reference?" Nina asked.

"Sorry," replied Raymond. "I'm afraid it's not here. But really, it's not important."

"No?" Nina was still smiling, although it was becoming more and more obvious how unnatural that smile was.

"Oh, no. If you knew about the hospitality industry, you'd understand."

"We would?" said Nina.

Raymond nodded. "Indeed. It all works by word of mouth in this business, you see. A sort of trust."

Raymond lifted his arms expansively. Tom had the distinct impression that if the manager carried on being this pompous, Nina's smile would be replaced by something very different.

"Mr Raymond," he said, hurriedly, "as I mentioned, we expect you'll be cooperating with our investigation, yes?"

Raymond nodded.

"In that case, it's vital we find out precisely when Josh McKenzie was last here. So please, can you find me your CCTV footage from the last week?"

"What CCTV footage, exactly? We have a number of cameras, both inside and out, for the comfort and security of our guests."

"All of it, please," Tom said. "We'll look through and download what we need. If I recall rightly, you keep it for a fortnight."

"Very well." Raymond stood. "I'll... Would you like to wait here?"

"No, thanks," Tom told him, getting to his feet. "I think we'll go for a wander."

Raymond frowned, but he glanced at Nina and must have seen something that made him think better of objecting. "Very well," he repeated, then strode to the door and out of his office.

"What an annoying prick," said Nina, before the door had closed behind him.

"True," said Tom. "But he's an interfering prick as well as

an annoying one, and now he's out of the way, we can have a chat with his staff, can't we?"

For the first time since they'd been in the room, Nina's smile looked genuine. "Good work," she said, nodding. "Very good indeed, Tom Willis."

CHAPTER SIXTEEN

IN THE BOSS'S OFFICE, Aaron outlined what he'd learned from the post-mortem.

"Nothing we didn't already know, then," said DI Finch. Aaron shrugged in agreement.

"Even Chris can't work miracles," he told her. "But the time of death allows for Susan Masters' noise and lights on Friday night. So she might have been telling the truth."

"That woman." DI Finch shook her head. "She's on the spot for one murder in the middle of nowhere and doesn't tell us anything about it, then manages to miss another one happening opposite her bloody window."

Her phone rang. She answered on speaker.

"Nina? I'm here with DS Keyes. Anything interesting?"

"Not yet, boss." Aaron could hear footsteps, and the sound of Tom muttering beside her. "Manager says Josh had been missing for a while. Up to a week. Doesn't know any more than that, but we've sent him off for CCTV while we talk to the other staff."

"Good work. Anything about Josh himself?"

"Previous place of employment. King George's Dining Rooms. Ah, looks like we're here. Got to go."

The line went dead, and DI Finch turned to Aaron.

"I saw you'd put in a request for Josh's phone records. Are you OK working on his background?"

"That's the plan. You want me to check out the King George's?"

DI Finch nodded.

"You know the place?" he asked her.

"No. Should I?"

"Not really. It's one of those small places with a big name. Middle of nowhere, but very posh. Makes Bassenthwaite Manor look like a Travelodge."

The boss looked blank. From what he recalled, her thing was curries, pizzas, anything that didn't take much effort.

"I'll follow it up," he told her.

Back in the team room, he tried the King George's Dining Rooms three times before giving up and examining the location. The place really was in the middle of nowhere, if the satellite image he was looking at was anything to go by, down a long track between Boot and Wast Water with nothing but sheep and trees for neighbours. Forty-five minutes' drive, maybe more.

He called again, got no answer again, and double-checked the website. The place was open, or would be that evening. Probably too busy prepping dinner service to answer the phone.

DI Finch was hoping to visit Carrie Wright later. Hopefully she'd find out more about the blackmail side of things while she was there, but there were other people who'd put blackmail on the team's radar nearly a year earlier.

Margaret Hooper, for one.

Aaron scrolled through the team mailbox, hunting down the details, reminding himself of the facts. Margaret Hooper was the head teacher at Norris Academy, and someone had found CCTV footage of her kissing another woman. She'd been sent a blackmail note, as vague as it was anonymous: *Margaret Hooper, we will be in touch with you in due course.*

Margaret Hooper was out and hadn't cared who knew it. She'd only reported the incident out of a sense of public duty, and had been apologetic even as she explained what had happened.

But Ellis Peters hadn't been so fortunate.

Ellis Peters had thrown himself off Scafell Pike, the September before last. No one had known why. The firefighter was married, had no kids but plenty of friends, and everyone, from his wife to his colleagues, insisted he'd been fine. Happy, even. But a note had been found in his personal effects at the fire station.

Ellis Peters, you can be sure we will contact you.

Which was unnervingly similar to the note Margaret Hooper had received.

Margaret Hooper was at work, in her office. The receptionist put him straight through when he told her he was with Cumbria CID.

But Margaret Hooper had never heard the name Josh McKenzie, and when he asked her if she'd spent any time at the Bassenthwaite Manor Hotel, she laughed and informed him that even head teachers didn't earn enough for a place like that.

Sally Peters, the fireman's widow, wasn't answering her phone. Aaron tried the King George's Dining Rooms one last time. Still no answer. He picked up his coat and headed out

CHAPTER SIXTEEN

of the team room, dialling Sally Peters again, and leaving a message.

Outside, the snow had stopped falling and everything was still. But it was icy underfoot, and the way the clouds were building to the east, it wouldn't be still for long.

More like an hour's drive, he decided, as he eased his Volvo out of the car park.

CHAPTER SEVENTEEN

Tom walked quickly out of Peter Raymond's office, and Nina found herself trotting to keep up.

"Take it easy, yeah?" she said.

Tom looked back over his shoulder and shook his head without breaking stride. "Don't know how long it'll take Raymond to get those files. Make hay while the sun shines."

He carried on, Nina a few steps behind and biting back a retort about the last time the sun had shone being weeks ago. Behind the reception desk, the dark-haired woman, Sarah, visibly flinched when she saw them.

"Have you seen Kate?" asked Tom.

The woman looked blankly at him.

"Kate," he repeated. "Blonde woman. Works here."

"Oh, Kate," said the woman. "Yes. She's not here. Not her shift."

"We'll try her room," Tom said, and off he strode again.

"For Christ's sake," Nina called after him, two minutes later. "This is ridiculous." They were walking along a corridor five floors up – for reasons he hadn't bothered sharing, Tom had decided to take the stairs rather than the lift.

He stopped, sixty feet and half a dozen numbered doors ahead of her, and turned around, puzzled.

"What?"

"Slow down."

"We've got to—"

"Yeah, yeah, make hay." She'd caught up with him. "We're CID, Tom. I know you want to speak to people before Raymond gets back, but he can't stop us. This is a murder investigation. If he makes trouble, we'll just fit him up."

"Nina..."

"Joke, Tom. It's a joke."

She followed him to a plain wooden door marked 535, and leaned against the white-papered wall while he knocked.

Nothing happened.

"You sure this is her room?" Nina asked.

"It was eight months ago," he replied. "This is where she showed me the footage of Laurence Eversholt and Harry Patel."

He stopped knocking and the two of them listened in silence.

Nothing.

"Follow me," Tom said, and walked back the way they'd come.

It wasn't until he'd reached the end of the corridor that he turned and realised Nina hadn't followed.

"What—"

Nina smiled and summoned him back with a single curled finger.

"Two things," she told him when he returned. "One,

slow the fuck down. Two, tell me where we're going before you set off. OK?"

"Yeah." He nodded. "Sorry. The bloke who works behind the bar, Leo. Worked there eight months ago, anyway. He was the one who said Josh was dodgy. If anyone knows someone else's business round here, it's Leo."

He began to walk away.

"Three," Nina called, and he stopped.

"What?"

"We take the lift."

The Bassenthwaite Manor Hotel bar was a glamorous affair, the bar itself long, all polished wood and brass, and the tables well-spaced with comfortable-looking sofas and leather wingback chairs that looked like they belonged in the sort of club Nina would never be allowed inside. Not that she'd want to hang out in that sort of place.

"DC Willis," said a voice from behind the bar as they entered, and Nina turned to see a crop-haired man grinning at them while he dried a glass. "I heard you were back. Who's dead this time?"

"Leo, this is my colleague, DC Kapoor. I was hoping you were here. I'd like to pick your brain."

Leo put down the glass and picked up another. "Fire away."

"What do you know about Josh McKenzie?"

Leo nodded as if he'd known where the conversation was heading. "He's not been around for days. I haven't seen him since... Let me see. Thursday. Rumour is, he emptied his room and disappeared that evening."

"Rumour from who?"

Leo frowned. "Not sure. You'll have to ask Kate, if you can find her."

"We've been looking for her."

"Might be hiding out in her room. Ever since Josh disappeared, she's been scooting back there as soon as she finishes her shifts. Doesn't talk to anyone."

"Do you know why?"

Leo shrugged. "No fury like a woman scorned," he said, and smiled.

Nina decided enough was enough. "Josh is dead, Mr..."

"Stanislaus. But people just call me Leo," the man replied. His easy smile was gone already, his expression serious. "Look, I'm sorry. When I said who's dead this time, I didn't mean..."

"I know," Nina said. "Don't worry about it."

"Fuck all in there," called a voice from behind them, and Nina turned to see Keisha walking in, pulling the net from her hair and shaking it loose.

"What?"

"Josh McKenzie's room. Here, you." Keisha turned to Leo and favoured him with a smile. "Couldn't do a girl a solid and knock up a Virgin Mary, could you? Heavy on the tabasco. I've got the hangover from hell."

Nina was torn between astonishment and admiration. "Nothing at all?" she asked. Leo was already busy slicing and squeezing a lemon.

"Bit of coke," Keisha replied, sinking onto a bar stool, "but you know these chef types. Coke's like paracetamol as far as they're concerned. Speaking of which, anyone got any paracetamol?"

CHAPTER EIGHTEEN

THE TEAM ROOM was quiet again. Nina and Tom were still at the hotel, and Aaron had just called to let Zoe know he was on the way to the King George's Dining Rooms. She'd taken a look at the place online, examined the menu, and decided it wasn't really her thing. The location looked spectacular, nestled between the fells and a tiny tarn she'd never heard of. But it was in the middle of nowhere, and from what she knew of Aaron's driving, she wouldn't see him again that day.

She'd just pulled up the scant details of Josh McKenzie's prior convictions when her phone rang.

"Mo," she said. "That was quick."

"When a job needs doing..." he replied. "I think I might know why Shona didn't want to give evidence against her ex-husband."

"Go on."

"Your dead man, Josh McKenzie. Around the time the charges were filed, he spent a little time in the Queen Elizabeth University Hospital."

She caught herself pulling a face: half grimace, half smile. It wasn't exactly an unusual name, but it brought back memories of a different Queen Elizabeth Hospital. One she'd hated, when she was in Birmingham. It was the place her dad had spent much of his last months, not to mention somewhere she'd had to visit too many times when attending postmortems.

"Feels like forever since I was last in Brum," she said. It was Mo she was talking to. There was no need to explain the link.

"You're missing the place?"

She sniffed. "No. It's beautiful in Cumbria. And this is where my life is now."

Silence.

"Mo?" she said. "You OK?"

"I'm fine. Just... I get a bit homesick, y'know?"

"I know." She shook herself out; there was a case to solve. "So, Josh McKenzie. Not a routine illness, I presume."

"Details are a bit light, but the snippets I got suggest he had a run-in with Shona's brother. Little chat that got out of hand."

"So..." Zoe rubbed her head as she thought. "So what, Shona figured that if she pushed the DV charges on Josh, he might push back with assault charges against her brother?"

"Four days in the hospital, Zo. More than just assault."

"Would be enough to make someone think twice."

"Exactly. And look, it's the same here as it is everywhere else. Too many old-school coppers who still don't take DV as seriously as they should. What's between a man and his wife stays behind closed doors, all that crap. Wouldn't surprise me if they weren't particularly supportive."

"Thanks, Mo. This is good. Look, I don't want to push things, but if there's anything more you can find out..."

"You only had to ask. I'll see if I can get anything out of the woman herself."

"You're a good man. Maybe I'll come up, actually."

She'd said the words before she'd really thought about them, and found herself filling the few seconds' silence that followed with reasons not to go to Scotland. She was working a new murder case; she'd just moved house; her team needed her.

"That would be wonderful," Mo was saying. "It's a fair drive, though. You'd have to stay here. Get Nicholas round. Eat haggis."

"Like you'd eat haggis," she snorted, and was still working her way through those reasons when they ended the call a minute later.

The fact was, a trip to Scotland, a visit to Josh McKenzie's ex-wife, might well move the case forward. She and Carl were settled in the new house, Carl would understand, and Yoda would be annoyed with her whether she was in the house or a hundred and fifty miles away.

As for the team, the DCs had demonstrated outstanding independent work for much of the last year, and she'd been watching Aaron like a hawk. He was as well as she'd ever seen him.

The only thing keeping her in England was the possibility of seeing Carrie Wright, and as if conjured by the thought, the next call she received was from the prison service.

"Zoe Finch?" said a female voice.

"Yes," she replied.

CHAPTER EIGHTEEN

"Yasmin Morgan, His Majesty's Prison Service. I gather you want to see a remand prisoner, is that right?"

"Yes."

"That's fine. They're expecting you. You're not that close, so any time before eight today will be fine. You... It's DI Finch, isn't it?"

The woman's voice had changed. Softened from businesslike to inquisitive.

"Yes," Zoe said, for a third time.

"You're the one who arrested Dean Somerville?"

"I am."

"I read about it in the papers. Up a hill, wasn't it? Well, you didn't hear this from me, but your Dean Somerville's obviously pissed off the wrong people."

"What d'you mean?"

"He's been attacked, hasn't he?"

Zoe frowned. "Attacked? Who by? Is he badly hurt?"

"We don't know, and yes, but he'll live. Wakefield Prison's not the sort of place you want to make enemies, DI Finch."

"Thank you," Zoe said, and Yasmin Morgan ended the call.

Dean Somerville had been running brothels staffed with women who'd been trafficked into the country by Myron Carter. It was Somerville's payments to Carter's company that might hold the key to finally pinning the man down.

And now Dean Somerville had been attacked.

It was always possible he'd made an enemy inside, but Zoe couldn't help wondering if he'd been attacked to send a message, or make sure he didn't talk. Wakefield Prison might not be the sort of place you'd want to make enemies, but

Myron Carter wasn't the sort of man to take threats against his liberty lightly.

Either way, Fiona Kendrick would need to know about it.

CHAPTER NINETEEN

AARON MADE it to Boot without incident, if slowly. In other circumstances he might have stopped and taken in the beauty of the place, the way it crouched in the shadow of the mightiest fells, the old narrow bridge over the beck. He'd been here before, of course. But never after it had snowed.

After Boot, things got harder. Twice Aaron found himself reversing and stopping to consult a sign. His satnav refused to accept the location he was heading for even existed, and his mobile signal had died long before he reached Boot. Beautiful it might have been, but the weather made everything harder.

He finally reached the King George's Dining Rooms an hour and a half after setting out, less impressed by the landscape than he had been, and in no mood to be messed around. If he hadn't been in his Volvo, Aaron might have turned back. At least the car park had been salted and swept clear of snow and ice.

The place wouldn't be open for another couple of hours,

but there were a handful of cars in the car park. He pushed at the main door, and it opened.

"Hello?" he called.

Nothing.

The building was low, made of stone and glass, a surprisingly modern style given the location, projecting a sort of laid-back coolness. Aaron stepped inside, onto a rug, where he stamped his feet before venturing onto the thick, pale blue carpet that led to an unoccupied reception desk. There was an open door leading to a bar on the right, and beyond that, he could see dark wood panelling and the crisp white of table linen.

"Hello?" he called again. He could hear voices to his left. There was another door, and again, it opened when he pushed it. The voices were loud – chatting, informing, ordering. Loud, but controlled.

"Hello?" He took another four steps, turned a corner, and there was the kitchen.

It was full of people, although given how much gleaming space there was between them, maybe 'full' wasn't the right word. Ten people, maybe twelve, all busy and then all stopping, looking up, and staring at him.

"I'm sorry," said a woman. She was wearing the same white as the rest of them, the same apron over the top, but her double-breasted jacket was monogrammed, the letters 'TH' embroidered in a repeating pattern along the lapels. "We're not open yet. Do you have a reservation?"

"I'm not a diner," Aaron replied.

The other chefs got back to work, and the one who'd addressed him narrowed her eyes to a cold stare.

"Who are you, then, and what the fuck are you doing in

my kitchen?" A scar ran down one of her cheeks, an inch from her left eye and down her jawbone.

Being a chef was probably more dangerous than being a copper.

"My name's Aaron Keyes," he said. He hadn't moved from the entrance to the kitchen, and with the rest of the chefs now talking amongst themselves again, he had to shout to make himself heard. "I'm a detective sergeant with Cumbria CID."

The woman nodded. She spoke quietly to the nearest man, then stepped away from the work surface and approached him.

"What do you want, DS Keyes?"

"We're looking into a serious crime involving one of your former members of staff, Ms..."

"Harding. Theodora Harding. I'm the head chef here. Did you say former staff?"

Aaron nodded. Theodora Harding wasn't a big woman – he was nearly a foot taller, he reckoned – but there was something about her presence that made him want to take a step back.

He forced himself to stay put.

"Josh McKenzie," he said.

Her face shifted at the name, a tiny curl of the lip, before she went back to staring at him.

"Josh McKenzie hasn't worked here for a couple of years, DS Keyes. Meanwhile, we're prepping for tonight's service and you're getting in the way."

"I can—"

"You can fuck off."

"Hang on," Aaron said. She'd stepped even closer, and he

could feel her breath, could smell mint and spices. "I just want to—"

"Have you got a warrant?"

"No, but—"

"And do we *have* to talk to you?"

"You're not legally obliged, but a man's dead, Ms Harding, and I—"

"Who's dead? Is it McKenzie?"

"Yes." He waited for her reaction.

"No great loss," she said, then turned and walked back to her station. She spoke again to the man she'd left there, then looked back up at Aaron.

"If you wouldn't mind fucking off, DS Keyes, I'd be most grateful," she called, and the sound of quiet laughter bubbled up through the room's conversations.

He turned and walked away, but not before he heard Theodora Harding say something about "Josh fucking McKenzie."

Chefs were a tough bunch. He knew that already. And if they were preparing service at a place like this, they wouldn't want to be distracted. He could see that.

But as he walked back out into the snow that had started up again and across the car park, Aaron couldn't help thinking that Theodora Harding was hiding something.

CHAPTER TWENTY

Fiona's assistant, Luke, stood in the corridor outside her office, silent as the enormous plant positioned outside her door to block any view of what was happening inside.

"Is she alone?" Zoe asked.

Luke nodded, then gave a pained expression. Fiona was alone, then, but not in a good mood.

"Sit down," Fiona told her as soon as she went in. This time, there was no hovering by the window. Fiona was sitting in her chair opposite Zoe, poring over a set of papers on her desk. There was a logo on the topmost sheet that Zoe thought she recognised, even upside down, but then Fiona looked up, followed the direction of Zoe's eyes, and turned the sheet over.

"What's up then, Zoe? You making progress?"

"I think so. There's multiple angles at the moment, so I..."

Fiona waved a hand dismissively. "Don't give me the details," she said. "Not yet."

Zoe nodded. "OK. We're looking into whether there's any connection with Carrie Wright, the woman who—"

"I know who Carrie Wright is, Zoe. Are there so many bent cops around you think I'd forget one who actually worked at this station?"

"Sorry," Zoe said. Luke had been right. There was definitely something wrong with the super.

"And you think there might be a link between your murder victim and Carrie Wright?"

"It's just one angle. I'll—"

"OK. I trust you to tell me if I need to know. Is that what you wanted to talk about?"

"No. I thought you should know that I've just heard there's been an incident involving Dean Somerville."

"Somerville? Isn't he inside?"

"Yes, Wakefield. He's been attacked. Badly hurt, but not dead. They don't know who did it and I doubt they'll make much effort to follow it up. They're assuming he's made enemies inside."

"Isn't that the most likely scenario?"

Zoe tugged at a fingernail. "Maybe. But I think there's a good chance it's someone from outside looking to make sure he doesn't talk."

"By outside, you mean..." Fiona tilted her head, as if pointing north.

North, and the Port of Workington, give or take ten miles and a few degrees.

"Yes," said Zoe.

There was a moment's silence before Fiona spoke again.

"Do you think this... this incident at Wakefield involves anyone at the Hub?"

Zoe pondered the question. "Unlikely."

The relief in Fiona's eyes was immediate and obvious.

CHAPTER TWENTY

"Tell me," she said, without missing a beat. "Are you still in touch with that journalist chap?"

"Jake?"

"That's it. Jake Frimpton."

Fiona watched her, waiting for a response. Why did the super want to know about Jake Frimpton?

"Yes," Zoe said. "I'm seeing him this evening, as it happens."

"Right." Fiona nodded, twice, and looked back down at the papers on her desk.

"Is there anything I need to know, Fiona?" Zoe asked.

"No. Nothing at all. Just keep me up to speed."

Zoe stood. Fiona was still looking down at the papers on her desk, frowning at them.

There was definitely something going on with the super. But whatever it was, it would have to wait. Zoe had a long drive ahead of her.

CHAPTER TWENTY-ONE

THE KING GEORGE'S Dining Rooms.

It had taken a few minutes for the name to sink in, and where Nina had heard it before. It was a famous place, of course. Everyone knew it. But it wasn't the sort of place you actually *went* to. No one Nina knew had eaten there. No one could afford to.

It was as she was following Tom back along the corridors and up the stairs that she remembered someone who had.

Huz had. The last time they'd worked together, when Jason Knight had been chucked out of a window by his wife. Huz had turned up late, wearing Armani, straight from an evening at the King George's, and it was yet another example of something obvious, something she'd missed. Because no one she knew could afford to eat at the King George's Dining Rooms.

Unless they were up to something, and it was far too late to do anything about that now.

"Fuck's sake, Tom," she called. "You've got to chill out."

He didn't even pause, moving up the stairs like they were

hardly there. He hadn't said where he was going, but she'd heard Leo's words, the same as Tom had. *Might be hiding out in her room.* Nina moved left, straight into an empty lift, and was standing outside room 535 a minute later, when Tom appeared from the top of the stairwell.

Tom ignored her, banging on the door and shouting, "Kate?" as he did so.

Nothing.

"He might be wrong, you know," Nina said. Tom frowned at her. "Leo. The barman. Kate might not be here."

"We need to speak to her," Tom told her.

Well, that's obvious.

"No," he went on, reading her expression. "I mean, we need to speak to her before someone else does. They all know by now."

"Who all knows? *What* do they all know?"

"They all know her boyfriend's dead. He might have been an arsehole, but he was still her boyfriend, and I don't think she should hear it from someone like Peter Raymond. Or Keisha."

Oh.

"Good point," Nina said.

Tom banged on the door again, then stopped.

Had there been a noise?

The two of them stood, holding their breath, straining to hear something against the silence.

"Kate?" Tom called quieter. Gentler.

"Go away," said a small voice from the other side of the door.

Nina tried to picture the woman inside. Blonde, Tom had said. It sounded like she'd been crying. She might not know her boyfriend was dead, but she knew he'd disappeared.

"Kate, it's Tom Willis. From Cumbria CID. Do you remember me?"

There was nothing for a moment, and then a quiet, "Yes."

"Can we speak to you?"

Again, a short silence, followed by the sound of a chain and the turning of a lock.

The door opened. Just a crack. Nina could see the corner of a bed, the edge of a skirt on the bed, a fragment of face. The expression on that face surprised her.

Kate didn't look like she'd been crying. She didn't look sad.

She looked angry.

"What do you want?" she said.

"I just want to talk to you," Tom replied, pulling gently at the door. It didn't move. The noise they'd heard, that hadn't been Kate taking the chain off. It had been the reverse.

"I don't want to talk to anyone."

"Is it—"

"Yes, it bloody well is. Since everyone seems to know my business, I don't see why you lot shouldn't too. Yeah, you too," Kate added, looking past Tom to Nina, almost snarling. "It's Josh bloody McKenzie. Bastard's walked out on me, hasn't he?"

"Hey," said Tom.

"I'm not interested," Kate added, and slammed the door.

"Come on," Tom called, tapping gently on the door.

Nina tapped a foot. *This was a waste of time.*

"Kate," he said. "Look, I know it's hard. When people lie to you. When they let you down."

"What the fuck would you know about it?"

CHAPTER TWENTY-ONE

"Everyone has someone, Kate. Usually, people hide it. But everyone has someone they've trusted, someone who's turned out not to be the person they thought they were. It's not just you."

Nina tried to work out who it was for her. There had been men, certainly, but no one she'd committed herself to. There'd been Huz, too, but it wasn't like they'd been good friends.

The door opened.

"What do you know about it?" said Kate. The chain was still on, but Nina could see her face again, and the question seemed genuine.

Tom shrugged. "Everyone's different. But I think I know what it's like. When you think you know someone, and it turns out you don't."

"I don't know what to do," said Kate. Her face withdrew from the gap, and the next thing Nina heard was the sound of the chain being removed.

"Come in," Kate said.

CHAPTER TWENTY-TWO

THE CLOSER ZOE got to the prison, the more her hands shook. She took a deep breath and forced herself to relax. The snow hadn't fallen so thickly elsewhere, had hardly fallen at all around Durham. If you lived around here, you wouldn't know what things were like in Cumbria.

But then, if you lived around here, you'd have your own problems. Everywhere did.

She gave her ID to the guard at the desk, handed in her phone, and waited to be processed. She was shown into the same room as last time, the same deal with the cameras, the sound muted, the guards watching from outside the room.

"What is it?" asked Carrie as soon as they'd both sat down. "Why are you here?"

"You wanted to see me," Zoe reminded her.

"Not now. Next week, I thought. What's happened? Is it Peter?"

"Peter's fine," Zoe told her. She'd called Carrie's soon-to-be ex-husband as she drove, not so much to enquire after his

CHAPTER TWENTY-TWO

health as to ask if he'd ever come across the name Josh McKenzie.

He hadn't.

"Look, there's been a development. It might be related to the blackmail. The people who threatened you, and Peter. We think we've identified one of them."

Carrie shook her head.

Zoe ploughed on. "I just want—"

"I'm not giving you names. Look, I know I'm not safe. And I know Peter doesn't want anything to do with me. But I can't—"

"Josh McKenzie is dead," said Zoe.

Carrie's mouth fell open. She stared at Zoe.

"Josh McKenzie. Chef at the Bassenthwaite Manor Hotel, someone we believe to have been involved in blackmailing members of the public, and possibly police officers. He held onto footage from the hotel. The bar, but probably other places too. I think he had footage of you and whoever it was you were with." Zoe watched Carrie's face for a reaction. "I think McKenzie's the one who blackmailed you."

"Dead?" said Carrie.

Zoe nodded.

"You're sure?"

"I've seen the body," Zoe assured her. "He's dead."

Carrie sat back in her chair and closed her eyes. Zoe could almost see the tension leaving the woman as she exhaled.

"He's dead," Carrie said. "That fucker's dead, then."

"So, it was him?" Zoe asked. "Josh McKenzie?"

Carrie opened her eyes and nodded. "You were right, what you said, just now. There was... It was just one night. Hen do, for a friend. Had too many drinks, things went a bit too far, next thing I knew, I was in bed with this bloke. He was perfectly nice about it all. Actually apologised."

"Who was he? Was he involved?"

Carrie shook her head and blushed again. "I don't think so. I don't even remember his name. He was there on some work thing. Whole gang of fit blokes. Mostly blokes, anyway. Everyone was drunk. It was ages ago. I went home and tried to forget about it."

Zoe waited.

"And then Josh McKenzie called," Carrie said. "I'd never met him. Never heard of him. Told me he was calling from the hotel and there was something he needed me to see. Then he sent me a video."

Zoe didn't want to ask, but Carrie told her anyway. "Not from the room. Bar, and the corridor. But me and... Me and this bloke, we were all over each other. You didn't have to be a genius to know what was gonna happen when we got into his room."

"Then what happened?"

"Josh called me back. Told me he knew who I was, knew what I could do for him and his friends, and if I did what they wanted, he'd hold on to the video and make sure no one saw it. Said he'd make sure Peter didn't see it. Used his name. That was when I got really scared."

"What did he have you doing?"

"Drugs. You know how it worked, DI Finch."

"You tell me."

"He'd tell me where I could bust a dealer. Always knew how much they'd have on them, but I had to do it right when he said, before they'd sold it or hidden it. Number of times I had to change shift at the last minute for those bastards. Couldn't believe no one figured it out. Once I had the drugs,

I'd pretend there was nothing there, and then I'd arrange a drop with Huz, and he'd take it from there."

"That was it, then? You did the busts, all of them? And passed everything onto Huz?"

Carrie shook her head. "Sometimes Josh already had the drugs. He'd call me with a location, and I'd go and pick up a bag, pass it to Huz, same from there."

"A drop? So Josh wasn't there?"

Carrie shook her head. "He was careful like that. Car parks, places where the light was bad. Bags under benches, that sort of thing."

"So you never actually saw him personally?"

Carrie stared at her.

"I did, actually. Once. When I decided I had to get out, before they told me they'd kill Peter. I turned up early and watched. Saw him drop the bag and walk away."

Zoe reached into her pocket and pulled out the folded photograph she'd printed earlier from the system. Josh McKenzie's mugshot from his last arrest. She smoothed it out and placed it on the table.

"Yeah, that's him," said Carrie. "He's definitely dead, yeah? You're not pulling something?"

"He's dead," Zoe said. "He's absolutely dead."

A smile formed on Carrie's face. "Good. Best thing that could have happened to him."

CHAPTER TWENTY-THREE

KATE SAT on her bed beside a pile of clothes. The room was sparsely furnished: a small double bed, a wardrobe, a desk, a chair, also piled high with clothes, and a tiny bathroom attached. It was smaller than Tom had suspected, but no doubt the paying guests experienced something very different. She'd agreed to them recording the conversation, although she'd been mystified as to why.

She wouldn't be mystified for long.

Nina gave Tom a small nod, but he didn't need her direction. He'd talked them into the room, hadn't he? He'd remembered how it had felt when the boss had told him Harriett was PSD, the sense of betrayal, of being lied to by someone you trusted. He'd thrown all that into what he'd said to Kate, and it had worked.

But the boss was wrong. Harriett wasn't PSD. She couldn't be.

"There's something I need..." he began, but Kate started to cry. She was shaking, too, and pale. Nina nodded at him, and he approached the bed, knelt down in front of her, and looked into her face.

He felt ridiculous.

"Kate," he said.

She sniffed, tried to smile. "I'm sorry," she said. "You wanted to talk to me."

"There's no easy way to tell you this, Kate. But I'm afraid Josh is dead, and we're treating his death as suspicious."

It took twenty minutes to calm her. Twenty minutes, with him sitting on one side of her, Nina on the other. They took turns grabbing a handful of toilet roll for her, uttering soothing words in low voices, trying to return her to a state where she might be able to talk.

"Is there someone you'd like us to call?" Tom asked when he thought she was finally capable of understanding the question.

She shook her head. "No," she whispered, looking down at her feet. "No, thank you." A tiny laugh. "I'm sorry. You must think..."

"It's OK," Nina told her. "I know it's a shock."

"People didn't like Josh, you know?" Kate said, her gaze fixed on her feet. "But they didn't know him. Not like I did."

"It's OK," Nina repeated.

"He could be difficult. I'm sure people have told you that."

Tom opened his mouth to agree, then let Kate continue.

"But he wasn't always like that. We used to..."

She looked up at Nina, then Tom, a weak smile on her face.

"Used to what?" asked Nina.

"We used to take a boat out. On the lake." Kate pointed towards the window.

Nina shivered. It was cold out there.

"Just the two of us. At night. It was... romantic." Kate shook her head and looked down again, wiping her eyes.

"Kate," said Nina, "I'm so sorry this has happened. But our job is to find out what happened to Josh, and we're hoping you might be able to help us."

"Me?" Kate looked up at Nina. "Why me?"

"Because you knew him better than anyone else. We understand he disappeared on Thursday night. Is that right?"

Kate frowned, and closed her eyes, then nodded.

"He... He got a call. From his mate. Must have been about six in the evening."

"This was Thursday?" Tom asked.

A nod. "He seemed scared. When he got off the phone, he told me someone was looking into things, and people might be talking."

"What did he mean by that?"

"No idea." She smiled weakly. "I didn't know what he was talking about. And then he said he had to get away." Her brow furrowed. "'I need to get away.'"

Kate looked back down. For a short while, she'd seemed calmer, but now she was shaking again. Tom looked questioningly at Nina, who was sitting next to Kate on the bed, stroking her shoulder. They stayed like that for a minute or two, Kate crying again, as the shaking eased off, and she muttered the words again and again under her breath.

I need to get away. I need to get away.

"I'm sorry," she said eventually. "It was all... It's so awful, isn't it? It's even worse than I thought. I was so upset. But he was really scared, and then he just grabbed a few things from here, a few from his own room, and took off in his car. He

CHAPTER TWENTY-THREE

was gone by quarter past. Didn't even take all his stuff. Look."

She stood and took two steps to the wardrobe. Inside, clothes were thrown over hangers, with no obvious order. "Here," she said, pulling out a suit. "This is his. And a shirt. And he's left his best shoes. I don't know what he was thinking."

"Did you ask him?" asked Tom.

"Yes. But he was in such a panic. I'd never seen him like that. He was always so in control. I'm sorry."

"It's OK," he told her. "Now, this friend, the one who called Josh, do you know who that was?"

She shook her head. "He just looked at his phone and said, 'it's my mate,' and then he answered. I think it was a male voice, but I'm not even sure of that."

Tom met Nina's eye, and knew they were both thinking the same thing.

Was Josh's friend another copper?

"Do you know Josh's friends?" Nina asked. "From outside the hotel?"

Kate shook her head. "He's... He goes to the darts club, at the Bothwell Inn."

Tom and Nina exchanged looks. The Bothwell Inn sat alone on a stretch of road between Bassenthwaite and Cockermouth and was known for fights, drugs, and drunk drivers. They'd both spent more time than they'd wanted to at the Bothwell Inn, back in their Uniform days.

"Now, Kate, I've got to ask you this, for the record, but please don't take it the wrong way. Can you tell me, since Josh left, have you heard from him or seen him at all?"

"No," Kate said, a sob catching in her throat. "No," she repeated after a moment.

CHAPTER TWENTY-FOUR

Zoe sat in her car, staring at her phone. She could feel eyes boring into her. She knew they knew who she was, who she'd been to see, and why. She'd felt the same thing last time, but now there was something different in it. Something more dangerous.

It wasn't until she'd recovered her phone and was playing back her messages that she realised what that thing was.

The first message was from Ryan Tobin, telling her to call him back.

It was bad enough getting orders from Fiona Kendrick. Being told what to do by a sneaky little bastard like Tobin would have been a step too far, if it wasn't for the fact that Tobin could help her. As long as she helped him.

It was the next message that triggered it. It was from Nina, explaining that they'd spoken to Kate Bellamy, McKenzie's girlfriend. McKenzie had disappeared on Thursday, having received a call from a friend, but Kate didn't know who that friend was or what they'd said. "Just that

CHAPTER TWENTY-FOUR

someone was looking into things, and people might be talking."

Zoe listened to the rest of the message, then played it back.

Someone was looking into things, and people might be talking.

Josh McKenzie had heard from his friend last Thursday. Nearly a week ago, now. Two days earlier, on the Tuesday, Zoe had received a call from His Majesty's Prison Service.

She couldn't remember who she'd spoken to. A man. Not Yasmin Morgan, the woman from earlier. This man had informed her that her request to visit Carrie Wright had been approved.

Someone was looking into things, and people might be talking.

She headed west towards Cumbria, still turning it over in her head. This was why Josh had run, possibly why he'd been killed. Someone knew Carrie was about to talk to Zoe. Someone knew Carrie might be about to reveal Josh's name.

She phoned Aaron.

"Boss?" he said. "I can hardly hear you."

"Yeah, I'm in the car."

"Me too. Just been to the King George's Dining Rooms."

"Anything useful?"

"Nothing, except they didn't want to talk to me, which might be."

She smiled. Aaron's suspicious nature sometimes got the better of him, but he could usually tell between the general wariness of the police, and something more sinister.

"Can you do me a favour and set up a briefing? Get Nina and Tom on. They're still at the hotel, but I want all four of us on the line together. Ten minutes, if you can?"

"Got it, boss. I'll be in the clear by then."

She hoped so. The line was awful.

The next call she made was to Ryan Tobin. For once, he answered immediately.

"It's Kev," he said, without preamble.

"What?"

"My mate, Kevin Downes. He's missing."

"Right. Have you reported—"

"Done all that. No one seems to care. You lot, you don't really waste your time on the likes of us."

Zoe slowed for a red light and tried not to let her frustration show in her voice.

"Where's he gone missing from?"

"He's been over at Elterwater. They're building a fucking theme park there, DI Finch. There's a protest camp, a whole bunch of them who aren't happy about it, and it turns out he fucked off weeks ago and no one's seen him since."

"Is he—"

"No. I mean, yeah, he wanders about a bit, but we keep in touch, me and him. But I can't get hold of him."

"And the other protestors?"

"They're like you lot. Think he's just popped off somewhere else. But I'd have heard from him if he had."

The lights turned green. As Zoe eased out onto a dual carriageway, a thought occurred to her.

"Sinead Conway," she said. "You asked me about her a few months back, didn't you?"

"Yeah."

"This theme park. It's one of her developments?"

"Yeah. Kev was asking. Didn't trust her. Thought I'd pick your brain."

CHAPTER TWENTY-FOUR

"And now he's disappeared?"

"Exactly. And I want you to find him for me."

Zoe took a moment to compose her response. "Look, the local police will be looking into it."

"The local police aren't taking it seriously."

"Fine. I'll get one of my team to look into it. I can't promise anything. And Ryan?"

"Yes?"

"I expect something in return."

For months, she'd been trying to get information about the Myron Carter company Ryan had previously worked for. This might be her opportunity.

And wasn't Aaron from Elterwater? He'd have contacts with the local police. Maybe Zoe's luck was finally turning.

Her last call was to Carl. He needed to know about Carrie. Josh McKenzie. All of it. If Carl was at the Hub, she'd catch up with him there, but if not, she'd have to do it over the phone.

He answered immediately. "Sorry, love," he said. "I'm busy right now. Can we speak later?"

"I'll call you," she said, biting back her frustration. It wasn't like Carl was sitting around doing nothing, after all. And it had been a good day, so far. They'd started off with nothing. They hadn't even known who the dead man was.

It wasn't even the end of the working day, and they had an ID, a criminal history, a link to Carrie Wright, and possibly even a motive.

All they needed now was a suspect.

CHAPTER TWENTY-FIVE

BY THE TIME Aaron had the call set up, more than ten minutes had passed, but at least the signal was clear.

"I've just met with Carrie Wright," said the boss. "She confirms that Josh McKenzie was the one blackmailing her. He had footage of her, at Bassenthwaite Manor. And there's something else. An idea I want to run past you all."

There was silence. Aaron spotted a dip in the road ahead and pulled over. The last thing he wanted was to lose the signal.

"I heard your message, Nina. For Aaron's benefit, can you repeat what Kate said to you?"

"Sure." Nina's voice was muffled, at first, then clearer. She and Tom were sharing a phone somewhere in the hotel. "She said Josh got a call around six last Thursday. Panicked, said he had to get out, packed a few things, and disappeared. She hasn't heard from him since."

"What did she say about this call, his response to it? I want to hear the words she used."

CHAPTER TWENTY-FIVE

Tom's voice came on the line. "He said, 'I need to get away.' She kept repeating that."

"What about the call, though? What had he heard?"

"Oh, yeah." Nina again. "That was, 'someone was looking into things, and people might be talking.'"

"Thursday, you say?" Aaron asked.

"That's right, Sarge."

"And I take it we don't know who the caller was?" the boss asked.

"Sorry. Male voice. That's all Kate could tell us. Hopefully the phone records will be more useful."

Even though he couldn't see her, Aaron could tell where the boss's thoughts were going. He waited for her to say it.

"As I mentioned," she said, "I've just been talking to Carrie Wright. Now he's safely dead, she's named Josh."

"You believe her?" asked Nina.

A pause. "Yeah, I do. And the first appointment I had with her was confirmed last Tuesday. Two days before Josh McKenzie got this mysterious call."

"Shit," said Nina. She'd got it, too.

A moment later, Tom said, "Oh, right."

Aaron thought he might as well spell it out. "So we're thinking that the someone who was looking into things is the DI, and the people who might be talking is Carrie Wright, and the person they might talk about is Josh McKenzie. Josh legs it before he gets pulled in. Someone else gets to Josh, possibly to make sure he doesn't become the next person naming names."

"Nicely put, Aaron," said DI Finch. "OK. I'm heading back to the Hub."

"Me too," Aaron added. "I've been to the King George's, where I was not-so-gently told to fuck off."

He heard Nina sniggering.

"We've still got some people to speak to here," Tom said. "And we need to get hold of the CCTV footage from the night Josh did his runner. But we should be back in a couple of hours."

"Good. I'll see you all later," said the boss. "Aaron, do you mind staying on the line?"

He waited for Nina and Tom to leave the call.

"Everything OK, boss?" he asked.

"Yes. But I need a favour. I've heard from Ryan Tobin."

"Oh." He sat up, suddenly interested.

"His friend's gone missing. Man called Kevin Downes. Ryan's worried no one's taking it seriously."

"Whitehaven?"

"No. That's why I wanted to speak to you."

Aaron had a sense of what the boss was about to say, and he could feel his heart sinking.

"He's been protesting one of Sinead Conway's new developments. Over at Elterwater. Your old neck of the woods. I was wondering whether you might be able to have a word with someone there. Maybe push things along."

Aaron closed his eyes and saw them again, Jasmine Woolley and Isaac Bateman. The sneers. The shaking heads. The *country cops*.

"I'll do what I can, boss," he told her. "But they don't like me very much over there."

"I can hardly believe that, Aaron," she said, and ended the call.

No sooner had Aaron started driving than his phone rang. He assumed it would be the boss again.

"Hello?" said a voice. Not the boss. Aaron slowed and glanced at the screen. He didn't recognise the number.

CHAPTER TWENTY-FIVE

"This is DS Keyes, Cumbria CID. Who's this?"

"It's Sally Peters? You called me, earlier?"

The woman sounded nervous. Aaron pulled over again to continue the conversation.

"Thanks for calling back," he said. It had started to snow heavily, his headlights picking out waves of white against the darkness. "I don't know if you remember, but we spoke—"

"I remember you, DS Keyes. You called me a few months ago, didn't you? Wanted to ask about my Ellis."

"That's right. And I'm sorry to bother you again, but a name has come up in connection with a separate investigation, and I was wondering if it might ring any bells. Josh McKenzie."

There was a short pause.

"Sorry," she said. "Never heard of him."

"You're sure?"

"Sure as I can be."

"How about the Bassenthwaite Manor Hotel?"

"Well, I've heard of it. Never been there, mind."

Aaron thanked her and ended the call.

Damn. Sally Peters didn't know a thing, but that didn't change the facts: her husband had been blackmailed. And there was no way of knowing whether the person who'd blackmailed him was McKenzie or someone else entirely.

But Aaron couldn't stop his thoughts returning to McKenzie. He'd blackmailed Huz and Carrie, had Carrie getting hold of drugs and Huz distributing them. But how had McKenzie known who to bust? How had he known where they'd be and what they'd have on them?

McKenzie had to have someone on the inside. A drugs operation, at the wholesale end. Someone who knew when the dealers were being supplied.

And whoever was supplying those dealers, they wouldn't have been happy with McKenzie. Yes, McKenzie's partners might have had him killed, but the people whose business he was spiking had just as much reason to take him out, if not more.

Blue lights ahead.

"Shit."

He slowed, crawling along until he spotted a uniformed officer he thought he recognised, standing by the side of the road in the snow, hair and face completely white. He opened his window.

"What's happened?"

"Car's come off the road. This side of Frizington. Oh." The man peered closer, recognising him. "Are you heading for the Hub, Sarge?"

"I am."

"You'll have to go north and come back that way, I'm afraid."

Aaron thanked him and headed north. Towards Workington.

It was half past five already. About the time Bobby Silver and her friends went for evening drinks at the Henry Bessemer.

Bobby had been a friend of Victor Parlick's, the man Aaron had befriended and begun to cultivate as a potential source at Myron Carter's Workington operation. When Parlick had been killed, Aaron had almost fallen apart with the guilt of it all.

But he was over that now. He liked Bobby Silver. He liked Bobby's friends. They might work for Carter, but Carter didn't just have a criminal empire, he had a legitimate business empire to cover it, and that was the part Bobby worked in.

If anyone was distributing drugs on a large enough scale to supply all the dealers McKenzie had ripped off, chances were that person was Myron Carter. In which case, Myron Carter would have wanted McKenzie dead. Maybe Bobby and her friends would have heard Josh McKenzie's name.

The road was taking him most of the way to Workington anyway. The boss was on the other side of the country, and Nina and Tom still had things to do at the hotel.

At some point, Aaron would have to phone Isaac Bateman and ask him about the missing protestor, but there was no urgency about that.

A quick stop at the Henry Bessemer was just the thing.

CHAPTER TWENTY-SIX

It was like the flick of a switch. East side of the country, no snow. West side, down it came, like it had been waiting for Zoe to cross the line.

They'd made progress. She'd briefed Aaron about Ryan's missing friend, although he'd sounded less than keen. The next item on the agenda was speaking to Carl.

She pulled over to make the call, then hesitated, her finger over the button.

Why am I so anxious?

Carl was her partner. They didn't tell each other everything, they couldn't go that far, but they made a decent go of it. They did their separate jobs, and when those jobs ended up crossing each other, they rubbed along as best they could.

A decent go of it. Rubbed along as best they could.

Was that good enough?

Zoe shook her head and tapped the button. She started the car and moved off while the call was connecting.

"How was it?" Carl asked. So he knew why she was calling.

"I'm on my way back now. Somehow, they don't have snow on that side of the country."

Carl laughed. "There's enough for both sides over here. Did Carrie Wright have anything to say?"

"Yes. I... Look, I'd rather actually see you, if I can. I'm meeting up with Jake later. Want to tag along?"

"Sorry, Zoe. Wish I could. But there's too much on, and it's not even interesting."

"I thought your job was always interesting."

"Not today. Branthwaite's got a bee in his bonnet about admin. Expenses, timesheets, allocations. Got to be done, I suppose. Just boring. So tell me about Carrie."

"Josh McKenzie was the man who blackmailed her."

Carl exhaled, slowly. "Bloody hell," he said. "So you were right."

"No need to sound so surprised. But there's more. She says McKenzie sometimes gave her the drugs, but more often than not, he directed her to the dealers. Knew which ones to bust, when, how much they'd be carrying, where they were."

"So he must have a source somewhere like... Somewhere like the port. Someone working there or watching the place."

"Exactly. But that's not all. Nina and Tom have been talking to McKenzie's girlfriend. He got a call last Thursday. Was told that people were asking questions, and someone might be talking."

"Shit," said Carl.

"Exactly," she agreed.

"That's two days after your appointment was confirmed. Someone knew you were going to see Carrie Wright, tipped McKenzie off, and he ran. Maybe the same person killed him."

"Or maybe the people at the port."

"Shit," said Carl again. Drug dealers stealing from each other was bad for the county, but it wasn't his problem. But if Zoe's meeting with Carrie had been leaked, it was all the more likely...

"There's another copper," he said, as if reading her mind.

Zoe slowed as a pair of high headlights bore down on her, and felt the wind push against her car as a heavy goods vehicle passed.

"Who is it?" she asked.

"Who's what?"

She sighed. "Who's PSD got working undercover at the Hub, Carl?" She tried to keep the impatience from her voice.

She shouldn't be having this conversation over the phone. It would have been so much better if she'd been able to see his face.

"Boundaries," he replied.

It took all her willpower not to punch the steering wheel.

'Boundaries' was their code word. They had boundaries, areas of work the other couldn't know about, and that was what they'd agreed on: if either of them pushed too hard, all the other one had to do was say 'boundaries.'

"Fine," she said.

It wasn't fine, it was a long way from fine, and she decided right then that she'd be speaking to David Randle later. Not that Carl would know.

Randle was her former boss, a detective superintendent who'd been in the pocket of organised crime in Birmingham and gone into the Protected Persons Programme when everything had come out. And then he'd started calling her, and Carl had got nervous, and the calls had stopped.

Only they hadn't. Zoe was still talking to Randle. Still soliciting his advice, much as she hated to admit it to herself.

CHAPTER TWENTY-SIX

Because Randle knew how people like Myron Carter operated, how people like Streeting did his bidding. Randle was a terrible man who was only interested in himself, whose sole motive for bringing down Carter was that Carter's network had previous form in tracking down witnesses.

But Randle's advice was sound.

"Listen," Zoe said, "are you sure you can't make a quick drink with Jake later? There's every chance I'm going to have to go to Scotland this week. Maybe as soon as tomorrow."

"Sorry. Wish I could. I'm probably away myself later in the week. Branthwaite's sending me on a course."

"What?"

"Interviewing police officers. Apparently, there's new advice on how to do it, written by people who've never interviewed a police officer but think they're qualified to tell the rest of us how to do our jobs."

Zoe tightened her grip on the steering wheel. "OK," she said. "I'll see you at home."

CHAPTER TWENTY-SEVEN

Workington had avoided the worst of the weather, but the streets were still quiet, even for a Wednesday afternoon in January. Approaching the pub, Aaron could hear nothing but the wind. For a moment he feared the place was shut. But then someone opened a door, and music and voices spilled out onto the street.

Inside, it felt like half the town had taken shelter in the pub. If anywhere was big enough, it was probably the Henry Bessemer. Aaron stood by the door for thirty seconds, letting his eyes adjust to the dim light, and scanning the crowd for familiar faces.

There. At five foot tall, Stacey wouldn't stand out, but her earrings were enough to draw the eye. Huge, shiny things that reflected the light in a thousand different ways. He could see her now, beams shooting off in every direction as she nodded at something the bald man she was talking to had just said.

The bald man was Miles. Bobby wouldn't be far away.

Aaron spotted a gap at the bar and got himself a

lemonade before heading over to where he'd seen Stacey and Miles. Bobby was with them by the time he got there. She saw him coming and grinned, pointing him out to the others.

"Alright?" he said.

"Great," replied Bobby. Miles nodded, and Stacey gave him a wink that he might have taken the wrong way if she hadn't known he was gay. They hadn't managed to land a table, but that was OK. Aaron wasn't staying long.

They chatted for a few minutes about the weather. Bobby had her usual tin of Vaseline on the ledge beside her, applying it liberally to her lips between sips of her drink.

"Wind on the docks dries your skin up," she explained. Aaron looked over at Miles, whose face bore a worrying resemblance to a dried-up river bed. Being a copper wasn't so bad, really. Even if you did have to talk to the likes of Isaac Bateman.

In this corner of the pub, the music wasn't so loud they had to shout, which was good, because what Aaron had to say wasn't suitable for public consumption.

"Listen, any of you lot heard of a man called Josh McKenzie?" he asked.

All he got was three puzzled frowns.

"Sorry," said Stacey. "Not me."

Miles shook his head.

"Nope," said Bobby. "Why? He owe you money?"

"No." Aaron gave a rueful smile. "Someone slashed the poor bastard's throat and dumped him in Ennerdale Water."

Miles and Stacey stared at him. Bobby, who'd just knocked back a mouthful of bitter, spat it straight out again, aiming down, thankfully, so most of it landed on the floor.

"Fuck," she said. "Sorry. Didn't mean to do that. What you asking us for, Aaron?"

"I don't know." He shrugged. He hadn't expected anything from these three. But there weren't so many people in Cumbria. Sometimes, paths crossed in the unlikeliest of places.

He decided honesty was the best option.

"I'm trying to figure out if he had any connection with the port," he explained.

"He work there?" asked Miles, almost the first words he'd spoken since Aaron had arrived. "Don't recognise the name, but there's enough of us there."

Aaron shook his head. "He worked at the Bassenthwaite Manor Hotel."

Stacey released a long, low whistle, and he grinned. Bobby was shaking her head.

"Do me a favour, Aaron," she said. "Will you stop being a copper, just for a minute?"

"I'll give it a go," he said. "But since I've got to head back to the station in a bit, it won't be easy." He drained his lemonade, checked his watch, and looked at the bar. "Come on, then. My round."

It took a few minutes, and he made his way carefully back to the three of them, drinks perched on a tray, spillage kept to a minimum.

"You coming next week?" Bobby asked, taking her pint.

"What's next week?" he asked.

"Drinks. For Victor. Here. Next Thursday at two."

For Victor? He ran through the dates.

"Shit," he said. "It's a year, right?"

"One year on Thursday, yeah."

A year since Victor Parlick's body had washed up. A year since his own decline had begun. But he was better. He was definitely better. If someone had mentioned Victor a few months ago, he'd have been floored.

Now things were different. He'd liked Victor. He was sorry Victor was dead, but he couldn't spend the rest of his life blaming himself for everyone else's misfortunes.

If he could make it, he would. In the meantime, the living needed him a lot more than the dead. It was time to get back to work.

CHAPTER TWENTY-EIGHT

NINA AND TOM left Kate in her room, insisting she would be fine and agreeing to speak to them again when she was ready. They'd explained that they'd probably need to go through her room and remove Josh's possessions, but she'd been there for nearly a week since he'd left; one more night wouldn't make much difference.

Tom still seemed anxious to avoid Peter Raymond, but Nina was keen to get the CCTV footage from the night Josh had left, and head back to the Hub. Tom, by contrast, wanted to talk to every employee of the Bassenthwaite Manor Hotel.

He started at reception, where he spotted the uniformed, straggly-bearded porter heading outside and called out to stop him.

But Stuart Sullivan didn't seem to know anything, and was keen to emphasise the point.

"I don't know anything," he kept saying. He looked nervous, but people often did, when the police were on the scene.

"How well did you know Josh McKenzie?" Tom asked.

"Who? Oh, that one. Not well," said Sullivan. "You wanna talk to Kate Bellamy. She were 'is girlfriend, you know."

Sullivan had heard McKenzie was dead. Keisha's loud mouth had achieved that much, at least. But even Tom seemed to realise they were wasting their time with the porter.

Nina started to walk towards the manager's office, then she realised Tom wasn't with her. She turned to see him heading down a corridor towards a door marked KITCHENS.

"Let's see who else is about," he said.

Nina shrugged and followed.

It was probably a waste of time. Chances were, Josh McKenzie had been killed by the people he'd been working the drugs operation with, or the people they'd been ripping off, and none of those people would be hanging around the Bassenthwaite Manor Hotel. But if there was one thing Nina had learned about murder since DI Finch had turned up, it was that the more you knew about a person, the easier it was to figure out who'd killed them.

"Yeah?"

There were two men in the kitchen, a tall one with a mane of hair swept into a net, wisps escaping down his face, and a short bald one holding a long knife and looking at them like he'd just eaten a lemon with a wasp in it.

"DC Tom Willis, Cumbria CID." Tom held out his ID, and both men ignored it. "This is my colleague DC Nina Kapoor. We'd like to ask you some questions about Josh McKenzie."

"I'd like to ask Josh McKenzie some questions myself, the

lazy fucker," said the bald man, still holding the knife. His taller colleague gave a small laugh.

"You'll struggle," Nina said. "He's dead."

Neither man looked particularly shocked. If anything, they seemed disappointed.

Nina raised an eyebrow. "You don't look surprised to hear that."

"McKenzie was a prick," the bald man said. "And he wasn't even that good in the kitchen. But I was hoping he'd turn up again. Six hands are better than four, even if two of the hands are a bit shit."

"Can you tell us anything about him, though? In what way was he a prick?"

"Look." The man put his knife down and approached them. "DC Kapoor, was it?"

Nina nodded.

"I'd like to help, I really would, but we're down a sous chef, sort of, and we've got dinner to prep."

"What do you mean, sort of?"

"I mean a sous should be able to run a kitchen, or most of it. I wouldn't have trusted him to run this place. I'm Max. Head chef. This one's David." He pronounced the name with a soft 'a' and a hint of an accent. "He's the commis. He's French, but he understands everything, don't you, David?"

The taller man nodded.

"Thanks," said Nina. "We'll come back when you're quieter."

She turned out of the room, dragging a reluctant Tom with her. These people didn't know anything.

"Here."

They both turned in the direction of the voice. Leo, the

barman, was beckoning them into a side room. Tom walked towards him.

For the second time in five minutes, Nina shrugged and followed.

Leo hadn't liked McKenzie any more than Max had. "I don't want to speak ill of the dead," he said, "but that one was trouble. Difficult. And you wouldn't want to mess with him."

"Someone did," Nina pointed out.

"Yeah." Leo nodded. "Tell you what, though, whoever it was, they might have got themselves bashed up a bit. Never saw Josh without his knife bag."

"His what?" Nina asked.

"Knife bag. He had, what, half a dozen knives, something like that? For the kitchen, not stabbing people, but you never know. Kept them in this grey canvas bag he'd roll up and take everywhere with him."

Nina turned to Tom, and saw her own thoughts echoed on his face. There'd been no knife bag on the body or near it. No sign of it in Kate's room, either.

They found Keisha in Josh's room, fully suited up and going through every inch in the sort of detail that would probably keep her there all night.

"Any sign of a knife bag?" Tom asked, outside in the corridor where Keisha insisted they remain if they weren't going to suit up.

"A what?"

Nina described the knives and the bag, and Keisha shook her head.

"I'll let you know if it turns up," she said. "And yeah, I know, I haven't forgotten about the phone, but if we get what we want out of the poor fucker's room, we won't need the phone, will we?"

Nina shook her head as they walked away. Keisha had a peculiar way with words, but she wasn't wrong.

CHAPTER TWENTY-NINE

Zoe hadn't expected Nina and Tom to be back already, but when she walked past the team room she could hear them arguing about the state of Nina's car. A disagreement that had been going on since long before Zoe had known them.

She paused, then carried on walking. Nina and Tom could wait. And the call she was about to make had to be done in private.

She hadn't wanted to save Randle's number in her phone, or write it down anywhere it could be found, and she made sure she deleted his texts and their call logs. Instead, she'd memorised it. Tapping it into her phone, she felt her anxiety rise.

This was what David Randle did to her.

"Zoe! How the hell are you?"

She clenched a fist, resisting a shiver. Even when she hadn't known he was corrupt, she'd thought him insufferable.

"Fine. There's been a development."

"I didn't think you were calling to pass the time, Zoe."

There was an edge to his voice now, arrogance laced with a hint of menace. The old Randle.

"I told you about the group that was ripping off local dealers. As well as the students, we had a CSI and a copper. The CSI's dead already."

"And the copper will be if Carter gets hold of her."

"We don't know it was Carter's customers they were ripping off," Zoe shot back, but they could hardly be anyone else's. "But anyway, we've had another one turn up dead."

"Another copper?"

"Chef. But he was part of the ring. He blackmailed the copper, and the CSI, that was how they got involved."

She heard a faint snort, followed by a laugh. "And I'm sure the money had nothing to do with it."

She was filled with an urge to defend them, Huz, Carrie Wright, the very people who'd made a mockery of the police.

"Well," Randle said, "I suppose it could be someone else in the op, cleaning house. Either that, or it's Carter. I did warn you this would happen."

There were lots of things Zoe could ask, but they were all half questions. Things she knew the answers to already. Or things that only took her part of the way.

She'd called Randle for a reason. She couldn't let pride or distaste get in the way.

"Any idea what I should do next?" she asked.

"Do your job. If it was Carter, he might have screwed up, left evidence. It's unlikely, but it's all you've got for the time being. How did you get on with your forensic accountant?"

She'd told Randle about all that. She'd told him everything, from Zhang the forensic accountant, through Olivia

Bagsby's photos and Elena's return, to the non-existent evidence regarding Victor Parlick's death that she'd planted in an abandoned unit near Stella's lab.

Zhang and the photos had got them so far, but not far enough, Elena couldn't remember any more than she'd remembered months ago, and the evidence had gone up in flames almost as soon as Streeting had found out about it. Randle knew all this.

Had she told him too much?

"We've linked the trafficked women to Carter's business. But there's nothing to prove Carter knew about it. If we move in now, he'll just throw us one of his staff and say they were doing it behind his back."

"I see. Very well, Zoe. Keep me informed." The line went dead.

She stared at the phone in her hand.

Did David Randle still think he was her boss?

It rang a few seconds later. Not Randle.

"Zo," said Mo when she answered. "You OK?"

"Nice to hear your voice." If anyone could be described as the opposite of Randle, it was her old DS.

"It's not like we didn't speak this morning. Listen, I've tried, but I haven't got anywhere."

"What d'you mean?"

"I went to see Shona. McKenzie's ex-wife. She wouldn't talk to me."

"Did you tell her Josh was dead?"

"I thought I'd leave that for you. If you're still thinking..."

She shut her eyes and considered it. They'd just moved in. Carl would be off on his course, soon. The bloody cat wouldn't like it.

The bloody cat could cope.

"Yes," she said. "Assuming we don't suddenly crack this case in the next eighteen hours, how d'you feel about cooking me a nice meal tomorrow night?"

CHAPTER THIRTY

"There he is."

Leaning over Tom's shoulder, Nina jabbed a finger at the corner of the screen. Tom tapped pause and checked the timestamp and location.

"Main lobby," he said. "Ten past six. And look, he's got a little bag."

"Same bag PC Collins found in his car. But no sign of the knife bag Leo was talking about."

"No." Tom rewound the footage and played it again, following the figure's jerky progress across the reception area towards the main doors. "No sign of it here, and no sign of it in the car. Might still turn up at the scene, though."

He glanced up. Nina's lip was curled. She didn't think it was very likely. He didn't either.

"Right. Car park. Here." He'd just opened another file on his screen when DI Finch walked in.

"What are you looking at?" she asked.

"Footage of Josh McKenzie leaving the hotel." He tapped again, and the images appeared on the room's big screen.

They stood and watched the footage of McKenzie coming into view, walking fast from the direction of the hotel, glancing more than once over his shoulder. It would have been dark, but the car park was well lit and the image clearer than the ones from inside.

The three of them watched as Josh McKenzie unlocked his Peugeot, dropped his bag in the back seat, and climbed in. By the time he'd started the car and was driving away, the sarge had appeared and was watching silently along with them.

"Recap," said DI Finch.

The sarge had nothing, except the possibility that Theodora Harding knew more than she was saying. "I'd like to speak to her again, boss," he said.

The DI bit her lip and sat in silence.

"I suppose his previous work history could be relevant," she said. "But only if nothing better comes up. What about you two? You've told us about Kate Bellamy. Did you speak to anyone else?"

"Yes," Tom said. "There's the manager, for a start. We spoke to him at the start and again at the end to get this." He pointed at the screen. "CCTV for the whole of Thursday night. He's still retrieving the rest of the week, but this is what we wanted. McKenzie leaving the hotel. This is ten past six, up to quarter past. Ten to fifteen minutes after Kate says he received that call."

"How's Keisha getting on with his phone?" asked DI Finch.

Nina shook her head. "She's at the hotel, going through his room. Said she'd get to the phone after."

DI Finch nodded. "Want me to have a word with Stella?"

"It's OK," Nina said. "I can handle it."

Tom looked at her. Nina had handled a lot in her time, but Keisha Middleton had the feel of something different.

"The manager," he said. "Peter Raymond. He's a slimy one. I don't think he's going to make things easy for us."

"Do what you can, Tom."

He nodded and went on. "We also spoke to McKenzie's boss in the kitchen, who didn't like him. And Leo, the barman, who didn't like him either, and says he was always walking around with his grey canvas knife bag."

"Don't tell me," the DI said. "No sign of the knife bag."

"Exactly."

"OK. You all know where I've been, and you all know what she's said. I'm working on the assumption that someone found out I was going to see Carrie Wright and tipped McKenzie off. The fourth man."

"Fourth man?" asked Tom.

The DI counted off on her fingers. "Huz. Carrie. McKenzie. And whoever this is. Anyone see any flaws in that?"

Tom shook his head, along with Nina and the sarge. It was depressing, because it meant yet another corrupt copper, or prison officer, or someone in the prison service. But it was all too plausible.

"We've got a lot to look into," she said. "But I think the priority is to identify the fourth man."

"Boss," said Nina, "there is something else."

"Yes?"

"We asked Kate about McKenzie's friends. She didn't know them. But she said he was part of the darts club at the Bothwell Inn."

The sarge muttered something. Tom knew what he was thinking.

"Is there something I should know?" the boss said.

"It's the Bothwell," the sarge replied. "Not a nice place. Flat-roofed hellhole where the only thing the punters hate more than each other is the police."

"So you don't fancy a quiet undercover drink there?" The boss was smiling. "That could be relevant, Nina, and we'll add it to the list. But in the meantime, we've got enough angles. I'm probably going to Scotland tomorrow, I want to find out why McKenzie's ex dropped the DV charges. There could be something there. Tom?"

"Yes," he said.

"Think you can handle this Peter Raymond?"

"I can, boss."

"Good. I want you back at the hotel tomorrow. Go straight there. Aaron, you carry on looking at McKenzie's background. Are the phone records in yet?"

The sarge shook his head. "I'm expecting them tomorrow."

"Good. You work on that. Nina, you can help him. And help me, too. I want to dig into connections. Anything that links any of the people we already know to the hotel, or McKenzie, or Carrie Wright. OK?"

"Got it," said Nina.

"Good," said the boss. "I'm heading off now. We'll keep digging tomorrow. There's something there, folks. And when we find it, we'll find whoever killed Josh McKenzie."

CHAPTER THIRTY-ONE

JAKE FRIMPTON WAS WAITING for Zoe at their usual table in the Anchor Vaults, the one furthest from the door, which meant they could avoid the chill wind every time someone stepped in or out. The place was busy – a cosy pub was just what people wanted on a cold, miserable day.

He stood as she entered and pointed to the table. There were two drinks there: a lemonade and Zoe's Diet Coke.

Zoe didn't drink alcohol, which limited the choices, but was she really that predictable? Maybe she'd try something different next time.

They clinked glasses.

"How's things?" she asked.

"Good." He was smiling. There was something different about him.

"Oh," she said. "Clark Kent has finally turned into Superman, has he?"

Jake laughed. "Not sure you can compare the *Whitehaven Chronicle* to the *Daily Planet*, but yes, well done. No specs."

"You're wearing contact lenses?"

He nodded. "With deductive skills like that, I can see why Whitehaven's criminals are so afraid of you, DI Finch."

"Piss off," she said, laughing. "You're looking well, though. How's your dad?"

"Good," Jake said.

Zoe examined his face as he spoke, but it looked like he meant it.

Jake had sacrificed a promising career and a marriage when he'd moved back to Whitehaven to care for his father, a retired miner suffering from advanced dementia. But Solomon Frimpton had finally moved into specialist accommodation, and Jake seemed genuinely relaxed, for the first time in over a year since Zoe had known him.

She was pleased for him. But, with Jake, there was always something else.

"Tell me," she said. "Why would my super have mentioned your name today?"

He nodded, smile dropping. "Vicky Speares."

"Who?"

"Victoria Speares. The—"

"Yes," Zoe said. "I know. The woman who attacked Roddy."

PC Roddy Chen had been beaten half to death by an addict armed with a metal bar. He'd survived, but she hadn't, or not for long. By the time the police caught up with her, she'd choked to death on her own vomit following an overdose.

"I wanted to know what really happened to her," Jake said.

Zoe opened her mouth to argue, then changed her mind. The man who'd found Vicky Speares was PC Tel

Cummings. The same Tel Cummings who'd run away when Chen was being attacked. The same Tel Cummings who'd beaten up Ryan Tobin, years earlier, and whose name seemed to crop up whenever there was trouble.

Maybe it needed looking into. And if the police weren't doing it properly, perhaps Jake would.

"I don't just mean how she died," Jake added. "The focus is her life, not her death. A proper feature. The sort of person she was, the person she'd been before the drugs got hold of her."

"Right."

"But, yes." He nodded. "I've been asking questions about her death, too. No doubt Fiona Kendrick's heard about it."

"She doesn't like you, you know," Zoe told him.

They paused for a moment as a crowd of young women pushed their way in from the street, bringing the snow and the sound of the wind with them.

"I know," Jake told her, and grinned. "Just proves I'm doing my job right."

CHAPTER THIRTY-TWO

AARON OPENED his eyes and blinked. Serge was smiling down at him, coffee in one hand and a plate in the other.

Whatever it was, it smelled delicious.

He sat up. Toasted bagel. Smoked salmon. Poached egg. He looked up at Serge and shook his head.

"Not hungry?" asked Serge.

"Oh, I'm hungry." He kissed his husband. "What's this all for?"

The last few months, things had been good between them. The way they'd been for years, before everything had gone wrong. Even the mention of Victor Parlick last night hadn't managed to ruin the sense that life was starting to fall back into place. But Serge still had a tendency to sugarcoat bad news with food.

"Happy anniversary," Serge said.

Aaron grabbed his phone and checked the date.

Phew.

"That's not till tomorrow."

CHAPTER THIRTY-TWO

"I know. And I've got plans for you." Serge arched one eyebrow.

"What sort of plans?"

"You'll find out soon enough. Meanwhile, yesterday was your first day off light duties, and I didn't get a chance to spoil you. Now I can. Thought you could do with a decent breakfast."

Aaron wasn't keen on surprises, but he couldn't help smiling as he drove to the Hub. Whatever Serge had planned, he was looking forward to it.

The smile lasted long enough for him to log in and check his messages. The boss was reminding him to follow up on Kevin Downes. Meanwhile, Josh McKenzie's phone records had come in, and there was almost nothing of them. The banking records were there, too, and it took all of five minutes to establish there was nothing of interest there. There was a note from Nina on his desk. She'd heard from Keisha late last night. The damage to McKenzie's phone had been too extensive, the combination of water and cold wrecking any chance of salvaging data from it.

Aaron printed out the phone records. Two sheets of paper, for three months' worth of calls and texts. And without the phone itself, no record of what those texts might have been.

McKenzie must have had another phone. A burner. No chance someone could run an operation the way he had without making a lot more contact than was printed on those two sheets of paper. If another phone turned up in his room, or his car, then great. But Keisha and a bunch of PCs had been through the room and the car already. If there had been a burner, he'd got rid of it.

Starting in November, Aaron moved through the

numbers. There were only three texts, all long before McKenzie's disappearance, and all to Kate Bellamy's number.

The rest were routine calls. One to a doctor's surgery, unlikely to mean anything. Several to and from a motor mechanic, but when Aaron pulled up the records for McKenzie's Peugeot, he could see that these were all around the time of the last MOT. There were three calls to a bar in Whitehaven, and Aaron called them, too, and was surprised to find someone answering so early.

He explained why he was calling, but before he'd finished, the duty manager had cut in.

"Yeah, I remember 'im. Left his jacket 'ere. Wouldn't shut up about it. We found it, though, called 'im up, 'e comes and gets it, doesn't even leave a tip for the cleaner who'd looked after it for 'im."

"Leather thing?" Aaron asked. "Belstaff?"

"Yeah, that's it."

Another dead end. Aaron thanked the woman and moved on, checking two more calls before he reached the one that mattered. One minute past six, last Thursday evening, just when Kate had said it had come in.

Two minutes. Long enough for someone to tell him he was in trouble.

But there was no number attached to the call. Completely untraceable. Aaron wondered, briefly, why the call hadn't come through on McKenzie's burner, and then remembered that the chef had been with his girlfriend at the time. Probably didn't have the burner with him. Whoever the caller was, they'd have tried the burner, then called on his main phone.

But who *was* the caller? And what, precisely, had they

said? Get out and run? Or get out and run to a particular place, at a particular time, where they'd waited for him, slashed his throat, and dumped him in the icy water?

There was one more call on the log. It had been made by McKenzie, at two minutes to nine, last Friday. The night Susan Masters had heard a car and seen lights. Right in the middle of the window for McKenzie's murder.

The number was familiar.

Aaron picked up his phone, dialled the number, and heard the door to the team room open while it was ringing.

A moment later, it was answered. He listened for a moment, then apologised and hung up. He turned to see Nina standing behind him, looking at his screen.

"Everything OK, Sarge?" she said.

"Yes. I think so. But look at this." He took her through the call log, and the number he'd just dialled.

"Who is it, then?" she asked.

"It's the Bassenthwaite Manor Hotel," he told her. "Earlier on the night he probably died, Josh McKenzie called the direct line for the reception desk at the Bassenthwaite Manor Hotel."

CHAPTER THIRTY-THREE

ZOE'S PHONE rang when she was still a few minutes from the office. With two inches of snow on the road, more coming down, and patches of black ice where the snow hadn't landed, driving took every ounce of her concentration. She pulled over to answer.

"Ma'am," said a familiar voice. "It's PC Collins. I'm over at Ennerdale, with the team looking at the crime scene."

"OK," she replied. "Any developments?"

"Yes. And sorry, I know we were supposed to call DS Keyes, but his number's busy."

"That's fine." Zoe looked up, the road a barely visible streak in the white blanket ahead. Further away, over the fells, it looked like the cloud was starting to break up. "What have you got?"

"His wallet. Credit cards, driving licence. All soaking wet. All with the name Josh McKenzie."

"Where was it?"

"Couple of hundred yards away, on the shore. Washed

up there, by the looks of it. Like it's been chucked into the lake separately from the body."

"Any cash?"

"No, Ma'am. Just the plastic."

Josh McKenzie wouldn't have run without cash. Which meant whoever had killed him had taken it. Trying to make the whole thing look like a robbery? Whoever they were, they'd have to try harder than that.

Rob Collins was still talking.

"The keys were close by, too."

"Keys?"

"For his Peugeot, Ma'am."

She closed her eyes, tried to visualise the scene, tried to make it fit with the footage she'd seen of Josh McKenzie leaving the hotel, with what she'd heard about him.

"Any sign of a knife bag?"

"A what, Ma'am?"

"It's a bag you can roll up, for carrying knives. Grey, made of canvas. The deceased was a chef."

"Ah. No. Sorry. We'll keep an eye out."

She thanked him, disconnected, and got back on the road. A few minutes later, she pulled into the car park and headed straight for the team room. Aaron and Nina were already there, poring over two sheets of paper on Aaron's desk.

"What's this?" she asked.

"Call logs," Aaron told her. "Looks like McKenzie called the hotel reception just before nine on Friday evening."

"And no one we spoke to admitted to hearing from him after he went missing on Thursday," Nina added.

"Interesting. Show me that CCTV again, Nina. McKenzie leaving the hotel."

She watched as the footage ran on the big screen. McKenzie walking across the lobby. McKenzie in the car park.

There was nothing that matched the description they'd been given of the knife bag. And Nina hadn't seen it among the items McKenzie had left in Kate's room, either. Zoe picked up her phone, noticing a missed call from Ryan Tobin, and dialled Stella Berry.

"DI Finch," said Stella. "What can I do for you?"

"Have you still got Keisha working at the hotel?" Zoe asked.

"No." Stella's voice was hard, even for Stella. "Stupid bloody girl."

Zoe frowned. "Why? What's happened?"

"I had to pull her out. There were complaints. From staff *and* guests."

Zoe didn't want to ask. "Is she with you, then? I want to talk to her about her examination of McKenzie's room."

"I'll put her on."

Zoe heard muffled voices. Even with Stella's hand over the phone, she could pick up the anger in the CSM's voice.

"DI Finch," said Keisha a moment later, her voice normal. Bright, even. "What can I do for you?"

Zoe described the knife bag.

"Yes, DC Kapoor mentioned that yesterday. Still no sign of it, I'm afraid."

"Who's there today?"

"Caroline Deane."

"Call her, will you?" Zoe said. "Tell her to look out for it."

"Sure," Keisha replied, then killed the call.

CHAPTER THIRTY-THREE

The woman had an attitude, and with Stella in the same lab, there probably wasn't room for two of them. Hopefully Keisha would calm down a little. As long as she did her job, it didn't really matter.

CHAPTER THIRTY-FOUR

THE DARK-HAIRED WOMAN, Sarah, was behind the reception desk when Tom walked in. He'd already exchanged greetings with Stuart Sullivan outside – the porter had seemed relieved at the more civilised state of Tom's car, having been exposed to the sight of Nina's the day before.

"Morning," Tom said, smiling.

Sarah didn't return the smile. He wasn't sure he could blame her.

"Your colleagues are on the sixth floor. In…" She frowned. "In his room."

Tom started to walk away, then turned back. The woman wouldn't even say his name. Was that because he was dead? Or something else?

"Did you know Josh McKenzie?" he asked.

She nodded.

"Did you like him?"

"I didn't know him well enough to have an opinion," she

replied. "Kate liked him. I prefer to keep my distance with colleagues."

She gave a thin smile and bent down to stare at her computer. Tom turned and walked to the lifts.

He'd expected to find Keisha in Josh's room. Not Caroline Deane. And he certainly hadn't expected Harriett Barnes.

"Oh," he said, taking a step back.

What's Harriett doing here?

She'd been at the crime scene. Combing over the shoreline, examining the ground for evidence. She'd have changed by now. Shower, fresh clothes. No risk of cross-contamination.

"Hello, DC Willis," said Harriett. Caroline looked up and gave him a silent nod.

"Erm, hi," Tom replied. "Don't suppose you've found the knife bag?"

"Sorry, no," said Caroline. "Keisha mentioned it on the phone just now. We'll keep an eye out."

"Right," said Tom. "I'll be... I'll be somewhere here."

He took the stairs back down, giving himself time to think.

He'd been convinced, at first, by the boss's suggestion that Harriett was PSD. But as the months had gone by, he'd changed his mind.

She was just a good copper. A great copper. Maybe she took things a little too seriously, drew too thick a line between her personal and professional lives, the same line that had put an end to their brief relationship. But she was good at her job.

She'd be in CID soon enough, and it wouldn't be long before she'd overtake him. Nina had better look out.

But why was she here? She'd been doing the grunt work. Coordinating the grunt work, maybe, but he'd done enough of it himself to know the difference between scouring the ground and poking around someone's room.

What had changed?

The boss had been to see Carrie Wright. Carrie Wright had named Josh McKenzie as her source. PSD was suddenly interested in McKenzie's death.

And now, Harriett was here.

He was so engrossed in these thoughts that it wasn't until he heard Peter Raymond saying, "What the devil?" that he realised he'd walked straight into the manager's office without knocking.

"Sorry," he said. "I was miles away. Look, I need more CCTV."

Raymond sighed. "Of course you do. What is it now?"

Tom checked his phone, the message from DS Keyes. "Reception area. Nine o' clock, last Friday. And if you can tell me who was on reception then, according to your shift logs, that would be great."

"Stupid bloody fool," muttered Raymond, as he slowly tapped out a command on his keyboard using a single finger.

Tom didn't like confrontation, but he couldn't let that go. "I beg your pardon?"

Raymond straightened up. "Sorry. Not you, DC Willis. Josh bloody McKenzie. All this trouble."

"The man's been murdered, Mr Raymond."

"Yes, I appreciate that, and it's a shame, and I hope you catch whoever did it. But him being murdered doesn't change the fact that he wasn't the most pleasant of individuals."

"What do you mean?"

CHAPTER THIRTY-FOUR

Raymond wrinkled his nose. "Oh, nothing much. He just had... a certain attitude. A way with him. Aggressive."

Tom nodded. "Any incidents?"

"Nothing I can recall, and nothing on the files. I checked them last night, see if we had anything useful I could tell you."

Tom narrowed his eyes. *Wanted to see if there was anything you needed to delete, more like.*

"Now then." Raymond squinted at his screen. "Friday evening, you say? I'll have the CCTV shortly, but it looks like it was Kate Bellamy on shift. Would you like me to send someone for her?"

Tom declined the offer, thanked him, and said he'd stop by later for the CCTV. And no, Peter Raymond hadn't seen the knife bag.

Neither had Max, or David, when Tom walked into the kitchen two minutes later. The two chefs had more time to talk now, but not much more to say. They agreed with Leo: the dead man and his knife bag had been all but inseparable. Max reiterated his views on McKenzie's personality and culinary skills. David, whose English was excellent, agreed with his boss. Unlike Raymond, they both said there *had* been incidents, but, as David put it, "There always is, in a kitchen. As long as the blood is cleaned up later, we simply forget about it."

"Neither of you had reason to—" Tom began.

Max laughed, loud and clearly genuine. "I'm sorry," said the chef, when he'd finally recovered. His face was red, and he was panting. "No. Neither of us had reason to kill the bastard. If I'd wanted rid of him I'd have just sacked him."

David nodded along with his boss. "I did not like Josh McKenzie, and I did not respect him either. But if I were to kill everyone I did not like or respect, the world would be a much less crowded place."

Nobody seemed to have liked Josh McKenzie very much. Nobody except Kate, at least. And Kate was next on Tom's list.

CHAPTER THIRTY-FIVE

"Still nothing?" Aaron asked. Zoe waited while he listened, shaking his head, then ended the call.

"That was Tom," he told her. "No one seems to know where this knife bag is. Have you read Dr Robertson's report?"

Zoe nodded. She knew what Aaron was thinking.

"Chef's knife is a possibility for the weapon," she said. "And the victim's own knives are nowhere to be found."

Aaron was staring past Zoe into the middle distance. It was a look she recognised.

"Out with it," she said.

His gaze snapped to her. "What do you mean?"

"You've got something on your mind. You can stand there looking like you're stoned, or you can tell me what it is."

Beside them, Nina looked up, interested. Aaron gave a shame-faced grin.

"It's the raid, boss."

"Raid?"

"On the hotel. There was a raid there, nearly a year ago. Drugs warrant. Last February. Quite a big deal."

"And?"

"And they didn't find anything. It was something I was looking into, alongside the blackmail. But then the Dean Somerville case took over, and it wasn't really a priority."

Zoe sank into the spare chair.

"OK," she said. "Look into it. Find out what you can. In the meantime, I—"

There was a knock on the door, and Fiona's face appeared.

"Zoe," she said.

Zoe stood. "Ma'am."

"Mind if I have a quick word?"

The super turned and walked away. With a bewildered shrug in the direction of Aaron and Nina, Zoe stood and followed her. She'd assumed they'd be heading upstairs, to the super's office, but instead Fiona led Zoe straight to her own office.

What was going on?

Inside the office, Fiona stood aside and gestured for Zoe to take her usual seat, behind the desk. The super sat opposite her, making Zoe feel uncomfortable.

This was Zoe's space. If she wanted privacy, she could ask people to leave.

But not Fiona Kendrick.

"Any developments in your case?" asked the super. On the desk in front of her, Zoe's phone buzzed. Tobin, again.

She hit the button to ignore it and nodded. "We're making progress. We've got a line on a possible motive, and I'm heading up to Scotland later to look into another angle. Slow, but steady."

CHAPTER THIRTY-FIVE

But whatever the super wanted, it wasn't the fine detail on the McKenzie case.

Fiona sat forward, her elbows on Zoe's desk, her fingers steepled. "Victoria Speares," she said. She'd narrowed her eyes and was looking directly at Zoe.

"What about her?"

"You don't happen to know anything about what happened to her, do you?"

"No," Zoe said, wondering if her confusion was obvious. "I mean, I was there in your office when Alan Markin came in and said they'd found her and she was dead."

"And that's all?"

This had to be about Jake Frimpton. But if Fiona wanted to know what Jake was planning, she'd have to ask the right questions.

And Zoe wouldn't answer them.

"I think so, yes," Zoe said. "She was found by Tel Cummings. OD. Choked on her own vomit."

Fiona frowned. "Choked on her own vomit?"

"That's what I understand."

"I don't remember Alan saying anything about that." Fiona was leaning even further forward now, her face uncomfortably close to Zoe's. And she was right. That had been later. Months later.

"I asked him later. I was just interested in what had happened."

"Why?"

This had gone on long enough. Did Fiona think she'd been leaking information to the press?

"I was interested, Fiona, because a woman who was the subject of a police investigation had died in unnatural circumstances. A woman who'd attacked and seriously injured one of our officers and was found by another one. It would have been unusual *not* to be interested. Is there anything else?"

"No." Fiona stood. "I hope your trip to Scotland goes well, Zoe." She walked to the door.

"Is everything OK?" Zoe asked.

Fiona ignored the question. "Thank you," she said, and walked out.

CHAPTER THIRTY-SIX

THE BASSENTHWAITE MANOR HOTEL wasn't enormous, but already Tom felt like he'd walked miles. He took the lift back up to the fifth floor, and Kate answered her door immediately.

"Oh," she said. "Hello."

"Hi." He smiled at her, and she gave a sort of smile back. "Mind if I come in?"

"Be my guest."

She stood aside, and he walked in. The clothes had been cleared from the bed and the chair, and the room looked neater. Larger, too.

"Mind if I record?"

"Sure." She sat on the bed.

He set the app running and put his phone on the desk. He sat down in the chair. "You said yesterday you hadn't heard from Josh since he left."

Kate looked down. "That's right."

"Are you sure? We know Josh called the hotel on Friday evening, around nine. We know the call came through directly to reception, and we know you were on shift at the time. I've asked Peter Raymond for CCTV footage of the reception area for Friday evening, but if there's anything you want to—"

"Yes," she said. "Fine. Yes. I did speak to him."

"Good."

"I'm sorry. I don't know why I lied. I won't go to prison for it, will I?"

He shook his head. "No, of course not. If you can just..."

Kate had wrapped her arms around herself and was shaking.

"It's OK," he said, and waited for her to calm down. He wanted more than anything to reach across, to touch her shoulder, but he knew he couldn't. So he waited.

"I'm sorry," she repeated, once the tears had subsided. "I just... I felt so terrible. I was..."

"You were what?"

"I was upset with him. He'd run off like that, and then he called, and I thought he was going to tell me where he was. I thought he was about to come back."

"But he didn't say anything like that?"

She shook her head. "He told me I was an idiot."

"Why?" Tom asked. "Why would he say that?"

The tears came, again. Once more, he waited.

"Because of you," she said, eventually.

"Me?"

"Remember when you came? Back in May?"

"Of course."

"I gave you that recording. The man."

"Laurence Eversholt. What about it?"

"Josh said he knew. He knew I'd given it to you. He said I

shouldn't have spoken to you. To the police. I'd got him in trouble. I was stupid."

"Why?"

"I don't know." She looked down at the bed, shaking her head. "But that was it, I swear it. He said I was an idiot, and he hung up, and that really was the last I heard from him."

"OK."

Kate frowned. "You don't believe me?"

"I do, Kate. But we'll have to search your room, I'm afraid. We're searching everywhere closely connected to Josh. I hope you can—"

"That's fine," she said, as there was a knock on the door.

"Hello?" said a voice. "Is DC Willis in there?"

Tom went to the door and opened it. Peter Raymond was there, holding a USB stick, and looking disapprovingly into the room.

"The footage you asked for," he said.

Tom took it. "Thanks. As it happens, I'm not sure we need it now, but—"

"I beg your pardon?" said Raymond.

"I'm sure it'll be useful. For corroboration purposes, if nothing else."

"This is not good enough, young man. I will be speaking to—"

For once, Tom's fear of confrontation took a back seat.

"You go ahead and speak to whoever you like, Mr Raymond. A man has died, and it's my job to find out how he died. A member of *your* staff, Mr Raymond. A man who worked for *you*." Tom realised he was jabbing his finger in Raymond's direction, and lowered his hand. "Now, if you're willing to cooperate, great, but don't expect gushing congratulations for acting like a human being. If you're not, we'll have to come back with warrants. Either way, we'll get what we need."

Raymond took a step back. "Yes, but—"

"Do you understand me?"

"Yes," Raymond said, then turned and stalked away.

When Tom turned back, Kate was staring at him from the bed, her expression part surprise, part glee.

He dropped into the chair.

"People don't usually talk that way to Mr Raymond," Kate said, smiling.

"Maybe they should," Tom told her. "Wouldn't do him any harm."

CHAPTER THIRTY-SEVEN

"How are you getting on?" asked the sarge.

He'd asked Nina to look into the failed drugs raid on the hotel, while he got on with 'something else.' 'Something else,' Nina thought, was probably the King George's Dining Rooms. She'd checked the menu online earlier, and had never seen so many words that made her feel less hungry. *Wood. Hay. Intestines.* If that was the sort of place Aaron wanted to carry out the investigation, good luck to him.

On the other hand, he might have got the better side of the draw.

"Not great, Sarge. Just found out whose intel was behind the raid."

DS Keyes stood behind her, looking at her screen. She heard him suppress a chuckle.

"Off you go, Nina. She won't bite."

Nina headed out of the team room, along the corridor to the stairs. On another day, she might have asked the sarge to do it instead, but he'd only just come off light duties. It wouldn't be fair to inflict this on him. The raid had been put together by DS Tracy Giller-Jones, who worked for DI Alan Markin, and both seemed to delight in making life as difficult as they could for everyone else in the station.

But if anyone knew anything about the raid that wasn't in the reports, it would be DS Giller-Jones. Sometimes, you just had to speak to people.

She won't bite, the sarge had said.

Giller-Jones was alone in the tiny team room she shared with no one else. She turned as Nina knocked and pushed the door open, grunted, and turned back to her screen.

"DS Giller-Jones," Nina said.

"Yes?" the DS replied, her back still to Nina.

"I was hoping you could help me. We're looking into a murder. Victim worked at the Bassenthwaite Manor Hotel."

"Good for him."

"He's dead, so not really," Nina shot back, remembering suddenly that she could give as good as she got.

Giller-Jones turned to look at her. "What's it got to do with me?"

"We suspect the victim was involved in criminal activity centred around the hotel," Nina explained. "Blackmail, amongst other things. You organised a drugs raid there last February. I wanted to ask you about that."

Giller-Jones nodded. "It was a bust. Got nothing."

"Nothing at all?"

"Traces. Probably just crumbs left behind by the guests. I was convinced there'd been a tip-off."

This was more like it. "Why?" Nina asked.

"You don't send twenty Uniforms to the middle of nowhere on a fucking whim, Nina. We had good evidence that there was something big going on at the hotel."

"What sort of evidence?"

CHAPTER THIRTY-SEVEN

Giller-Jones stared at her. "Cars."

"Cars?"

"Cars, Nina. They go vroom vroom. Sometimes they go too fast and they get pulled over and searched, and sometimes, when they're searched, we find drugs. There was a lot of that, back end of the year before. Suggested a centre of activity. The random searches got a bit less random, some of the people in question got scared, and the hotel got named."

Why hadn't Nina heard about this? Why hadn't DI Finch, or the sarge, or any of them?

She supressed a sigh. It wasn't any sort of conspiracy. It was just that Markin and Giller-Jones cared more about marking their territory than they did about solving crimes.

"Did any individuals get named?" she asked.

"Yeah. Hang on." Giller-Jones turned back to her keyboard and typed for a moment. "Josh McKenzie. Mouthy bastard, but he was clean, and so was his room. Works in the kitchen."

"Worked. Past tense."

"Eh?"

"Josh McKenzie is dead. He's the body we found in Ennerdale. If we'd known he was a suspected dealer, it might have helped. Why didn't you put his name in the system?"

"Didn't you hear what I just said, Nina? He was clean." Giller-Jones was on her feet now, her bored expression replaced with a sneer. "He. Was. Clean. If you can't figure out who killed him, we're not going to do your job for you."

She turned and sat back down. Nina walked away, shaking her head.

CHAPTER THIRTY-EIGHT

While Nina complained about Tracy Giller-Jones, Zoe tried to dismiss the growing unease since her conversation with Fiona. She couldn't get it out of her head. She had the sense that the super had chosen to talk in Zoe's office to make her uncomfortable, to pressure her into saying things she didn't want to.

"Sounds like she's right, though," Aaron was saying. "Giller-Jones, I mean. There must have been a tip-off."

Zoe checked her watch. She'd need to be on the road soon.

"OK," she said. "Let's talk through where we are. Nina, get Tom on the phone, will you?"

She waited while the call was connected, and a moment later Tom's voice filled the room.

"Hello? Everyone there?"

"Yes, Tom," Zoe replied. "I wanted to catch up before I head to Glasgow."

"I was about to call, actually. I've just been speaking to

CHAPTER THIRTY-EIGHT

Kate Bellamy, and she's admitted she was the one who took the call from McKenzie on Friday evening."

Nina shook her head. "So she lied to us?"

"She was scared. He called her, she was hoping he'd come back, but it sounds like he was having a go at her for speaking to me back in May, when we got the footage of Laurence Eversholt. He said she shouldn't have spoken to the police, said it was dangerous, and she'd got him in trouble."

"In trouble?" Zoe asked.

"That's what she told me."

Zoe thought through the implications, and how they tied in with what they'd already learned that morning.

"OK," she said. "To me, that suggests we're on the right track and this whole thing is connected to McKenzie's criminal activities. He was worried Kate had put his name on our radar. Worried I'd mention him to Carrie, and everything would come out without her having to say anything first."

"Why does that matter?" asked Nina.

"When you're scared, it's much easier saying yes to a name you're given than naming names yourself. And Carrie Wright was scared. Tom, we've got more news here. There was a drugs raid at the hotel last February. McKenzie was the target, and they had good reason to believe they'd nail him, but he came up clean."

There was a brief burst of static before Tom spoke. "So, what, a tip-off?"

"Exactly. And we've got to assume it was Carrie. I wish I could see her now, but I've got to hit the road shortly. In the meantime, Tom, while you're at the hotel, try to mention the raid when you can. Check people's reactions. For all we know, McKenzie might have had an accomplice there."

"OK," said Tom.

Zoe turned to Aaron. "What about you?" she said.

"I'm still interested in the King George's Dining Rooms," he told her. Behind him, she could see Nina rolling her eyes, but Aaron had good instincts. And Zoe could hardly object, given she was about to drive to Scotland.

"Fine. You look into that if you think it's worthwhile, but drop it as soon as it becomes clear it isn't. *If* it becomes clear it isn't. At the same time, I want you and Nina to follow up on this raid and see if you can confirm Carrie was involved in the tip-off."

Nina nodded.

Zoe continued, thinking out loud now. "From what McKenzie said to Kate, it's likely he ran because I was going to see Carrie. If that's the same reason he was killed, it was either someone inside his op, or someone they'd crossed. If it was someone inside, Carrie and the tip-off are our best leads. If it was someone they'd crossed, then..."

She fell silent. Aaron gave a small nod, and Nina looked from one of them to the other.

"Then what, boss?" Tom asked.

"Then we're probably looking at Myron Carter," Aaron answered.

CHAPTER THIRTY-NINE

KATE BELLAMY STOOD in the corridor, leaning against the wall, while Tom and Caroline searched through her room. They'd donned full forensic suits, even masks, but Tom knew that was a waste of time. Kate had been there for a week since McKenzie's disappearance. He'd been in there with Nina. Peter Raymond had been there. Anything they found would be contaminated.

But sometimes, even if you couldn't use evidence in court, it might point in the right direction. Tom thought of the photos the boss had got from that artist, Olivia Bagsby. No use in court, without the woman who'd taken them, or the women who were in them. But still useful.

Which was more than could be said for Kate's bedroom. There was nothing he wouldn't have found in any other staff bedroom in any hotel in the country. Kate's clothes. Some of McKenzie's, which they slid into evidence bags to be looked at later. Books and electronic devices. Toiletries and personal items. Tom had carried out enough searches not to be embarrassed by what he found, but it was weird, rooting through a woman's underwear while she was standing outside watching you.

Kate had calmed down. The tears had dried up, and the shaking had stopped. She wasn't watching them because she was worried about what they'd find. She was watching them because she wanted to get back in as soon as they were done. She had nowhere else to go.

He'd asked about her family and friends. The family were in Stockport. As for friends, she didn't seem to have any. Tom couldn't see why.

Next to him, Caroline was scraping something into an evidence bag. He turned towards her, using his body as a shield so Kate couldn't see what they were doing, and looked down.

There was residue in the bedside drawer. So little of it he probably wouldn't have noticed it himself, but this was Caroline's job.

He bent down to whisper in her ear. "What is it?"

She shrugged. "Don't know, not until I test it. Could be coke. Could be crystal meth. Just traces, really."

He nodded. Kate's boyfriend had been a dealer. It wasn't surprising something like this would turn up.

They were done five minutes later, and Kate was back in the room, sitting on her bed again, looking around. Now they'd been through everything, the room seemed somehow emptier, as if, having been examined and catalogued, Kate's possessions were no longer really there.

Or perhaps it was just that there weren't that many of them, especially now McKenzie's items had been removed. The whole search had taken less than half an hour.

"Do you remember a drugs raid, here?" Tom asked.

To his surprise, Kate laughed. "You mean last winter?"

He nodded. "February."

"Of course I do. Bunch of pigs... Sorry, bunch of police running around the place in the middle of the night, waking everyone up? Not likely to forget that."

"What happened?"

"Not a lot, really. Mr Raymond was furious. I was half-asleep, most of us thought it was funny at the start, but it went on a bit."

It was like she was describing a movie. Did she think drugs raids were supposed to be fun?

"What about Josh? Was he worried?"

She shook her head. "I know what you're getting at. Everyone knows Josh was the man if you wanted to get hold of something."

"He was a dealer, then?"

"I wouldn't go that far, DC Willis." Kate's face crumpled, and she took control of herself. "He just knew where to get what people wanted. But no, Josh wasn't worried. He was very relaxed, if anything."

"And you say Peter Raymond was furious?"

"I know he's a bit of a dick, but you can't blame him, can you? There were guests. Not many, not that time of year, but you should see what some of them wrote on TripAdvisor."

Tom thanked her and made his way downstairs, thinking. Did Kate Bellamy really think her boyfriend had been that innocent?

CHAPTER FORTY

"Right," Aaron said. "This raid."

"Yes, Sarge?" Nina replied.

"We need to find out if Carrie Wright tipped off McKenzie."

"Should we arrange to see her?"

He shook his head. "It'll take too long. And she probably wouldn't tell us anyway. DI Finch is the one she trusts. What else can we do?"

A frown. "We can check her phone logs?" Nina suggested, straightening.

"How can we get hold of them?"

She slumped back into her chair. "PSD, maybe, but it'll take a while. Oh, I know!" She was nodding now. "Inspector Keane."

He smiled. "Well done. OK, I'll have a word with him."

Two floors down, he knocked on Keane's door, heard the man shout "Yup," and entered.

Morris Keane was just one of several inspectors, but when you wanted something done, he was the one you went

CHAPTER FORTY

to. He'd have been the one who'd put together the raid. More importantly, he'd help Aaron without making things difficult.

Aaron explained what he was looking for.

"Shift patterns, eh? Well, I can find out if she was on your raid, I suppose. But even if she wasn't, it doesn't exactly put her in the clear, does it?"

"We're just trying to put together a picture. It's a start."

"Here you are." Keane turned his screen around and leaned across his desk to point at something, his stomach knocking over a pile of papers. "That's her. When are we looking at?"

"Eighteenth of Feb, Guv," Aaron told him. "Early hours."

Keane frowned. "That's not... Oh. Yes, I remember."

"Remember what?"

Keane pointed to a line on the screen, and Aaron scanned across it.

Shit.

"It's not her, Aaron. I'm sorry."

According to the shift log, Carrie Wright had been ten days into a sixteen-day holiday when the raid had taken place.

"Do you remember where she was? It might be—"

"Not local, no. She was in the middle of a two-week cruise."

Aaron was working through the implications. "She couldn't have known about it before she went. Bloody hell."

Inspector Keane was shaking his head.

"What is it?"

"She was off with her husband. Caribbean, it was. Said it was an anniversary present."

Aaron's mind flicked back to that morning. The breakfast

Serge had brought him, and whatever it was his husband had planned for them for their own anniversary.

"And?" he asked.

"I should have realised. What sort of copper can afford a two-week cruise in the Caribbean? I just assumed her husband was loaded. But no. It was her. On the fucking take." Keane ground his teeth together. "I should have bloody realised."

CHAPTER FORTY-ONE

"She might have been lying, Sarge," Nina said.

The sarge didn't look convinced. "She was away, Nina. On leave. It doesn't matter where she was, does it?"

"It does, though. If she wasn't where she said she'd be... Hang on."

She'd done this before. Tom had shown her the Exit Checks database, something that hadn't existed when they'd been through training. There was supposed to be a system for requesting API data, with forms to fill in and hoops to crawl through, but if you knew where to look, there was always a way to get things done quicker.

"There," she said. When you had a name like Carrie Wright, there would probably be more than one of them. But there was her passport photo, blonde hair, small features, the sort of face you wouldn't notice.

She tapped the screen and the exit data appeared.

"Yeah, it's true," she said. "She left from Heathrow on the ninth. Flew to Barbados, back on the twenty-third. It wasn't her, Sarge."

"Which means it was someone else."

He looked grim. Bad enough knowing there was one rotten apple in the barrel. Worse realising that you'd dug it out and there were more still in there.

But this was what they'd suspected. The boss, and her partner, DI Whaley. Now they might have a way of finding out who it was.

The sarge was on the phone already.

"I'd like to speak to Ops Command... Yes, I'll hold for the chief superintendent."

Chief superintendent? Whatever happened to starting low and working your way up?

Her thoughts were interrupted by her phone. She answered immediately.

"Elena? Is everything OK?"

"It's all fine," Elena replied, but Nina could hear the noise of the wind, or the sea, or—

"Are you outside, Elena?"

"Yes."

"Where are you?" Nina asked, trying to keep the tension out of her voice.

"You will not like it, but it is fine, Nina," Elena replied.

Nina frowned. "Where are you?"

"Workington."

Shit.

Elena had been hiding out at Nina's for more than six months now, and that was too long to stay inside the house.

But they had an arrangement. *Be careful. Go outside briefly. Stay in Whitehaven, away from the main streets. Avoid daylight.*

Most of all, avoid Workington.

"What are you doing?" Nina asked. Even she could hear the fear in her voice.

"Really, it is fine."

Of course it wasn't fine. The people responsible for trafficking Elena and murdering her friend would do anything to find and silence her before she could remember more than she already had.

A warehouse. The smell of ammonia. If Carter and his friends only knew how little Elena could recall, they probably wouldn't bother coming for her.

"Elena, you need to get out of Workington."

"No, Nina. Listen to me. Listen."

"You need to—"

"No! *You* need to listen!"

Stop shouting. Her accent. It was so obvious. If anyone heard her...

Nina could hear the sarge on the phone beside her. "Yes," he was saying. "We need the details of everyone who knew about it."

"I am not doing anything useful," Elena said. "I am not worth my keep."

"What do you mean?"

"I mean, I am not *earning* my keep."

"You don't have to pay, Elena. You're welcome—"

"No! I have been with you more than half a year. I remember a building and a smell, but what building is it? I do not know. This is not good enough. I should find out or I should leave you and not waste more time."

"Don't do anything stupid, Elena."

"I do not do anything stupid. You know I am not stupid, yes?"

"Yes." And that was true. Even in her second language, a language of which she'd hardly known a word before she'd been smuggled into the country, Elena was interesting and engaging. And, since they'd started to relax around each other, fun.

Just a few feet away, the sarge was still talking. "I appreciate this is sensitive information, but as you'll see, Sir, we're working on a murder investigation."

"So I put on hat," said Elena. "I put on big hat."

"A hat?" Maybe she *was* stupid after all. "You put on a hat?"

"It covers much of my face. It is January. Cold. People expect big hats, yes?"

Nina supposed that was true. The sarge was still on the phone with Ops. "That's right," she heard. "Both during the raid, and beforehand, Sir."

"So I put on big hat and get bus to Workington. And now I walk through Workington and I see if I can remember building."

"Jesus Christ," said Nina. "Listen to me, Elena. Get out of there, now."

"No!" Elena sounded angry. "You do not understand. I am wasting time."

But Elena wasn't as angry as Nina.

"For fuck's sake," she said, keeping her voice low. "Just get the fuck out of Workington and go home, Elena."

"I thought you would not understand," Elena replied. "I should not have called."

The line went dead.

CHAPTER FORTY-TWO

"Of course I bloody well remember it," said Peter Raymond.

Tom was standing by the door of the manager's office, watching his face, but Raymond made no effort to disguise his feelings.

"It was a bloody disgrace." He narrowed his eyes. "I made a complaint at the time."

Fine. Let him complain.

"Why?" asked Tom.

"Why? Because it was obvious someone had put them up to it to disrupt our business. Probably Glovers or Whately Park."

"Who?"

"You've never heard of Glovers? Whately Park?" Raymond shook his head. "Hotels. Our rivals, or at least, that's how they see themselves. Not really in the same league."

Tom decided to ignore the hotel industry angle and focus on the raid.

"And there was some disruption, then?"

"What do you think? You can hardly have fifty coppers stomping around the hotel at two in the morning without some disruption, can you?"

"Fifty?"

"It might have been fewer. I wasn't counting."

Raymond was still furious about the raid nearly a year later. Tom could well imagine the manager being incandescent at the time.

He went to speak to Leo, the barman, who still found the entire event amusing.

"Middle of the night, and they're all down here in the bar. After a while I thought, who knows how long this'll last, might as well get some drinks going."

"And the guests were happy with that?"

"Most of them, yeah. What else are you gonna do in your dressing gown at two in the morning? We weren't exactly full at the time, with it being February, but it was still the drunkest crowd I've seen outside a hen night. Best tips I've ever got, too."

But other than the drinks and the tips, Leo had little to offer.

Sarah, behind the reception desk, hadn't been working for the hotel at the time, but the porter, Stuart Sullivan, had. Tom found him in the entrance lobby.

"Fucking carnage, I can tell you that," he said. "Don't tell Raymond I said that, though."

"I wouldn't even consider it."

"Listen, DC Willis, right? There's something else."

"What is it?"

Stuart looked nervous, a sheen of sweat glistening on his brow. At the sound of footsteps on the gravel behind them,

CHAPTER FORTY-TWO

his expression shifted to terrified.

"In here." He led Tom back through the lobby to the semi-hidden door in the wall behind the reception desk. Sarah watched impassively as they walked past, through the door, and into a narrow corridor with doors on either side.

"Break room," announced Stuart, and pushed open a door. Inside was a small, dark space; a dirty sofa, two old wooden chairs with stained cushions on them, and a metal table that looked like it belonged in Interview Room Three back at the Hub. All the items of furniture were pushed up against each other, with hardly any space between them.

"What is it?" Tom asked.

Stuart sank into the sofa, pulled a vape out of his pocket, and slowly inhaled and exhaled half a dozen times. "Fuck, I needed that. Look, sorry. I just didn't want anyone hearing what I'm saying, right?"

"Yes, of course. What is it?" Tom asked.

"It's the taxi. Look, I don't want to get anyone in trouble, right?"

Tom resisted a sigh. "What taxi, Stuart?"

"Right, it's like this... Hang on, what you doing?"

Tom had got out his phone and was about to ask Stuart if he could record their conversation.

"No way, fella." Stuart shook his head. "No recording."

"OK, OK." Tom put his phone back in his pocket. "Just tell me what you wanted to say."

"It's like this, right? Friday night, late, this taxi shows up. Like midnight, or something."

Tom's pulse quickened. "OK. Is that unusual?"

"Yeah. I mean, no, we get taxis, but this one, it comes round the back."

"And that *is* unusual?"

Stuart stared at Tom. "Well, yeah, that's the staff entrance. Staff don't take taxis, do we? Don't get paid enough." He giggled, took a drag from his vape, and coughed a few times.

"Did you see who was in it?" Tom asked.

"That's the thing, right? I'm leaning out my window, smoking – that's how I see it coming up the drive – and I can see inside, and there's just the driver. No one else. So I figure it's picking someone up, right? But it doesn't stop out the front, just carries on round the back. And then I sort of forgot about it and crashed out. Heard it leaving again a few minutes later. Figure it must be staff, right? But who's leaving from the staff entrance in a taxi at midnight? No one's got a shift ending then. I don't know. And I'll tell you something else, DC Willis."

"What's that?"

"Round the staff entrance, yeah? No CCTV there. Cameras all over the place at the front. But round the back? Nada."

No CCTV, then. And something else that had been on Tom's mind since the moment the porter had said *midnight*.

Midnight tallied with the vehicle Susan Masters had heard idling an hour or so later.

CHAPTER FORTY-THREE

THE DRIVE to Stirling seemed to go on forever. But at least Zoe could talk as she drove. Carl was home, tucking into beer and a jumbo sausage from the fish and chip shop down the road. Even though she was only going to be away one night, it was nice to hear his voice. She'd got in late last night after her chat with Jake, and they'd barely exchanged greetings before he was asleep. And they'd not had much chance to catch up today.

"Oh," she said, as her satnav warned her that she'd overshot the turning. "I'm in danger of getting lost. I'd better go."

"Love you," Carl said.

"Love you too," she replied. And it was true. For all their talk of *boundaries*, she was sure of it.

The front door was open before she'd got out of the car, and there was Catriona, hugging her and leading her inside.

"Look at the size of you!" Zoe exclaimed. Mo and Catriona's daughters were standing in the hallway, lined up as if preparing to greet royalty. Isla was eight. Fiona was already a teenager.

She bent down to give Isla a hug. Bending wasn't necessary for Fiona. She could sense a little reserve – at that age, chances were they hardly remembered her – but as she straightened up and smiled at them, she could see the shyness begin to melt away.

"My boss is called Fiona," Zoe told the older girl.

"Is she nice?"

"She's very good at her job," Zoe said. Standing behind her daughters, Catriona raised an eyebrow. "Actually, I think she *is* nice. But you've got to watch it with Fionas. The only way to tell if they're not actually demons in disguise is to do this."

She reached out and tickled the older child under her chin, prompting shrieking and laughter.

"Hmmm," Zoe said. "Definitely human. Can't do that to the super, though."

She looked up to see Nicholas in the kitchen doorway, Mo behind him. She felt her face break into a wide smile.

"Two of my favourite men," she said, pulling Nicholas into a hug; she still found it odd, thinking of him as a man. He'd stopped growing a few years ago, but he was still tall, four inches taller than Zoe. It was wonderful to feel him, to smell him.

"Mum," he muttered.

"I know," she replied. "It's been too long." She pushed him away and held him at arm's length. He'd lost weight. "Are you eating?"

He rolled his eyes, and she bit her lip; stop nagging. Nicholas was a better cook than she was, and had been since he was fifteen. She shouldn't worry.

"We feed him up when he visits." Mo stepped around Nicholas and wrapped her in a hug. She was struck by how familiar he smelled. How could the smell of one man somehow be the smell of home?

The next three hours passed in what felt like minutes. There was so much catching up to do, so much news to share, but every now and then they'd fall silent, all of them, and grin at each other.

She was relieved to see that Mo seemed to be more settled now. He was starting to appreciate the differences up here, in particular the views. She knew how he felt, though; it would always be slightly alien, living and working in the countryside.

"How's your new boss?" she asked him. "Not as good as the last one, I imagine."

He chuckled. "Jade's good. It took her a while to find her feet, but... yeah. I like her. And not so much of the new. It's been three years."

She raised an eyebrow. "I'm not being replaced, I hope."

He laughed. "Never."

Nicholas was chatting with the girls, helping to set the table. He'd made himself at home here, she could see.

Good. She didn't have to feel quite so guilty. And Mo had been there at Nicholas's birth; he was practically the boy's dad.

She shuddered. The less said about *him*, the better.

Shaking away the memories, she clapped her hands, making Fiona jump. "So, what's for tea?"

"Bolognese," said Nicholas. "Cat and I made it earlier."

She exchanged a glance with Mo's wife. *Cat*, eh? But that was good. She shouldn't feel jealous.

Even so, she needed to get Nicholas home to Cumbria, and soon.

The meal went by so fast that by the time Nicholas

pointed out he had to be back in his digs soon, Zoe realised she'd barely caught up with him. She stood and insisted on driving him back.

In her Mini, they fell into a companionable silence, as the lights of the suburb receded, giving way to more dense clusters and the occasional patch of darkness. It felt as if they'd said everything they needed to, but the journey was short, and there was something else Zoe needed to tell him before it was over.

"You know I miss you, don't you?" she said. She glanced over and caught the beginnings of a smile.

"Of course I do, Mum. And I miss you. Look, turn here and you can pull up there." He pointed. "That's my building."

She parked and took a deep breath. When she looked around, Nicholas had already unstrapped himself and was reaching to open the door.

"Thanks, Mum. See you soon," he said, leaned over to peck her cheek, and disappeared into the darkness.

She waited a minute, hoping for a sight of him silhouetted against one of the buildings, but he was gone.

Why had he gone so quickly? She'd thought he would invite her in, show her his digs. He'd always lived neatly, cleanly; there wouldn't be the sort of squalor other students might be ashamed to show a parent.

So what was he hiding?

CHAPTER FORTY-FOUR

"What is it now?"

Peter Raymond glared at Tom through tired eyes, but there was an air of defeat about the man now. He'd been tamed. Resentful, maybe, but docile.

"I'm sorry," Tom began. A little grace in victory never hurt. "But I've got to go through that CCTV footage you gave me." He held up the USB stick. "And I might need more. How far into the evening does it go?"

Raymond sighed. "Ten, I think. Maybe..." He tapped on his keyboard and frowned at his screen. "Eleven." He looked up. "That good enough for you?"

Tom almost felt sorry for him. "I need footage around midnight. Every camera. So, let's say from eleven through to one. I'm going to want everything you've got from that day and night. But for now, I want to look at eleven till one."

"Right." Raymond bent down, typed again, and stood. "Wait here, please."

While he waited, Tom flicked through the files in the team inbox, checking updates from Nina and the sarge, who seemed to be looking into the raid from the previous February. Ten minutes later, Raymond was back with another USB stick, dropping it into Tom's hand as he walked past.

"Are you getting anywhere?" the manager asked, slumping into his chair.

Tom shrugged. "We have some leads, Mr Raymond. I'm sorry to have to ask you this, but I'd like to go through some of this footage now, if you don't mind. Which means I'll need a computer."

Raymond nodded. "Follow me," he said, and led Tom down the corridor, back to reception, then through the door behind the desk, past the room in which Stuart Sullivan had told Tom about the taxi, to another room, which Raymond unlocked with his key card. This room was equally small, but tidier: two chairs, one desk, a computer.

"For visiting staff. From the parent company."

Tom hadn't realised there was a parent company. Even managers had people to answer to. No wonder Raymond was looking tired. He made to leave, but Tom wasn't letting him go that easily.

"Do you mind waiting a moment?" he asked, and Raymond all but fell into one of the chairs.

It took two minutes to find the taxi Stuart Sullivan had seen, and it was exactly as the porter had described: a vehicle entering the grounds just before midnight, driving past the main entrance and around to the back of the hotel, where it disappeared. It returned six minutes later.

The CCTV images were grainy, the light poor on the driveway. There was no way of knowing what colour the vehicle was, but its shape suggested a people carrier. Stuart

CHAPTER FORTY-FOUR

Sullivan hadn't been able to identify the cab company, and neither could Tom.

There were plenty more files from the same time period. Tom flicked open one that showed the car park, the same camera from which he'd seen Josh McKenzie leaving the hotel.

To his surprise, there was movement. A car drove in and parked a little way back, in an unlit area of the car park.

A figure emerged. Tom squinted.

He couldn't see their face, or much of them at all. Probably a woman, but that was a guess based on movement, body shape, hair length.

She stood facing the hotel. After a couple of minutes, she turned to her right, and he could see her in profile, just, but there was nothing remarkable. Probably a woman. That was it.

And then she got back in her car and drove away.

Tom emailed the external footage to the team inbox, then pulled up all the other files, from both inside and out, covering the rest of the night. He sent them to the same destination, forming a slow but orderly queue.

It would take a while.

"Please come with me," he told Raymond.

The manager didn't even ask where they were going.

"I'd like to see all the routes to that exit, please."

"What exit?"

Had Raymond not even been looking at the footage?

"The staff exit, I think it is. Round the back."

"Oh, that. It's this way."

Tom expected to be led back to the reception desk, but instead, Raymond turned right. They continued along the corridor, which turned to the left and ended in a black fire exit door which was ajar, the cold air streaming in.

"I've told them to keep this bloody thing shut," said Raymond, reaching for the metal bar. Tom held out a hand. "Hang on." He pushed the bar and stepped out.

There was hardly any light. A faint glow emanated from windows above and behind him, but nothing illuminated the space itself. Tom waited for his eyes to adjust to the darkness.

It was a narrow space, enclosed on three sides by the building, but with no windows at ground level as far as he could see. Above, rows of windows had views out to the deer park, once you got to the higher levels. Nothing to make you look down. Nothing to see. And no cameras.

Tom had seen no cameras in the corridor, either. He turned and re-entered the building, where Raymond was waiting.

"No cameras along here?" he asked, as they walked back the way they'd come.

"No," Raymond agreed.

"But if you're coming out this way, you've got to go through reception, right? And there's cameras there."

Raymond shook his head, walked back a few steps and pushed on a nondescript brown door. Tom poked his head through the gap, to see a bare floor and a basic linoleum staircase.

"Staff stairs. Serves every floor. No cameras here either. There's a separate staff lift, too, but that does have cameras."

Tom nodded. "So someone could leave the hotel, from any floor, coming out through the exit you've just shown me, and the only time they'd be caught on camera is on the long driveway?"

The manager nodded. "Never really thought that would be a problem."

CHAPTER FORTY-FIVE

It wasn't until Nina heard the sarge muttering yet again about not trusting them that she'd decided she'd had enough.

"Don't trust who, Sarge?" she asked, even though she knew what he was about to say.

"That Theodora woman. The chef at the King George's Dining Rooms. Her and her mates."

"Right. Heard back from Ops yet? With the list?"

He stared blankly at her.

"The names. Everyone who knew about the raid."

"Oh, right. No, not yet."

"Right. And you're not actually doing anything about the King George's Dining Rooms, are you?"

"No, you're right." He stood. "Maybe I should—"

"Sarge, I could do with a hand here," she said, fighting back her irritation. She'd managed to get hold of Elena, who was safe, back home, and refusing to talk in more than angry grunts. Part of her wanted to get back and apologise, and part of her wanted to get back and yell at the woman. It was probably best she was stuck here for a while.

CHAPTER FORTY-FIVE

She was stuck here for a while because Tom had just sent through several gigabytes of footage from cameras inside and around the Bassenthwaite Manor Hotel from Friday night.

Apparently, someone had taken a taxi. It didn't seem like much of a lead to Nina, but while they waited on Ops and couldn't speak to Carrie, it was all they had.

She navigated to the file Tom had highlighted and found the footage of the taxi. If Sullivan hadn't said it was a taxi, she wouldn't have known, but it was the right sort of shape, and it did come and go the way you'd expect a taxi to come and go.

"It didn't seem right," she heard. "Like they're hiding something."

"Sarge?"

"The—"

"I know who you're talking about, Sarge. Just... Please, can you help me find out who got in this bloody taxi?"

He came to stand behind her, frowning at her screen.

"How do you even know that's a taxi?" he asked.

She sighed and went through it all again.

"Right," he said. "If you can ID the vehicle, you can find the driver and they might be able to help."

"Footage isn't clear enough, Sarge."

"Have you looked up ANPR in the area? Might have triggered a camera as it drove past."

Nina smiled. Even working with only half his mind, the sarge was good. She tapped in a series of commands and returned to the footage while she waited for the ANPR camera results.

"Thing is, Sarge," she said, "we might be able to catch them inside the building. On one of the other cameras."

DS Keyes looked at her, then at his watch, then back to

her. He nodded. "Fair enough," he said. "I'll take the first two now."

The two of them worked in silence for ten minutes or so, Nina glancing over at his screen from time to time. She could see pretty much the same thing there as she could see on her own.

"This is pointless, Nina," he said. "It's a decent-sized hotel with a few guests in it, and everyone in the bloody place seemed to spend most of Friday night walking up and down corridors and stairs and doing things."

"Too much noise, then," she said. "Too much to follow everyone."

"Precisely. It would be helpful if you could work out who was where. You could put them in a room or a corridor at one or two and be confident they hadn't left in a taxi at midnight. But the quality..."

"It's shit," she agreed, as the notification came through on her ANPR search. "No results on the ANPR either," she said. "Only one camera in the area and it's been out of action for weeks."

The sarge glanced at his watch again, then back at his screen. "Might as well finish the one I'm on."

"Same," Nina agreed. "I've got the car park here. Quiet as... Oh. Hang on."

A car had just parked, almost in the dark.

Nina checked the time stamp. Just before midnight. Tom had mentioned something about this, hadn't he?

As she watched, a figure emerged, looked at the building for a few minutes, then turned so her face was just visible in profile. She waited, got back into her car, and drove away.

What had the woman seen? Why would someone drive

CHAPTER FORTY-FIVE

all the way out to the Bassenthwaite Manor Hotel, and just stand there for a few minutes before driving away again?

She rewound the footage and watched it again.

There. The registration was visible for a moment, as the vehicle left the car park. She tapped in what she'd seen, waited, then checked the results.

"Oh."

DS Keyes, who'd returned to scanning his screen, looked up. "What?"

"That fireman, the one who killed himself, remember him?"

"Of course. Why?"

"What's his widow called, again?"

"Sally," he replied. "Sally Peters."

"Right." Nina nodded. She turned to the sarge. "Any idea why Sally Peters might have driven out to the Bassenthwaite Manor Hotel the same night Josh McKenzie was murdered?"

CHAPTER FORTY-SIX

Zoe slowed down, looking for the turning to Mo's house she'd missed the first time round, when her phone rang.

Unknown number. There were any number of people it could be. Not Ryan Tobin, at least. His number was all too familiar, and she'd already ignored it once this evening.

"Hello?"

"Zoe," said a voice she'd only heard a handful of times but knew instantly.

"Olivia. Have you—"

"I sent you the photos. Have you arrested Carter?"

"Not yet."

Zoe could hear Olivia breathing short, sharp breaths. Panicked breaths.

"You've got to arrest him, Zoe. I sent you the photos."

The turning was just ahead, but the signal was weakening already. There was a dip in the road before it rose again just before Mo's house. She pulled over.

"Look, the photos are great. Really helpful. We just need more."

CHAPTER FORTY-SIX

"What? What is it you need?"

"I can't—"

"Whatever it is, Zoe, I need you to find it. Fast. I can't keep ahead of him forever."

"Why?" Zoe gripped the steering wheel, a sense of foreboding sweeping over her. "What's happened? Has he found you?"

A short, bitter laugh. "I wouldn't be talking to you if he had, would I? But I can't carry on like this. One day I'll make a mistake."

"I understand. We just need—"

"Whatever it is you need, Zoe, find it."

The call ended. Zoe checked the display again. Nothing. No way of calling back. If Olivia Bagsby was making mistakes, Zoe couldn't see them.

Mo was waiting for her by the front door when she emerged from her car a minute later. He led her into the kitchen, sipped from a mug of tea he picked up from the counter, and offered her a coffee.

She shook her head. "It's too late for coffee."

She accepted a Diet Coke and followed him into the living room.

"Catriona's got an early start," he said. "She's settled the girls down and gone to bed. She said to tell you goodnight and hopes to see you in the morning."

"You've both been very hospitable," Zoe replied.

Mo laughed. "It's me, Zo. You don't have to thank me for my bloody hospitality."

She echoed the laugh, closed her eyes, and sank back into the sofa. She was immersed in friendship and comfort, and the need to do nothing except relax. Was this how other people felt when they'd been drinking?

"How's it been?" she asked, opening her eyes again.

Mo shrugged. "It's OK. Sometimes the work feels like it's too much. Not even the work, really. Just the bloody drive. And I'm not going to pretend it's been easy with Catriona's mum. And the girls... Well, they're settled in school now, but there's been plenty of tears and tantrums along the way. And we're not out of the woods yet."

Zoe nodded. She'd been spared most of that with Nicholas. Sometimes, when she heard other people describe the difficulties they'd had with their children, she couldn't believe how lucky she'd been. And then she'd remember how Nicholas's boyfriend had been captured and nearly killed by a man who'd been terrorising Birmingham's gay community. How, for weeks, she'd been unable to shake the knowledge that it could have turned out differently. Could have been Nicholas, could have ended in....

"Do you think Nicholas is OK?" she asked.

"Why? Don't you?"

"I've hardly spoken to him," she said, and it felt good, admitting it. "I can't get hold of him, and when I do, he's too busy and says he'll call me back. I mean, it's fine, I'm his mum, he doesn't need to tell me everything, but tonight, well..."

"Well, what?"

"It was wonderful, Mo. But it reminded me how much I miss him."

Mo stood, walked over to her, and took her hands in his.

"He loves you, Zo. He really does. He's a young lad, and he's away from home, and he's had his ups and downs, like everyone. But I think he's happy. You've just got to let him find his feet again."

CHAPTER FORTY-SIX

She nodded. "Tell me about your job," she said. "Take my mind off things."

Mo obliged. She'd already heard all about the murders at the G7 Summit back in September, or at least, the public version of events, but now she got the inside track, and it was even more extraordinary than it had seemed at the time. But the Complex Crimes Unit sounded precarious. Always on the verge of getting shut down, always pulling off a high-profile arrest at the last minute to keep the wolves at bay. He'd been working with Petra McBride, the forensic psychologist she'd called on in Birmingham years earlier. And DI Tanner sounded like a decent boss. But she knew he missed Birmingham and CID.

There was an elephant in the room, but neither of them was going to bring it up. She'd mentioned David Randle in a phone call with Mo months earlier. He hadn't wanted to talk about it.

"And you?" he asked. "This case, this McKenzie. You getting anywhere?"

Zoe shrugged. "Sort of. We keep finding leads, and every time we follow them, they open up another can of worms. We're working on the basis that McKenzie was part of a blackmail ring, with police and others working for him, busting dealers and selling the drugs. He might have been killed by one of his own, or one of the dealers. Or it might be something else entirely. He had a girlfriend, but I don't think she can tell us anything useful. No one who worked with him has a good word to say about him, but there's nothing suspicious. I'm hoping his ex will be more forthcoming."

Mo smiled. "Let's hope you have better luck than me," he said, and drained his mug. "Right. I'm having another cuppa.

Allow me to introduce you to our fabulous selection of soft and fizzy drinks."

CHAPTER FORTY-SEVEN

"I'M SO SORRY, LOVE," Aaron said, leaning over to kiss Serge goodbye.

"Huh?" mumbled Serge, opening one bleary eye.

"Happy anniversary," Aaron replied. "I'll see you later. Looking forward to this surprise of yours."

"What?" Serge sat up. "What time is it? Where you going?"

"I'm sorry," Aaron repeated. "It's half six, but I've just had some news. Got to go in early. Kiss Annabel goodbye for me, will you?"

Serge looked disappointed. "Happy anniversary."

Aaron bent over him, lifted his chin, and kissed him again. When he pulled away, his husband was smiling.

"I really am sorry. Look, I've got your card and stuff here, but—"

"Save it till later." Serge squeezed Aaron's hand, fully awake now. "I know, I know, it's the job. We'll open everything together. Oh, make sure you've got spare clothes with you."

Aaron nodded.

"Nice clothes," Serge said. "Not your usual manky jeans. I'll drop you a line later to sort out the arrangements."

In the car on the way in, Aaron caught sight of himself grinning in the mirror. A few months earlier, he'd been on the verge of getting murdered, and he'd hardly cared.

Funny how quickly things could change.

The news that had dragged him out of bed was a report from Ops Command, detailing who had access to information on the drugs raid. It had come from the very top, the chief superintendent himself, and Aaron could see why. There were names, phone numbers, access terminal details, the lot.

You wouldn't want this sort of information getting into the wrong hands.

He'd spotted the email on his phone when he'd woken at four, and instead of going back to sleep, he'd stupidly opened it and started scrolling through. It wasn't just a list of who'd been told about the raid; it detailed when they'd been told, by whom, and when they'd accessed further information about it, either in person or through the system.

Whoever had tipped off Josh McKenzie had to be on that list.

There were names he recognised, access terminal registrations that sounded vaguely familiar, but it was all too confusing, in the dark, his husband sleeping beside him. He'd thought about sending it straight over to Kay Holinshed, because Kay more than anyone would be able to make sense of it all, sort the columns and rows into things that actually meant something.

But Kay had been fired. Kay had made her own mistakes,

CHAPTER FORTY-SEVEN

and they'd been enough to have her thrown out, but she'd been framed for someone else's sins, too.

Maybe the same person who'd tipped McKenzie off over the raid.

As he drove, Aaron dialled a number. It was early, but she'd have her phone switched off if she was asleep.

"Who is it?" said Sally Peters. Not nervous now, but full-on afraid, which made sense: a call at seven in the morning could do that.

"Mrs Peters, it's DS Keyes," he said.

"Oh. Right. You. You scared me," she replied.

"I was wondering if we could have a chat, Mrs Peters."

"Erm, yes. Do you mind if I just make myself a brew? I'm—"

"I was hoping you could come in, actually. This morning, if at all possible. I'd like to ask you some questions about our previous conversation, and whether you've had any contact with Josh McKenzie."

A pause.

"That's the name you said the other day. I told you, I've never heard of him."

"OK. Well, if you don't mind coming in, I'd be grateful. It's entirely up to you. It's a voluntary interview, but it will be under caution. Do you know—"

"I know what that means, DS Keyes. I read enough crime fiction."

"And you're entitled to legal advice if you—"

"I've got nothing to hide. You at that new place, out near Frizington?"

"Yes."

"I'll be there in an hour."

CHAPTER FORTY-EIGHT

"What time is it?" asked Zoe, rubbing her eyes with one hand while she held the phone in the other.

"It's half seven, sweetheart. Thought you'd be up by now."

As the morning took shape around her, the image of Carl on her phone formed into something recognisable. He was up, dressed, and grinning at her.

"Half seven? Really?" She'd stayed up late with Mo, catching up, exchanging successes and failures, worries and joys. Mostly worries.

Carl nodded. He'd missed a tiny patch while shaving, but curiously, it made him look even better.

"I miss you," she said.

He smiled. "Miss you too, or I wouldn't have called. And I wanted to tell you I'm away tonight. Maybe tomorrow as well. This stupid bloody course. But also, someone's got an apology for you."

The camera panned around to the sofa, where Yoda was perched, watching warily.

"What's she done?" asked Zoe.

There was a moment's silence before Carl's voice cut in.

"Well, looks like she's too ashamed to tell you, so I'd better step in. Last night, our favourite feline decided to graduate from fighting over scraps and managed to steal a whole portion of fish."

Zoe gasped, torn between shock and admiration. "No!"

"Yes, I'm afraid. Poor woman, she turned her back, and when she turned back a moment later, her medium cod and chips was just chips. And there's a streak of grey bolting down the street to our place."

"What happened?"

"Showing the sort of instinct that might find her a place in Cumbria Police, the victim followed the thief, knocked on the door, and told me what had happened."

Zoe stifled a laugh. "Did she want the fish back? After Yoda had..."

Carl shook his head. "She was just being public-spirited, I think. Alerting the authorities to a known menace. And the fact that our house would be stinking of fish if we didn't locate the stolen property. Yoda here," Carl turned the camera to the cat cleaning her paws and looking bored, "had already managed to hide it, but we tracked it down a few minutes later. And this is why she owes you an apology."

Something moved into view in front of the camera. Was that...

"That's one of my shoes!" Zoe exclaimed.

"Yes," agreed Carl. "She found one of your most expensive shoes and slid a piece of fried cod into it. I've given it a good clean, though. Should be OK. And I bought the victim a fresh portion of cod."

"Yoda!" The cat looked up from cleaning her paws, and

gave a little movement that Zoe could have sworn was a shrug.

She chatted with Carl for another few minutes; he wanted to hear about Mo and Catriona, and most of all, about Nicholas.

"Good thing you woke me," she said, after filling him in on her concerns. "I've got to get myself going."

Downstairs, Mo had dragged the coffee machine out of a cupboard and by the time Zoe entered the kitchen, he was already spooning coffee into the top.

"I remember that machine," Zoe told him. "And a decent coffee is exactly what I need right now."

She sat in the kitchen sipping coffee while the organised chaos of the morning unfolded around her. Last night, they'd chatted until nearly one, running through their own lives, and then work. They'd talked through the McKenzie case, and Mo had shown her the reports he'd seen. The write-up of the domestic violence allegation made by McKenzie's then-wife Shona was almost embarrassing in its lack of detail. The report into McKenzie's injuries at the hands of a mystery assailant, who the police were convinced was Shona's brother, was a lot more thorough. But nothing had come of either.

Mo had looked pensive as they talked, but he seemed fine now, and remarkably calm. That was more than could be said for Isla and Fiona, who were running late for school, or for Catriona, who was already late for work, and couldn't spare more than a brief hug before racing out the door.

"I've got to get these two off," Mo said a few minutes later. "I can nip back here before heading to work..."

"It's OK." Zoe smiled. "I want to drop in on Shona before she's up and about."

CHAPTER FORTY-EIGHT

"From what I can tell, she doesn't have a job, Zo. She'll be there."

"Catch 'em early, catch 'em out, Mo. The sooner I'm there..."

Mo nodded. The two of them embraced. Then Fiona and Isla threw themselves at her, and she found herself swept into a four-way hug that she didn't want to end.

But it had to.

CHAPTER FORTY-NINE

"Shit," Aaron muttered.

He was alone in the team room, crouching under the spare desk. Kay's desk. Following the wire from the terminal on the desk to the docking point in the floor, where the access terminal code was written.

He'd recognised that code the moment he'd seen it on the report. He'd spent enough time under those desks, reconnecting wires when they came unplugged.

"Shit," he repeated with feeling. Someone using this terminal had accessed information on the raid, on the seventeenth of February. Less than twelve hours before it had taken place.

Kay had been with them at the time. Part of the team. Helping to sort out the aftermath of the Bernard Dearborn murder, putting the case together against Alice Winstanley.

Kay had denied any involvement with organised crime. Aaron had known the straightest people who turned out to be crooks, and the dodgiest turn out straight. But she'd admitted accessing other information, digging up details on

CHAPTER FORTY-NINE

her daughter's new boyfriend, Davey Grant. And there'd been enough information on the system about Davey Grant to keep her busy for a while.

That alone had been enough to lose Kay the job she loved. She hadn't tried to deny it. But she was insistent that she'd accessed nothing else.

Returning to his desk, Aaron scrolled through the data until he found what he wanted.

There. The time and date. He tapped on the terminal reference and checked it against what he'd just seen. He tapped again, and the login details came up.

Just as he'd expected.

The information on the raid had been accessed from Kay's terminal using DS Harry Oldman's login, which should have raised some flags, given Oldman had retired years earlier. Oldman hadn't cared much for password security, which meant anyone might have had his details. Other sensitive information – the images used to blackmail Margaret Hooper, for example – had been accessed via Oldman's credentials.

But Aaron had been trying to figure out who was behind it all for months, and he'd got nowhere. He sat, eyes closed, and tried to think of another way in.

There was nothing else. And the thing he'd been putting off for days now couldn't be put off any longer.

To his surprise, Isaac Bateman answered the phone immediately.

"Isaac? Aaron Keyes. I was wondering—"

"Bloody hell, Keyesie. A visit, then a phone call? Not thinking of moving back, are you?"

"No," Aaron said. "I was hoping you could help me out. You've got a missing person. Kevin Downes."

"First I've heard of it," replied Bateman.

"Protestor. Down at the quarry."

"Oh, the dosser. Yeah, he's just gone walkabout. You don't need to worry about him, Keyesie."

Aaron fought back his irritation. "It's quite important that we find him, Isaac. I was wondering—"

"Listen, pal. If you've got actual information, feel free to share. If not, leave us alone, will you?"

The line went dead. Aaron was still staring at his phone when a call from downstairs pulled him from his amazement.

Sally Peters was here.

She'd come without a lawyer, and he went through the formalities: her rights, the caution, what was about to happen. She sat, impassive, a tall, solidly built woman whose shoulder-length black hair framed a surprisingly delicate face.

"When we spoke on the phone, Mrs Peters, I asked if you'd ever been to the Bassenthwaite Manor Hotel."

"Yes, I remember."

"Your response was that you'd heard of it, but you'd never been there."

"That's right. What's this about, Sergeant? I thought you might be able to tell me something about what happened to my Ellis."

"I'm sorry, Mrs Peters, but do you mind looking at this?"

He opened the file on the laptop he'd brought down with him, and watched Sally Peters' expression as she saw herself and her car in the car park of the Bassenthwaite Manor Hotel. The very place she'd just claimed she'd never been.

"Can you confirm that's you, Mrs Peters?" Aaron said.

Sally Peters said nothing.

"As you can see, the registration plates on the car are

CHAPTER FORTY-NINE

quite clearly visible. They match your Nissan Micra, Mrs Peters."

Sally Peters stood up.

"We haven't finished here," Aaron said.

"I have," she told him. "I'm going home."

He watched as she walked to the door, opened it, and walked away.

Sally Peters didn't strike him as the sort of person who'd slash a man's throat and drop him in a frozen lake. But you never could tell.

And there was one thing he was certain of: Sally Peters had just joined Theodora Harding on the list of people who knew a lot more than they were telling.

CHAPTER FIFTY

AN HOUR after leaving Mo's house, Zoe stood in a very different kitchen, in a third-floor flat in a depressing-looking low-rise block in Pollokshields, not far from the heart of Glasgow.

"Thanks for seeing me," she said.

"Yeah."

Josh McKenzie's ex-wife had her back turned to Zoe. She was busying herself with two mugs and instant coffee, and Zoe had the sense that she didn't want the coffee any more than Zoe did. She just wanted a reason to look away.

Shona Murray was in her mid-thirties but looked maybe two decades older. She moved slowly and awkwardly, like someone not used to moving at all.

"You sent the other cop, did ya?" said Shona. Her accent was thick, but easy enough to understand. "Asian fella, yeah?"

"I did. I—"

"Yeah. I might a been a bit rude to 'im. But I don't like some fella turnin' up like that, you see?"

CHAPTER FIFTY

"I understand. I just wanted to know about Josh."

She'd already explained that McKenzie was dead. Murdered. She'd done it gently, but it soon became apparent that she needn't have bothered. Shona Murray wasn't sorry her ex-husband was dead; she'd said as much. She wasn't celebrating, but she wasn't mourning, either.

"Sit down," said Shona, pointing at the kitchen table. Zoe sat. "What do you want to know, then?"

"I suppose the obvious, like can you think of anyone who'd have wished him harm, and—"

Shona laughed, a surprisingly melodic, gentle laugh. "Sorry."

"And what he was like in general," Zoe continued.

"What he was like in general was nasty," Shona told her. She took a sip from her coffee and grimaced. "It's shit, this. Don't mind me if you don't wanna drink it. Yeah, he were violent, nasty, selfish, mean, if you got a... Not a dictionary, you know..."

"Thesaurus?" suggested Zoe.

"Yeah. If you got one of them, look up 'nasty.' He were all that. Manipulative," she added.

Zoe had never met Josh McKenzie. But anyone who'd been able to control Huz, Carrie Wright, the rest of them... Manipulative sounded like the right word.

"As for anyone wishing 'im harm, I don't know. Not these days. Probably everyone who met the bastard. Sorry."

"Nothing to apologise for."

Zoe eyed her coffee, but didn't drink. She looked at Shona.

"I know you made a complaint about him. Domestic violence. But it didn't go ahead. And something happened that meant Josh ended up in hospital. I was wondering..."

Shona looked past her into the hallway, her face paling.

Zoe turned. There was a man standing behind her. Short, sandy-haired, wearing glasses and the expression of someone contemplating violence.

"Who the fuck's this, Sho?" he said. His accent was stronger than hers.

Zoe stood carefully, and turned to face him.

"DI Zoe Finch," she said. "West Cumbria CID. I was just talking to—"

"The fucking police in 'ere?" said the man. "What you let them in for, Sho? I thought you told the last one to leave you the fuck alone."

"Sorry, Iain," said Shona, her voice low.

So this was Iain Murray. Shona's brother.

Expression aside, he didn't look the violent type, but appearances could be deceptive, and Mo had shown Zoe the hospital report on Josh McKenzie. Facial injuries. Abdominal. Back. Head. Indicative of blunt instruments, but hard ones. It had been serious, but it could have been worse.

"Get the fuck out," said Iain Murray, his voice menacing.

Zoe turned to Shona. "Do you want me—"

"I think you should, yeah," said the woman, not meeting her gaze. "I'll be fine with Iain. You'd better go, right."

"Get the fuck out," repeated Iain Murray.

Zoe sized him up. No sign of a weapon. He might be strong, a skilled fighter, but she was bigger than him and her karate skills had seen off tougher men than Iain Murray.

"You sure?" she asked Shona, ignoring her brother.

"Yeah," said the woman, with an apologetic half-smile. "Yeah. That'd be best."

"Fine." Zoe paused by the door, turned, and met Iain

Murray's gaze. They locked eyes for a full ten seconds. "If you change your mind, Shona, just call me," she said, then turned and walked away.

CHAPTER FIFTY-ONE

WHEN TOM WALKED into the team room at nine on the dot, the sarge was sitting in his chair, eyes closed, mouthing the same word over and over again. *Oldman*. Harry Oldman, then. The logins that Kay had denied using, and the boss had been so keen to prove were the work of someone else.

Hadn't they given up on all that?

Tom cleared his throat and the sarge's eyes shot open.

"You OK, Sarge?"

"I'm fine. Good work on that footage, by the way. I've just had Sally Peters in to—"

Tom's phone was ringing. He turned apologetically to the sarge before answering.

"Harriett?"

"Tom, I'm at the hotel with Caroline Deane."

"I know. Any developments?"

"You could say that. Your knife bag has shown up."

"Hang on," Tom said, as the door opened and Nina walked in. "Just putting this on speaker. Harriett, I've got Nina and the sarge here. Say that again, will you?"

CHAPTER FIFTY-ONE

"We've got Josh McKenzie's knife bag."

Nina paused on the way to her desk. "Where was it?"

"That's the thing," Harriett replied. "It was in the manager's room."

Nina and Tom stared at each other in surprise.

"In his office?" asked Tom.

"No, his bedroom. Wasn't us who found it," Harriett added. "The cleaner says she found it first thing this morning."

"In his bedroom? That's... Where was it?"

"Under the bed, apparently. She saw it when she was hoovering, recognised it as Josh's – he never went anywhere without it. She didn't want to pick it up and take it, she knows about contaminating evidence, but she was worried that if she left, he'd get rid of it. She'd been waiting in Raymond's room for about three hours when she saw me pull up in the car park fifteen minutes ago and shouted for me out the window."

Nina nodded, her eyebrows raised in appraisal.

"This could be an important development, Harriett," said the sarge. "You and Caroline know what you're doing. Hold on to the evidence, keep it clean, keep it out of Raymond's hands. I'm sending Tom and Nina over now."

Tom ended the call and turned to the sarge. "What was it you were saying, about Sally Peters?"

"Probably not important, if it turns out Peter Raymond's in the frame, but remember that woman who turned up in the car park Friday night and just stood there?"

Tom nodded. He'd wondered about that.

"That was Sally Peters. Or at least, it was someone driving Sally's car. Sally told me two days ago that she'd never been to the Bassenthwaite Manor Hotel. I had her in for a voluntary interview just now, under caution. Showed her the footage."

"What did she say?"

"Nothing. She walked out. So whatever we have on Peter Raymond, I'll still be following up with Sally Peters."

CHAPTER FIFTY-TWO

ZOE PASSED the sign for Moffat as she ended the call with Aaron. Just a couple more hours, and she'd be back. As long as the weather held off.

It had been a waste of time, as far as the investigation was concerned. But she didn't regret it for a second, not when she'd got to spend time with Mo and, most importantly, with Nicholas.

From what Aaron had just told her, things were hotting up back home. They'd made all kinds of progress, with all kinds of leads to follow up: a mysterious taxi, a woman who'd lied about being on the hotel grounds, and best of all, the discovery of the elusive knife bag.

Aaron had still been on about the King George's Dining Rooms. Yes, it was always possible he had something there, but what he'd discovered about the raid was more interesting, even if it didn't point them in any particular direction. It was the same person, all of it: someone accessing the raid information in advance and tipping off McKenzie, someone accessing the stills that had been used against Margaret

Hooper. The same person, and not Carrie Wright, because she'd been halfway across the world at the time.

Could it be Kay? It was always possible.

But Zoe didn't think so.

Her phone rang, and she smiled at Nicholas's name on the display.

"Wotcha," she said. "Long time no see."

"Yeah."

"Yeah? That's all you've got for me?"

Nicholas laughed hesitantly.

"Are you OK?"

"Fine, Mum. I'm fine. Just wanted to check you were OK. See if you're still around."

"Ah. No, I told you, didn't I? It was just a flying visit."

A short silence. She gripped the steering wheel tighter. *I should have reminded him.*

"Fine," he said. "That's what I thought."

She gritted her teeth. She *had* told him she was leaving. And this went both ways.

"Nicholas, love, can you tell me something?"

"Sure, Mum." He sounded almost absent.

"Why didn't you invite me in last night?"

"What?"

"I wanted to come in. I've not even seen where you live. I thought it would be—"

"Mum, I didn't even know you were coming until yesterday. You can't expect me to turn my whole life upside down at the last minute, just because you suddenly decide to turn up."

It felt like a kick to the gut.

"I only wanted a coffee, Nicholas. And to spend a little time with my boy."

CHAPTER FIFTY-TWO

She could hear the defensive note in her voice.

"That's not fair, Mum. I'm always happy to see you. But if you're just going to squeeze me in around work..."

There was a short silence. *Be the grown up*, she told herself.

"I'm sorry," she said. "You're right."

"I am?"

"I can't blame you if my sudden visit doesn't work for you. And you came out to Mo's to see me. I should be thanking you."

"Right," he said, quieter now.

"Look, why don't you come down here? I can't promise I'll be around the whole time, but you've got a much better chance of catching me."

She tried to laugh, but it sounded hollow and forced.

"Don't worry, Mum."

"I mean it, Nicholas. Come down. I'll... I'll take some time off, OK? I'll clear it with Fiona, get the team sorted. I'll switch off my phone. How does that sound?"

Her son laughed. "You'll switch off your phone? I'd like to see that. Listen, I've got to go. Love you, Mum."

"Love you," she said, to silence.

Her shoulders slumped as her Mini ate up the miles towards England. As she passed Gretna Green, her phone rang.

"Zoe Finch, Cumbria CID," she said, glancing at the *England* sign as it passed.

"DI Finch, is it?" said a man with a familiar thick Scots accent.

"Yes. Is that Iain Murray?"

"Aye, it is. Recognise me voice, did you?"

Zoe let her nose wrinkle. "What can I do for you, Mr Murray?"

"Look, I'm sorry, OK?"

Her nose unwrinkled. "You are?"

"I shouldnae been like that. Shouldnae been so... I dunno. Threatenin', like."

"Apology accepted, Mr Murray."

"I'm nae usually like that, DI Finch. I'm nae a violent man."

Zoe thought back to the report on Josh McKenzie's injuries, but said nothing.

"And I shouldnae taken it out on you. I just... She's fragile, ye know?"

"You mean Shona? She didn't seem fragile to me, Mr Murray." Tired, ill maybe. But not fragile.

"She's put a face on, ye know? It's that bastard. He ruined her life."

"You mean Josh McKenzie?"

"Aye, that's the bag of shite."

"You're aware that Josh McKenzie's dead, aren't you?"

There was a short silence before Murray spoke again.

"Sorry, yeah. She told me. It doesnae change it, though. The man was nasty. World's better off without him."

Zoe narrowed her eyes. "How do you mean, nasty?"

"Shona doesnae like to talk about it. He was a clever bastard, McKenzie. Pulled people's strings, see? Women, mostly. Picked ones he could control, and by the time he were done with them, they needed him. Dependent, like."

"You mean emotionally dependent?" Zoe asked.

Murray grunted. "Aye. That, and the rest. Let's just say when she met McKenzie, our Shona liked a drink or two. She was a normal lass. Twenty-five years old, and she looked eighteen. By the time they were done, seven years have gone, she's like an old woman, and she can't start the day without a few cans."

"And you think—"

"He did this to my sister. Josh McKenzie did it. And you mark my words, DI Finch. If he did it to her, he'll have done it to others, too."

CHAPTER FIFTY-THREE

AARON CURSED. Kay would have been able to find the number in seconds. Tom or Nina, too, but they were on their way to the hotel. He tried the internal directory, tried online, tried friends in other departments, and got nowhere.

He pulled his chair to the corner of the team room, where a CCTV camera stared out at him. He climbed onto the chair and manoeuvred himself until his head was level with the camera.

There was a phone number on it.

Parkers Security directed him to their parent company, Willow Security, who directed him back to the Hub. A Sergeant Brigham, the name he'd been looking for.

Sergeant Brigham seemed pleased to hear from him. She sounded like someone who didn't hear a lot from the *outside world*, as she called it. "All day in the basement," she said. "Watching you lot *do* things."

"I didn't know we had a basement."

"We don't. I'm exaggerating. And I'm sorry, DS Keyes, but I can't help you."

"No?"

"There would've been footage from the camera in your team room, and it would've captured the person who accessed your colleague's terminal. But it gets deleted after four weeks."

"All of it?" he asked.

"We keep it longer in the custody areas, obviously. But if you're after something in your team room, you're almost a year too late."

Damn. It had always been a long shot.

Theodora Harding from the King George's Dining Room was another long shot, one who didn't sound pleased to hear from him at all.

"Listen," she said. "I've just got in, roads are fucked, got a full service tonight. Last thing I need is you wasting time I don't have."

"If you could just tell me everything you know about Josh McKenzie, I won't bother you again."

"Everything? He was just a piece of shit. That's it. Look... He was murdered, right? Someone finally got rid of the fucker?"

"That's right, yes."

"Well, I'm sorry. Not for him." Her voice softened. "But yeah, I'm sorry you've got to waste your time figuring out who did it."

Aaron's phone buzzed, a text. Serge had booked them a taxi and would be picking him up from work. He smiled as Theodora Harding spoke again.

"I know you're just doing your job," she said. "And I wish I could help you. But McKenzie wasn't even that good a chef. He wouldn't have lasted here if he'd been the nicest person in the world. The fact that he was a piece of shit just meant I got rid of him sooner."

"In what way?"

"What do you mean?"

"In what way was he a piece of shit?"

"He was just trouble. Didn't get on well with anyone. Mean. I've got to go now, DS Keyes."

Aaron sat with the phone in his hand and ran through what he'd just heard. He picked up the phone and dialled DI Finch, who answered immediately.

"Boss, your chat with Shona Murray. How did she describe McKenzie?"

The boss laughed. "Nasty, selfish, mean. She wanted a thesaurus."

Mean. That was the word Theodora Harding had just used. But there was something else. Something DI Finch had reported from her conversation with Shona.

Sorry. That was it.

"Boss, one more thing. Did she say something like she wasn't sorry he was dead?"

"That's right. Exactly that."

"So did Theodora Harding."

"I think you're wasting your time there, Aaron."

He sighed. "So does she, boss. And you're probably right. I'm sure it's nothing. Which is all I have to report on Ryan Tobin's friend, I'm afraid."

"Keep on it, will you?" she told him.

He'd been afraid of that.

He'd been sitting another minute with the phone in his hand when it rang, and he almost dropped it.

"DS Keyes? It's Sally Peters."

"Oh," he said.

CHAPTER FIFTY-THREE

"I'm sorry I walked out."

He stood up and walked across the room, shaking himself into alertness. "You can come back in."

"No thanks. But I'm sorry. It *was* me, in the footage."

"Mrs Peters, I really think this conversation—"

"I just want to say it now. I don't want to come in and sit down and have my conversation recorded under caution. I don't want all that. I just want to tell you what happened and then forget about it, OK?"

"OK," he replied. It wasn't like he had much choice.

"He did say something to me, you know. Ellis did. Before he died."

She paused. He waited.

"He mentioned that place. That bloody hotel. Said he wished he'd never been there. And I didn't really think anything of it. It was just a comment, right?"

"So Ellis *had* been there?"

"Some charity thing. For the fire station. God, must have been a couple of years ago now."

"Do you know when, exactly?"

"I'll need to check my diary."

"I can wait."

He heard the sound of the phone being put down and, after a moment, her voice again.

"October," she said. "Just over two years ago. He didn't stay over or anything. Got a taxi back, they all did. And then a few months later he said he wished he'd never been. Out of the blue. I asked why, and he said forget it, and that was it. I forgot it. Time went on, no one's thinking about the Bassenthwaite Manor Hotel. And then he..."

Aaron heard the catch in her breath, a tiny gasp.

"I'm sorry," she said. "I just... I couldn't stop thinking

about it. After he died. After that note turned up. I know something happened there."

"Why didn't you say anything, Mrs Peters? Why didn't you tell us?"

"Because whatever happened there, I don't think I want to know what it was. It can't be good, can it? My Ellis killed himself. So I go there every few weeks, and I park the car, and I get out, and I look at the place, and then I get back in my car and go home again. I've even been in a couple of times, got a drink at the bar. Keep telling myself I'm going to talk to someone, ask someone if they know anything, but I don't have the nerve. Stupid, really. It's just a big posh hotel, isn't it?"

Aaron felt for her. "It is," he agreed.

"What does a place like that have to do with my Ellis, DS Keyes?" she asked, crying again. "It's just not fair."

Sally Peters was convincing. And so was Theodora Harding. They'd both come clean, eventually. Both played hard to get, then softened, and finally broken.

But if you were hiding something, that was exactly what you would do, wasn't it?

CHAPTER FIFTY-FOUR

"Bloody hell," Nina said from the passenger seat. Tom had insisted on taking his car, and she'd been too tired to argue.

"What?" Tom asked.

"The lake. Look!" she pointed. A cat had just walked across the ice, stopping a few feet from the fountain and placing one paw into the water. It was all Nina could do not to shout out a warning.

"It's just a cat, Nina," Tom told her. The cat retreated, and she turned her open mouth into a yawn. Tom frowned at her as he stopped the car. "You OK?"

"Yeah," she said. "I didn't sleep well last night."

Elena had been up when she got back, still angry. She hadn't actually ignored Nina, but she'd spoken in one-word sentences, pretending not to understand when Nina asked simple questions, which she'd understood perfectly well before.

Nina could see why Elena was angry. But she'd found herself awake half the night, worrying. And now there was a black cat walking across a frozen lake. *Talk about the universe sending signals.*

Good thing she wasn't superstitious.

There was no sign of the porter, Stuart Sullivan, but Peter Raymond himself was standing in the reception area when they entered.

Lucky. He hadn't seemed the sort, but there was always a chance he'd have bolted.

"Mind if we have a word?" Nina asked, walking straight past him towards his office. Tom followed and Raymond fell into step alongside him.

"Look," he said, closing the office door and standing with his back to it. "If this is about that bloody bag, I can tell you right now it's a load of nonsense."

Nina eyed him. "Let's take this slowly, Mr Raymond. We'll talk to our colleagues as soon as we're done here, but in the meantime, can you tell me precisely how Josh McKenzie's knife bag has turned up in your room?"

Raymond nodded. He took a few breaths, then walked around Nina and Tom and took a seat behind his desk, gesturing for the two of them to sit at the same time.

Back in control. It didn't take much.

"I don't know for sure, DC Kapoor," he said, with an insincere smile. "But I think I have an idea. Do you know who found it?"

"I don't—"

"It was Sophie Lambert. One of the maids."

His voice was rich with contempt. Nina didn't need to see the sneer that accompanied it.

You bastard.

"And how is this relevant?" Nina asked. Beside her, Tom was gesturing. She knew what he wanted.

CHAPTER FIFTY-FOUR

This conversation would be best conducted back at the Hub. Under caution. Ideally with a lawyer in the room, or so Tom reckoned.

"Because Sophie bloody Lambert's set me up, hasn't she? It's just the sort of thing she'd do. Bet you anything she was the one in that damn taxi, too."

Nina nodded. Nothing they could use so far, nothing incriminating, no need to caution. Just a chat.

"Do you have a photo of Sophie Lambert?" she asked.

"Yes. I—"

"Just the photo, Mr Raymond," she said, anxious that he might be about to say something he wouldn't get round to repeating when they wanted him to.

"Here." He spun his screen around. Staff records. There was Sophie Lambert, a moon-faced woman in her twenties, with long jet-black hair and glasses.

"Thank you, Mr Raymond. We'll be back shortly."

She'd left the room before Tom stood, and waited outside for him to shut the door and get a safe distance before she spoke.

"It wasn't her in the taxi. I recognise her from the footage you sent us. She was in the corridors. Working."

Tom nodded. "We can't talk to him any further without cautioning him, you know."

She nodded. "I agree. I think the taxi's a red herring and I want to know why he thinks Sophie Lambert set him up, but this isn't the place. Might be time to take him in."

Tom looked relieved. "Do you want to call the boss and check?" he asked. "I'll go and have a look at this famous knife bag."

CHAPTER FIFTY-FIVE

Peter Raymond's room, on the fifth floor, was very different from Kate Bellamy's just down the corridor. *More of a suite than a room*, Tom thought, as he stepped carefully inside, wearing a forensic suit and anxious not to disturb any potential evidence.

Caroline and Harriett were crouched with their backs to him, looking down at something by the bed.

"Hello," he said.

They rose as one, Caroline reaching for something on the floor in front of her.

A large clear evidence bag. Inside it, something made of grey canvas, rolled up, that could only be the knife bag.

"Where was it?" he asked.

Caroline pointed. "Just here. Almost poking out. I'm thinking the maid probably moved it, although she swears she didn't."

Harriett's mouth was covered, but he could see the scepticism in her eyes.

"Would be odd," she said. "Just leaving it there, almost in

plain sight. I've taken a statement from her. Sophie Lambert. She didn't strike me as a liar, but it's the sort of thing you might forget doing."

Would you? If you'd found something that linked your boss to the murder of a fellow employee, you might pick it up, shift it, do something with it before you realised what it was. But wouldn't you remember doing that?

"Yes," he said. "Maybe." He coughed, realised he'd been staring into Harriett's eyes, and looked away, to Caroline. "Have you looked inside?"

"Yes." Extracting it carefully, she unrolled the canvas bag onto a strip of white plastic.

Inside were flaps of material to hold the knives in place. One section for each knife. Four knives, of varying lengths. And one gap, where the largest of the knives would have been.

Tom bit back his disappointment. It would have been too much to hope the murder weapon would turn up that easily.

"May I?" Caroline gestured at the bag, and he nodded. "I'll get everything tested, of course."

"Good," he said. They were looking at him, as if they expected him to say something.

Those damn masks.

"I'll see you in a bit," he said, and left the room.

Pulling off his own mask and forensic suit, he turned a corner and knocked on Kate Bellamy's door.

"Come in," she said. He pushed it open and stepped inside. "Oh. You."

Kate was sitting up on her bed. There was a book open beside her, face down. Tom squinted to read the title upside down, then shook his head.

He looked back at Kate. She was pale, but not as starkly

as she had been the other day. And her hair – she'd dyed it again. It looked more alive. *She* looked more alive.

Probably just the makeup. You didn't recover from what she'd been through this quickly.

"What brings you back here, DC Willis?" she asked. There was a brightness in her voice that hadn't been there before.

"We've found Josh's knife bag," he said. He watched for her reaction. A hint of surprise, perhaps? Nothing else.

"Where was it?"

"Peter Raymond's room," he told her.

"The office?"

"No." He shook his head. "His bedroom."

She frowned. "But why..." She looked away from him, then back again, biting her lower lip. "Was it.... Is it there? The knife that killed him?"

Tom shook his head.

"Sorry," she said. "I didn't think... But if that's where the bag was, then Mr Raymond..."

She looked away.

"What is it, Kate?"

"I just... You remember those videos? The ones I gave you?"

"Of course. Are there more?"

"I only knew about that lot, with Laurence whatshisname, and one other set."

"What other set?"

"Mr Raymond. He was sleeping with one of the housekeeping staff, a French girl, Sophie something. She's about twenty years younger than him, too."

"Sophie Lambert?" he asked.

A nod.

CHAPTER FIFTY-FIVE

"And Josh had evidence of this?"

"A video. He showed me on his phone. Ages ago. Like, six months or something? I don't know what he did with it or where it is now, but I know Josh had a video of Mr Raymond with Sophie. Do you think maybe Mr Raymond found out about it?"

Tom fought to keep the smile off his face. With the exception of Kate, no one at the hotel had liked Josh McKenzie, but none of them really had a motive to kill him. Until now.

Peter Raymond had some explaining to do.

CHAPTER FIFTY-SIX

BACK IN THE TEAM ROOM, Zoe answered the phone to hear the word "Shit" being muttered by Nina.

"Hope that wasn't addressed at me, Nina," she said.

"Sorry, boss. Just seen Peter Raymond leaving his office. I wanted to keep an eye on him, make sure he doesn't go walkabout."

Zoe nodded. The last thing they wanted was to get themselves a suspect and then lose him. "Did you speak to him about the knife bag?"

"We did. He denied it, of course. Said he was being set up by the maid who found it. Said it was probably her in the taxi, which is bollocks, because I saw her in the footage from that night, and she's still moving around the hotel cleaning rooms."

"So it sounds like you're not convinced. What about the evidence?"

"Tom was going to take a... Oh, hang on. He's here now."

"Put it on speaker," Zoe said. "I want to go through this with you both."

CHAPTER FIFTY-SIX

"One minute, boss." There was a muffled conversation, then Nina came back on. "We'll go to Tom's car. No privacy here. I'll call you in two minutes."

Ninety seconds later, Nina called back.

"Tell me about this knife bag, Tom," said Zoe.

"Er, sure. So, it's a grey knife bag, matches what the others have said. Four knives in it, but the biggest one's missing."

"That would've been too much to hope for."

"There's something else, though, boss. I spoke to Kate Bellamy. She says she's seen footage of Raymond and the maid he accuses of setting him up."

"What do you mean, footage?"

"Together, boss. Like—"

She rolled her eyes. "I know what 'together' means, Tom. So, what, is Kate suggesting McKenzie blackmailed Raymond too?"

"She's just saying he had the footage on his phone. She doesn't know what he did with it, hasn't seen it for about six months. But if McKenzie had something on Raymond..."

"Then Raymond has a motive," Zoe said. "Nina, did you see Raymond in the footage from Friday night?"

"No, but I didn't get the chance to go through all of it. There's a lot of cameras there. And boss, the way things are going with Raymond, I'm worried he's going to let something slip."

"And we haven't cautioned him yet. Understood, but I think this video, if it exists, puts us beyond cautioning. Are Uniform there?"

There was a short pause before Tom replied. "Yes, boss. Harriett's upstairs, and Roddy's around somewhere."

"Good. I think it's time to arrest Peter Raymond. Get

Uniform to bring him in. Keep an eye there, then head back here, and we'll figure out a strategy to get the truth out of him."

Zoe put the phone down and turned to Aaron, the smile dying on her lips as she saw his frown.

"Everything OK?" she asked.

"Yeah. I mean, yes, boss. I just..."

"You're worried about this login, aren't you?"

He nodded. She could see why. They'd made an arrest, and there was every chance they'd arrested the right man. But it didn't feel like the time to celebrate. Not yet.

Someone had tipped off Josh McKenzie about a drugs raid nearly a year before he'd died. Someone had logged into the system, accessed information, and shared it with the man who was supposed to be its target. And they'd done that in this very team room.

It was all feeling uncomfortably personal.

CHAPTER FIFTY-SEVEN

"Nice one," said Tom, and Nina grinned.

They'd shared the arrest. It was his turn, technically: they'd tried to even things out lately, taking turns on everything from whose car they were driving to who pulled off the big arrest. But Tom had insisted she play her part. He'd delivered the crucial lines because only one person can do that. But she'd been there. She'd been part of it. It was her arrest as much as his.

He was an annoying sod sometimes. Weird around people, weirder around women, weirdest around Harriett Barnes. But he was a good mate.

They watched from the main entrance of the hotel as Raymond ducked and slid into the back seat of the patrol car. Harriett was driving – she always seemed to drive. Roddy Chen might have got in next to Raymond, but that would have been uncomfortable, and possibly grounds for complaint, given the size of Roddy Chen. So Roddy was riding shotgun, and Raymond was all alone.

Time with his thoughts. It wouldn't hurt.

"Pint to celebrate?" said Tom, and Nina was on the verge of agreeing when she remembered the boss's words.

Keep an eye there, then head back here and we'll figure out a strategy to get the truth out of him.

There wasn't anything left to keep an eye on as far as she could tell. It wasn't like Caroline needed someone watching her while she went through rooms and pulled out evidence.

Time to head back.

"DI Finch has work for us, Tom. We'll celebrate later, yeah?"

"Actually, it wasn't really a celebration I had in mind. More, a little digging."

"What?"

"The Bothwell Inn."

She turned to look at him, her mouth falling open. He looked straight back at her, serious as anything.

He wasn't joking.

"You know how to woo a girl, don't you?" she said, shaking her head. "A pint and a bag of pork scratchings at a flat-roofed murder pub where the locals can sniff out police like pigs with truffles."

"Don't you want to know who McKenzie's mate was?" Tom asked.

The laugh that had been forming in her throat withered away. "Come on," she said.

It took twenty minutes to get to the pub, Tom driving carefully through freshly laid snow. Nina talked most of the way. The alternative would have been Tom's latest musical obsession, prog rock, and even silence was better than that. He'd vetoed her Elvis the other day, too. He could listen to Nina, or the sound of the wind.

CHAPTER FIFTY-SEVEN

"So you reckon there's more to this blackmail thing, right?"

"Yeah," he said, face screwed up in concentration.

"We've got Carrie, Huz, Ellis Peters, Margaret Hooper. Someone at the top who knows where the drugs are, and someone else, or the same person, who knows when a raid's about to happen."

"Exactly."

"And when the boss is about to visit a potential source in prison."

"Yup."

"Let me get a word in edgeways, will you?" she said, and heard a faint chuckle in response. The last five minutes were spent in silence, just the wind and the snow, and Nina's own thoughts.

McKenzie's friend had tipped him off about the raid *and* the boss's visit to Carrie Wright. McKenzie's friend had set up Kay Holinshed, someone Nina had liked. McKenzie's friend was the fourth man, and the fourth man was another dirty cop.

The car park was almost empty, which was a good sign when it came to getting out of the place in one piece, but meant McKenzie's friend wasn't likely to be there. They fought their way through the snow to a door whose ancient green paint was almost entirely gone, and had to kick the thing to get it open.

Inside, the place was as dark as she remembered. Low lights over a pool table, a couple of fruit machines, and one small bar that hadn't changed in all the time she'd known it. There were two men and a woman standing at the bar, spaced apart and silent. All of them were in their seventies, but with that mean look that said they could fight people half their age and probably win.

Behind the bar stood an overweight, middle-aged woman with curly blonde ringlets and a pierced nose.

"What do you want?" she barked, before Nina and Tom were even in the room.

"Just a drink and a friendly chat." Tom smiled at her, looking braver than Nina imagined he felt.

"Not interested in a friendly chat, and don't serve coppers," she said.

"That's fine," replied Nina. "Just a quick word, then."

She took another step towards the bar and felt a tug on her arm. Tom was pulling her backwards.

"What?" she asked, irritated.

He pulled her around to face the wall to their right.

There was a dartboard there. And beside the dartboard, a series of five framed photographs.

Tom pointed to the one in the middle, and Nina gasped.

The legend *Bothwell Inn Darts Club 2023–4* was printed across the top. Below the words, seven men were standing scowling at the camera. Three in the front row, four behind them.

In the back row, one man had his arm around another, and these two had the closest thing to a smile on their faces.

"Bloody hell," said Tom.

"Yeah," agreed Nina.

The man on the right was Josh McKenzie. And the man with his arm slung around McKenzie with the familiarity of long friendship was someone else they knew. A man who was closer to fifty than forty. A bald, long-faced bastard who'd made so many enemies, it shouldn't have come as a surprise to see him there.

CHAPTER FIFTY-SEVEN

The Bothwell Inn was his natural habitat, really. The perfect environment for PC Tel Cummings.

CHAPTER FIFTY-EIGHT

"Right," said Zoe. "And you're sure..."

"It was him, boss." The signal was poor, Nina's words broken by static, but Zoe could hear her excitement. "I've sent a copy to the team inbox. Josh McKenzie was with Tel Cummings."

"Christ," Zoe heard from behind her. She turned to see Aaron rubbing his head and staring at the image on the screen.

"What's wrong?" she asked.

He shook his head. "I should have known."

Shit. She didn't have time for him to have a relapse. Peter Raymond was on his way in. And now, finally, they had a name for the fourth man. Perhaps.

"Nina, Tom, I'm going to follow this up, and Aaron and I will interview Peter Raymond. There's not a lot left to do here. Why don't you head home?"

She ended the call and turned to Aaron. "I need to speak to PSD," she said, and left the team room.

In her office, she tried Carl twice, but each time it went

CHAPTER FIFTY-EIGHT

straight to voicemail. The course. He'd be in some windowless, white-walled room listening to someone tell him how to do things he knew better than anyone else alive.

There was no answer from DCI Branthwaite, either. Zoe hesitated, then tried DS Denise Gaskill, but her phone went straight to voicemail too. Chances were, she was on the same course as Carl.

She'd made it halfway up to Fiona's office before she stopped and turned back.

This had to go through PSD. Not Fiona. She wasn't sure if Cummings was their man, but Zoe was going to find out, one way or another. And she was going to do this the right way.

She returned to her office, looked up a number, and dialled.

"PC Barnes," said a voice. Zoe could hear noises in the background, another voice, plaintive, whining. And the sound of the wind.

"Harriett, it's Zoe Finch. I'd like a word."

"I'll be back in ten minutes," Harriett replied.

Of course. She was with Roddy Chen in the car. Bringing Raymond in.

"Excellent. I'll see you then."

Harriett hadn't sounded worried, the way any normal PC would be worried if they'd just been asked for a word by a DI. Did she know what Zoe suspected?

Zoe sat behind her desk, opened her screen, and scrolled through the latest in the team inbox. She couldn't concentrate. All she could see was that car, with Harriett Barnes driving and Peter Raymond in the back, and Roddy Chen wherever he could fit.

Come on. Just get here.

She returned to the team room, where Aaron had Raymond's image up on the big screen. *Good.* Aaron needed to be thinking about this side of the case. Peter Raymond. The knife bag.

"Can you make sure we've got an interview room set up and check if he's got a lawyer coming in?"

"He's got a lawyer coming in, boss," Aaron replied, shaking his head.

Zoe felt her shoulders dip. "Basham?"

"Basham."

"OK," she said. "We've handled Stan Basham before. I'll see you down there."

They'd be bringing Raymond straight in through the custody suite, so Zoe positioned herself there, standing by the desk and trying to make small talk with Clive 'Ilkley' Moor, the custody sergeant, while she checked her watch every thirty seconds, and ignored another call from Ryan Tobin.

They should be here by now.

"Everything OK, DI Finch?" asked Ilkley.

"Yes, why?"

"You seem on edge. Oh, here's your package," he said, looking up and past her as three figures walked in through the main doors.

Harriett hesitated as she spotted Zoe, apparently unsure what to do. Zoe pointed to the desk and said, "Book him in, then hand over to Roddy. I'll wait."

The ten minutes of formalities seemed to take an hour, but eventually Roddy Chen and Peter Raymond were gone.

"My office," said Zoe. They walked there in silence, Harriett two steps behind her the whole way. In her office, Zoe pointed to a chair, shut the door, and turned, her back against it.

"I've got to interview Peter Raymond now, so I'll keep this brief."

"Yes, Ma'am," replied Harriett. She still looked a little confused, but not worried.

But you'd need that composure, if you'd been doing what Harriett Barnes had been doing for nearly two years.

"I know who you are, Harriett. I know the truth."

"I... I'm not sure I understand what you mean, Ma'am." For the first time, Harriett looked anxious.

"I don't have time for games, Harriett," Zoe said, opening the door and stepping out into the corridor. "I want you to wait in my office while DS Keyes and I interview Peter Raymond."

She walked away, closing the door behind her, and praying that Harriett would still be there when she got back.

CHAPTER FIFTY-NINE

"Christ almighty, she's not letting you run this all by yourself, is she?" said Stan Basham.

They'd been sitting in the interview room for nearly five minutes, Aaron on one side of the table, Basham and his client, Peter Raymond, on the other. Those were the first words Basham had spoken.

"DI Finch will be here shortly," Aaron replied. He hoped it was true.

Basham snorted and turned to Peter Raymond. "If they're dragging out the likes of DS Keyes here, you don't have much to worry about," he said.

Aaron ignored him. He was used to this.

But where the hell was the boss?

She walked in a minute later, short of breath and a little flushed. She'd run from upstairs, then. But why?

He pushed it from his mind, read the formalities, and prepared to kick things off.

"This is ridiculous," said Raymond, before Aaron could

ask his first question. Basham nudged his client, and Raymond turned to the lawyer. "What?"

"Why don't we listen to what the lovely police officers have to say, Mr Raymond?" Basham suggested.

"Well, we know what they have to say, don't we?" Raymond snorted, and Aaron realised with a start that they were remarkably alike, Stan Basham and Peter Raymond. "They think I killed Josh McKenzie because that little slut's put McKenzie's bag of bloody knives in my room."

Aaron revised his assessment. Whatever Basham was, he wasn't as stupid as Raymond.

"Mr Raymond," he said. "You've just referred to 'bloody' knives. Do you mean that literally, or—"

"I didn't see the damn things, did I?" Raymond said. "I've got no idea if they're clean or covered in McKenzie's organs! Why don't you ask her?"

"Her?"

"Sophie Lambert. Stupid bitch who put them there."

"Ah," said DI Finch, looking up from her notes, the first time she'd spoken since she'd sat down. "This would be Sophie Lambert, the woman who you claim framed you, yes?"

"Yes. Her."

"And the 'little slut' you've just referred to, this is the same Sophie Lambert?"

"Erm, yes."

"And why d'you think that she put the knives there?"

"I'll tell you why," said Raymond, ignoring Basham whispering in his ear. "It's because she thought she'd got her claws into me, that's why." He leaned forward, brushing Basham away, and pointed at the DI. "Have you checked this taxi that was ferrying people about in the middle of the night? I'll bet you anything she was in it."

"She wasn't in the taxi, Mr Raymond," said Aaron. "We have video evidence that proves it."

Raymond sat back and turned to Basham, a look of confusion on his face.

Is that real? It certainly looked real.

"She thought she'd got her claws into you," Aaron said. "Do you mind expanding on that, Mr Raymond?"

"My client—" began Basham.

"Yes. Fine," interrupted Raymond. "I slept with the woman. She'd been all over me for months. Couldn't do any harm, I thought. Only happened once. Maybe twice. I don't remember the details."

Aaron turned to DI Finch. He hadn't expected this, not quite so easily. It led neatly into the video footage McKenzie supposedly had of the two of them.

DI Finch was staring ahead, as if she wasn't really listening.

"And you think she planted the knives in your room because..." Aaron began.

"Because she'd hoped for more, hadn't she?" Raymond fired back. "Probably thought she'd end up marrying me. Not my type." He chuckled. "She didn't get what she wanted, so I suppose she was after revenge. Woman scorned, you see?"

He looked expectantly across the table. After a moment, and no response, he continued.

"And she had access to my room. I don't care if she wasn't in the damn taxi. It was her. And you know what?" he added, sitting back again.

"What?" said Aaron.

CHAPTER FIFTY-NINE

"I think we're done here. Bring in Sophie Lambert and see what *she's* got to hide. Until then, I've got nothing else to say to you."

CHAPTER SIXTY

Zoe made her way back to her office, her phone to her ear. Still no answer, from Carl, or Branthwaite, or Denise Gaskill.

The interview had been a waste of time, and for once, that hadn't been Stan Basham's doing. But Peter Raymond could wait. He wasn't going anywhere.

Unlike Harriett Barnes, potentially.

Zoe pushed open the door to her office and breathed deeply.

Harriett was still there, sitting in the same chair, now turned so it was facing the door.

"Ma'am," she said, rising. "I'm sorry. But I really—"

"Sit down," Zoe said, and Harriett sat down. "Listen to me. Don't say anything until I've finished. OK?"

Harriett nodded.

"Good." Zoe made her way around the desk and sat. "You're aware we've suspected for some time that we haven't reached the heart of the Carrie Wright operation, aren't you?"

CHAPTER SIXTY

Harriett nodded. On the desk in front of her, Zoe saw her phone light up with an incoming call. She ignored it.

"And you're probably aware that Carrie has now admitted Josh McKenzie was blackmailing her. Passing her drugs, and information on who to bust, and when. Which implies a presence on the supplier side, something we haven't yet got to grips with."

Harriett had opened her mouth to say something. Zoe shook her head, firmly, and Harriett closed her mouth.

"More pertinently, we've been working under the assumption that there was an additional operation here, at the Hub, or somewhere within the police. McKenzie had a call last Thursday, two days after I put in my request to see Carrie, warning him that someone was talking. And then he fled. We believe someone tipped him off that I was going to see Carrie, and that his name might come up. He was already on our radar, thanks to something his girlfriend mentioned a few months ago. But we needed Carrie to confirm it. Do you understand?"

Another nod. This was going well, so far, but this was the easy bit.

"Last February there was a drugs raid," Zoe continued, "on the Bassenthwaite Manor Hotel. McKenzie was the target, but it seems he had a tip off in advance."

Another nod.

"Everything I've said so far, you either knew or suspected. What I'm about to say may or may not be news. Whoever it was that tipped off McKenzie, they accessed their information right here in the Hub, Harriett. In my team room. Using the terminal that had been temporarily assigned to Kay Holinshed, with login credentials from a retired DS, Harry Oldman. Until now, we've not had the faintest idea who that person is." Zoe took a breath. "However, it's just come to our attention that Josh McKenzie was an associate of PC Tel Cummings."

She unlocked her phone and showed Harriett the photo. There, in the back row, were Cummings and McKenzie.

Harriett nodded again, her face impassive. She wasn't giving away a thing.

"We believe Tel Cummings is the man we've been after, the man who tipped off McKenzie about both the raid and my visit to Carrie Wright, and framed Kay in the process. It's also quite plausible that Cummings killed McKenzie. Cleaning house."

Harriett was frowning. Zoe's phone lit up again. She ignored it.

"I'm sorry, Ma'am, but haven't we just arrested Peter Raymond for that murder?"

"Yes, and Raymond is still a likely candidate. But we can't rule out the possibility that it was Cummings. It could also have been someone at the port, the main supplier, getting revenge on the operation that busted his dealers. If that's the case, Cummings could be the next victim. In the meantime, all we have on Cummings is a photo of him with McKenzie. It's useful, but it's hardly evidence."

"I'm sorry to ask, Ma'am, but why are you telling me all this?" Harriett asked.

She was good. She was *very* good. She still hadn't caved, after all this. She wasn't admitting a thing. The urge to applaud was overtaken by a weight in the pit of Zoe's stomach.

Maybe there was nothing to admit. Maybe Harriett was playing ignorant because she *was* ignorant.

Maybe Zoe had got it all wrong.

CHAPTER SIXTY

No. She hadn't got it wrong. She couldn't have got it wrong.

"I'm telling you this," she said, "because after what I've said, it should be clear we need to bring Cummings in, and I don't have enough evidence to do that. If anyone does have that evidence, they need to produce it now."

"But Ma'am—"

"And if," Zoe said, "you are what I think you are, and you've been looking into individuals here at the Hub, then you might be able to do that."

Harriett blinked back at her. "What do you think I am?"

Zoe smiled, swallowed, and said it.

"PSD, Harriett. I think you're PSD."

CHAPTER SIXTY-ONE

AARON STOOD in the team room, looking at the empty desks, and wondering what was going on.

Where was the boss?

She'd walked straight out of the interview room, leaving him to terminate the interview formally. Basham had suggested his client could go home now, and Aaron had rather enjoyed the expression on Raymond's face when he'd made it clear he couldn't.

But there was no sign of the boss.

He picked up his phone and dialled her number. It rang half a dozen times, then went through to voicemail.

He called the station at Elterwater, hoping no one would answer, and was disappointed when someone did.

"DC Hedley," he heard.

Hedley?

"Lynn?" he asked. "Lynn Hedley?"

"Yes, who's that?"

"It's Aaron Keyes," he told her. He was sure he could hear the smile in her answer.

CHAPTER SIXTY-ONE

"Aaron? DS Keyes? I heard you'd been in, but I didn't know if Isaac was just... Well, you know what Isaac's like."

Aaron knew what Isaac Bateman was like. Lynn, though, was a very different story. She'd just started at the local primary school as he'd been finishing, and he'd seen something in her that reminded him of himself. A certain sensitivity that meant she'd been the target of the bullies before she was even five years old. A resilience that meant she'd survive it and come out on top in the end.

He'd heard, over the years, that she'd done well at school, and gone on to join the police. He hadn't realised she'd ended up back home.

"I thought you were based in Yorkshire or something," he said.

"Position came up here. I couldn't resist," she told him. "It's so lovely to hear from you."

Aaron didn't have time to reminisce.

"You've got a missing person," he said, finally. "Kevin Downes. We've got an interest in finding him."

"Kevin Downes," she repeated. "The protestor, right?"

"That's right."

"Isaac says he's just gone for a wander," she told him.

"Isaac might be right, for once," he said, and heard her chuckle. "But he might not be. I know you've got your own chain of command and I can't tell you what to do, Lynn. But as a personal favour, would you mind keeping me informed of any developments?"

"Of course. Although I don't think there's going to be any developments," she replied. "Isaac and DI Woolley would have to actually look into it for that to happen."

Lynn Hedley was a junior officer. He didn't want to get her in any trouble. He couldn't really ask her to...

"I'll tell you what, though," she said. "I'll see what I can find out. Have a chat with the other protestors. Check the file. I'll let you know."

He thanked her and ended the call. That had certainly gone better than expected.

But now he couldn't get the other things out of his head. Peter Raymond. The way the boss had behaved, after the interview, and before it.

Had he missed something? Was it because he'd been on light duties?

He checked his messages, then opened the team mailbox, looking for something that might have slipped by, something that explained why DI Finch didn't seem particularly interested in the man they'd just arrested for murder.

He read through his notes, from Sally Peters, Theodora Harding. The forensic updates. Call logs. Messages from Keisha about the phone data she'd been unable to recover. The boss's notes from her meeting with Shona Murray and the subsequent call from her brother Iain. The Carrie Wright meetings. Nina, and Tom, talking to Kate Bellamy, the chefs, the barman, the other receptionist.

There was nothing new. Maybe Nina would know. Or Tom. He tried them both and got their voicemails.

The boss would tell him, in her own time. He'd just have to wait until she was ready. Which meant...

He picked up his phone and brought up Serge's number.

"What the hell am I doing?" he said out loud.

Had he really been about to cancel his plans? To duck out of whatever it was Serge had planned for him?

Idiot.

He tried DI Finch again. This time, he left a message,

checking everything was OK, and explaining that he'd be heading out shortly, but would see her tomorrow.

Then he tapped the screen again for a video call to his husband.

"Hello, gorgeous," said Serge. "Oh, I see you haven't changed yet."

"Just about to. And I see *you're* intending to make a statement."

"What, this old thing?" Serge pulled at the Vivienne Westwood shirt he was wearing. "Well, if I'm walking in on the arm of the handsomest man in Cumbria, I need to make an effort, don't I?"

"If you're swanning about with the handsomest man in Cumbria, I'll deck the bastard," Aaron laughed.

"With you in fifteen," said Serge.

Fine.

He'd go out and have a lovely meal with his husband, and DI Finch's disappearing act could wait until tomorrow.

CHAPTER SIXTY-TWO

Harriett stared at Zoe.

"I need to make a call," she said.

No denial. No admission, either.

"Fine," Zoe replied. "Speak to whoever you need to, but remember, this isn't something we can just come back to when it suits us."

Harriett nodded and left the room. She'd be trying Carl. Trying Branthwaite when Carl didn't answer. Maybe she'd talk to Denise Gaskill, maybe not. Zoe wasn't sure even Denise knew who Harriett really was.

They wouldn't answer. Zoe had tried all of them minutes earlier.

She resisted the urge to stare at the clock, instead pulling up the recording of the interview they'd just done and trying to convince herself it was important.

Of course it was important. The man down there was probably a murderer.

Possibly a murderer.

Definitely a bastard.

CHAPTER SIXTY-TWO

She heard footsteps outside, then a knock on her door.

"Come in," she called.

Harriett walked in and sat down.

"Did you get hold of anyone?" Zoe asked.

Harriett shook her head.

Zoe nodded. "So you've got to decide for yourself. Cummings is either in danger, or he's a killer, and either way, we need to bring him in. If you're willing to help me, I'd—"

"I've decided, Ma'am," said Harriett. "And yes. It's true."

"Sorry?" said Zoe. She'd spent so long thinking about this, it didn't seem real.

"I'm PSD, Ma'am. I've been undercover at the Hub for nineteen months. And it's just possible I've got what you're looking for."

CHAPTER SIXTY-THREE

AARON SHOULD HAVE EXPECTED IT. Everything nice always had a sting in its tail. It was typical that this should be their destination.

For the first twenty minutes, he hadn't paid much attention to where they were heading. Serge had got them a limo, not a taxi, and Aaron had bitten back the objection. Serge was making good money with his drone video business. And they were celebrating. Just getting a babysitter Annabel would tolerate had been enough of a challenge. It wasn't like they did this sort of thing regularly.

It wasn't until the headlights picked out the sign for Boot that Aaron began to suspect. His heart sank when they took the turn for Wast Water.

There was nothing here. Nothing except the King George's Dining Rooms, anyway.

Beside him, Serge was squeezing his hand, grinning in anticipation. He'd be expecting Aaron to sit up in amazement when they pulled into the car park and he realised where they were going.

CHAPTER SIXTY-THREE

He looked away, out of the window, feeling sick. She'd be there, Theodora Harding. Maybe he could feign illness. Ask the driver to pull over, pretend to vomit into the snow. He could probably do it for real, the way his stomach was churning.

No.

He'd make an extra appointment with Dr Filey. In the meantime, he was going to celebrate his anniversary with his husband. He reached into his pocket and switched off his phone.

This was a happy night.

Aaron made what he thought were the right noises, exclaiming when the sign came into view, cooing over the lights in the car park and the elegantly dressed staff who rushed out to the limo, umbrellas aloft, to usher them inside.

At the table, he allowed himself to relax. The descriptions on the menu were vague, but their waitress, a woman in her twenties with long red hair, filled in the gaps in mouth-watering detail. The prices matched the descriptions, but this was a one-off, Serge reminded Aaron. And the drone business was going very well indeed.

"Here's to you," Serge said, smiling.

"To us," replied Aaron, and they clinked glasses.

After the second of the eight courses, Aaron stepped away to the gents. It was in the small corridor on the way back that he saw her, walking determinedly in the direction of the kitchen. He watched as her expression changed from friendly, to neutral, to puzzled, to furious.

"You," she said, marching back towards him.

He took a step back.

"What the fuck do you think you're doing?" she asked. "You stalking me, DS Keyes?"

"I'm not—"

"I was being friendly when we spoke earlier, but I'm not feeling friendly now. Do I need to make a complaint?"

He took a step past her and pointed to the table, where Serge was sitting, twirling a wine glass thoughtfully in his right hand.

God, he looks good in that shirt.

He turned back to the chef. "That's my husband," he said. "It's our anniversary, and he's brought me here as a surprise. He has no idea I've ever been here. No idea I've met you. My work – well, you know all about tough hours. It doesn't make things easy, for him. So I'd rather you didn't—"

A look of horror passed over the chef's face.

"I'm sorry," she said. "I didn't realise. I've never spoken to a customer like that. Please accept my apologies, DS Keyes."

"Aaron."

"Aaron. I don't know what to say. If one of my staff had done what I just did..."

"It's fine," he assured her. He was about to walk away when he realised there was an opportunity here. "Ms Harding, you must know everyone in this industry."

"I wouldn't put it like that, but yeah, I keep my ear to the ground."

"What do you make of Peter Raymond?"

She looked up, right into his eyes. "I thought this wasn't an official visit," she said.

"Well, yes..."

"Maybe try being a husband and stop being a cop for the evening?"

He couldn't help smiling. An image passed through his mind, Bobby Silver, in the Henry Bessemer, putting down her glass and shaking her head.

CHAPTER SIXTY-THREE

"Someone else said something very similar to me, just the other day," he told her. "Maybe you've got a point."

He'd started to walk away when he felt a tap on his shoulder, and stopped. She was there, behind him.

"Yes?" he said.

"But for the record, everyone in hospitality's heard of that creep."

The rest of the meal was a delight. Aaron knew he'd drunk more than he should have done when he found himself laughing as Serge picked up the remains of the lobster, and made it perform a complex dance on the tablecloth. Their red-headed waitress looked on with an indulgent smile. She'd have seen it all before.

Aaron looked up as the bill came, and found himself forcing a grin onto his face. Theodora had brought it herself.

What's she doing?

"I hope you've enjoyed your evening," she said.

Serge turned. His jaw dropped and his eyes widened.

"Oh," he stammered. "Yes. Yes, it's been marvellous."

"Well," she said, "I just wanted to say, this one's on us."

"What?" said Serge and Aaron at the same time.

"Happy anniversary," she replied, and walked away. Serge picked up the bill she'd just left. Aaron could see numbers on it, all of them crossed out.

Serge turned to him. "What the fuck just happened?" he asked.

"Search me," replied Aaron. From across the room, Theodora Harding threw him a wink. He shook his head. "I guess we've just got lucky."

"And if you play your cards right, DS Keyes," Serge said, "you might just get lucky again later."

CHAPTER SIXTY-FOUR

IN THE SIXTEEN months she'd been in Cumbria, Zoe hadn't once had cause to lock her office door.

Until now.

She stood, walked past Harriett, and clicked the lock. By the time she returned to her desk, Harriett had produced a USB flash drive and was holding it out.

"What's this?" Zoe asked.

"Footage. From inside the Hub."

"From when?"

"Eighteen months, Ma'am."

Zoe sat back and stared at the woman in front of her. "What's your actual rank?" she asked. "Should you even be calling me that?"

"I'm a DC, Ma'am. So yes."

"Is Harriett Barnes even your real name?"

"It's all real. My cover's pretty much the whole truth, except I'm two years older than I'm supposed to be. I was with West Yorkshire Police for a year, in Uniform, but Branthwaite spotted me in training when he came to deliver a short course on counter-corruption. He had an opening, thought I might be suitable. I worked with him on the quiet for a few months, and then, well..."

"Then you got dropped in here."

"Exactly. May I?" Harriett gestured to Zoe's laptop.

Zoe nodded. "I don't mean to sound negative, but have you actually achieved anything in all your time here?"

Harriett paused in the act of inserting her USB drive, and sat up to face Zoe.

"Not yet. I'm aware that we didn't find Huz until it was pretty much too late, and it was your team that found Carrie. And believe me, I'm not happy about it. But," she continued, bending over and opening a series of files, "I think I might be able to help you now. Look."

She spun the laptop round to face Zoe. There, listed by location and date, were thousands of video files.

"How come you've got this?" Zoe asked.

"I've been copying the internal feeds. They delete them after four weeks, but I had a feeling we'd need more than that. It's your team room, right?"

Zoe nodded, and Harriett entered a series of filters. The thousands of video files shrank to a few hundred.

"Bloody hell," whispered Zoe. "Is that—"

"Everything. Eighteen months, twenty-four seven. What's the date we're looking for?"

"Aaron's got it. Hang on."

Aaron's phone went straight to voicemail.

"Shit. OK. It'll be in the team inbox." Zoe pulled up a file, scanned and closed it, pulled up another. "Here it is. The raid was on the eighteenth of February, last year. Two in the morning. I think Aaron said the login was the previous day. Maybe the day before that."

"Right. Shall we go from the sixteenth, then?"

It was slow work. After ten minutes, the two of them side by side, watching footage of the team room at eight times normal speed, Harriett stood and left the room. She returned five minutes later with her own laptop and moved on to the next file.

Zoe watched as the room on her screen brightened and darkened and brightened again. She watched Tom enter and leave, Nina, then Tom again, then Aaron, then Zoe herself, none of them ever settling before they were up and gone again. Kay seemed to disappear every two hours, for exactly seven minutes, which was presumably how long it took to get outside, smoke a cigarette, and get back again. Aaron, she could see, was hardly smiling. It should have been obvious how unhappy he'd been even then. But Victor Parlick was dead, by that point. Aaron was already blaming himself.

She stared at Tom, paused the footage, then returned it to normal speed, watching his movements. He'd been recovering from his ordeal in the mine, held at gunpoint by Alice Winstanley. He was stick-thin. Pale. But he was always stick-thin, and they all looked pale in February, under that sort of lighting.

Zoe finished viewing the file, clicked open the next, and sped the footage up again. And again.

Halfway through the seventh file and well into the evening of the seventeenth, the team room emptied. An evidence review. All of them presenting what they had for the case against Alice.

The door opened, and a figure crossed the room.

Zoe paused the footage, rewound it, and played it back at normal speed.

There.

The door opened. A man walked in and went straight to Kay's desk. He tapped away on the keyboard for five minutes, pausing to look at the door, standing, ready to move should he need to. Then he checked around him, looked right at the camera, frowned, and left.

Zoe rewound it again.

"Got him," she said.

Harriett stood behind her as she played the footage twice more until they were certain.

The women looked at one another in silence.

"Tel Cummings," Zoe said. "No doubt about it."

CHAPTER SIXTY-FIVE

IT WAS close to midnight when Carl finally called back, but Zoe was still in her office.

She'd spent the last ninety minutes going through the rest of the files with Harriett. They'd seen Tel Cummings come and go twice more, each time waiting until the team room was empty, going straight for Kay's desk, doing whatever he needed to, and disappearing within minutes.

He'd have known he was running a risk with the cameras. But he'd have assumed the footage would be deleted within weeks. A calculated risk, then.

"About time," she said, picking up the phone.

"Missing you too," Carl replied. "How's my favourite—"

"You're on speaker," she said. "I'm in the office, Carl."

"Oh?" There was a question in his voice.

"I'm with Harriett."

"Oh."

"And – listen, Carl, are you sober?"

"Of course. Went out after the training sessions. But I stuck to the non-alcoholic stuff."

CHAPTER SIXTY-FIVE

"Good. Because I know about Harriett."

There was a short pause.

"I don't understand," Carl said. "You know what about Harriett?"

Harriett leaned towards the phone. "She knows I'm PSD, Sir. She confronted me, and I tried to get hold of you and DCI Branthwaite, but neither of you were available, and the circumstances meant—"

"It's OK," said Carl. Zoe heard him sigh. "If it's out, it's out. Does anyone else know?"

Harriett looked at Zoe questioningly.

"Not yet," Zoe said. "Tom suspects. But listen, we've found something. We know who tipped off McKenzie about the raid last year. It's Tel Cummings. We've got him accessing files in my team room, using Kay's desk and Harry Oldman's logins."

"Really?"

"We've got him, Carl."

She smiled as she said it, could see Harriett smiling. Carl would be smiling too.

None of them liked Cummings. None of them had suspected he'd be capable of anything as complex as this. But now it was out there, it suddenly seemed obvious.

"Excellent news," said Carl. "We'll bring him in when I'm back tomorrow."

"Good," said Harriett, at the same time as Zoe said, "No."

"No?" repeated Carl.

"Either Cummings killed McKenzie, or whoever did kill McKenzie will be going after Cummings as soon as they figure out he's involved. He needs to be brought in now, Carl."

Zoe waited. Beside her, she could see Harriett's knee jogging up and down.

"OK," he said. "I'll make the arrangements. But no one's questioning him until morning."

"Why not?"

"Because I want to do this one myself."

Zoe opened her mouth to object, then closed it again. They had enough evidence now to charge Cummings the moment they arrested him. Once they brought him in, he wasn't going anywhere.

"OK," she said. Beside her, Harriett nodded.

"And don't tell anyone about this," Carl warned.

"Carl, it's my team that identified him. Nina and Tom found a photo of him with McKenzie. They might not have the proof, but they know—"

"Please, Zoe. Just keep it to yourself. For tonight."

Again, Zoe found herself biting back an objection. Maybe Carl was being paranoid.

But being paranoid was probably sensible, in the circumstances.

CHAPTER SIXTY-SIX

IT WAS HALF past eight when Tom entered the team room. He was surprised to find everyone else there waiting. Even Nina, who winked at him and looked at her watch.

"Nice of you to join us," said DI Finch, rising from the spare desk.

"What?" he said. "I mean, sorry, boss. I'd— Did I miss a note or something?"

"We've got a murder suspect waiting to be interviewed downstairs, and there's still too many pieces missing from the jigsaw, Tom," she replied. "You shouldn't have to be told to come in early in this sort of situation."

He frowned.

"It's OK," the sarge told him. "You're fine. Nina's only been in two minutes. And I've only been in ten."

"Saaarge," complained Nina.

"Enough," snapped DI Finch. She looked tired. The sarge looked rough – he'd been out for his anniversary the night before, hadn't he? And Nina had announced she was heading to the Miner's Yard for a drink and a bit of karaoke. But DI Finch was the only one with dark shadows under her eyes.

"Here's what's happening this morning," she said. "Tom, like I say, there's too many pieces missing from the jigsaw. So I want you back at the hotel today."

"Right," he replied. He forced a smile, but he was disappointed. They'd brought in a suspect. They'd arrested him for murder. Surely the hotel was...

"I know what you're thinking," she said. "The hotel's done. But it isn't, is it? Caroline hasn't finished with Raymond's bedroom, or his office. We may have to bring this Sophie Lambert in for an interview. And maybe you can get more out of Kate Bellamy. If she's willing, perhaps she can come in too. I don't like the way we've been getting information out of her. It's too piecemeal."

Tom nodded. "She's nervous, boss."

"Neurotic," added Nina.

"Her boyfriend's just been murdered," Tom pointed out. "But I'll have a go at persuading her."

"Good. And we'll let you know if there's any need to bring in Sophie Lambert." The DI turned to the sarge. "Aaron, you can take the lead on Raymond this morning. Interview him with Nina. See if you can get a confession out of him. Then maybe we won't need Kate Bellamy at all."

She walked to the door and turned to face them all. "OK, everyone?" she said, and without waiting for an answer, she walked away.

Nina was the first to speak. "She OK?" she asked.

The sarge was frowning. "I'm not sure. Did she say where she was going?"

"What's happened with Tel Cummings?" Tom asked. "Did she do anything about that?"

The sarge shook his head. "She couldn't get hold of PSD. But Cummings can wait. Come on." He looked at Nina. "We've got a murder suspect to interview."

CHAPTER SIXTY-SEVEN

"Look," said Peter Raymond. "This is all just a stupid mistake. Surely you can see that?"

Beside him, Stan Basham was whispering. Raymond shook his head.

"See what?" asked Aaron.

Basham's whispering grew more urgent. The standard Stan Basham operating procedure: keep your mouth shut long enough, and they might just give up. It was crude, but occasionally it worked.

You had to have a client willing to cooperate, though, and Peter Raymond liked the sound of his own voice far too much to keep his mouth shut.

"All of it," Raymond replied. "I suggest you just let me go, apologise, and we'll forget about the whole thing."

They'd hoped a night in the cells might soften him up. At least he was talking.

"Mr Raymond," said Nina. "I'd like to pick up on some of the things you said yesterday."

"DC Kapoor's one of those experiments they throw into

CHAPTER SIXTY-SEVEN

a situation, see if it changes anything," Basham said. "You don't have to answer her questions any more than you have to answer his."

"DC Kapoor's put away enough of Mr Basham's clients for him to be familiar with her methods," Aaron said.

Basham scowled.

"Look, enough of this," said Raymond. "I just want to go back to the hotel, have a shower, put all this behind me."

Aaron glanced at Nina, whose eyes had gone wide.

The man was under arrest for murder. Did he really think it was going to be that easy?

"If you've got something to tell us that allows us to release you, Mr Raymond, we'll be very interested to hear it," she said, smooth as anything.

Aaron smiled. She was getting good at this.

"Look, I've already told you I slept with the woman. Sophie Lambert. If it's a crime to have sex with a moderately attractive female, then fine. Throw away the key."

Across the table, Basham's scowl had turned into a look of horror.

"And I made it eminently clear to the woman that this was never going to be a proper relationship. I assume you've asked her about this?"

"Not yet, Mr Raymond," Aaron said. "I'd like to—"

"Not yet?" shouted Raymond. "I don't have time to sit here all day waiting, while you—"

"You are under arrest for murder, Mr Raymond," Aaron reminded him. "If you have anything useful to tell us, then do so. But you will not be directing the conduct of this investigation any more than I will be directing the running of your hotel. Is that clear?"

Raymond sat back and shrugged.

"Now," Aaron continued. "We have information that the victim, Josh McKenzie, had evidence of your affair with Sophie Lambert."

"I keep trying to tell you, it wasn't an affair. It was a meeting of bodies. Once, maybe twice. Brief, convenient, not unpleasurable, certainly, but—"

"Fine," interrupted Aaron.

Basham had shut his eyes and sat back in his chair. Aaron was impressed by how quickly Raymond had managed to alienate his own lawyer. Basham rarely gave up this early.

"Whatever it was," Aaron said. "Josh McKenzie had video evidence of it. Are you aware of this?"

"Yes," replied Raymond. "He showed it to me. Horrible man. Do you know, he insisted that I pay him for it? Said he'd show it to the board at Benson's."

"Benson's?" asked Nina.

"Oh, do keep up," replied Raymond. "Benson's Leisure Hotels and Hospitality Incorporated. Our parent company. Based in America. Usually leave us alone to do our own thing, but McKenzie said he'd show them his tawdry little videos."

Aaron eyed him. "And what was your response?"

"Well, I paid him, didn't I? He asked for five thousand pounds, and I cashed in a little investment and gave it to him. As far as I was concerned, that was the end of it, only Sophie Lambert seemed to have got it into her head that there was still something going on between us."

"Do you recall when you made this payment?" asked Aaron.

They hadn't seen anything like that in McKenzie's banking information. But they hadn't seen any evidence of his other activities there, either. There had to be another account somewhere.

"I don't know. Four months ago? Five? I can probably find out. But that's not the point."

"What is the point, Mr Raymond?"

"Sophie Lambert. I will not be made to suffer as a result of that woman's absurd delusions."

At least she was a 'woman,' now. Yesterday she'd been a 'little slut.'

"Returning to McKenzie, Mr Raymond. Did he at any point ask you for—"

"I'm not interested in talking about Josh McKenzie and his horrible little schemes. The important thing is that I made it eminently clear that my brief liaison with Sophie was over. If she claims otherwise, I may have to consider my position."

"Consider your position?"

"Well, I could sue her, couldn't I? For slander, or libel, or whatever it's called. You're the lawyer." Raymond turned to Basham. "You'll be able to see I've got an excellent case here, even if these flatfeet can't."

Beside Aaron, Nina was biting her lip, hard, to stop herself from laughing. Across the table, Basham was shaking his head. Aaron wasn't sure they'd ever had a suspect quite like Peter Raymond, and there was something enjoyable about watching him reduce Basham to a horrified, helpless bystander.

Raymond had admitted to being blackmailed. It was a good start, even if he didn't want to talk about it now. Maybe he'd be more inclined to answer their questions after a break.

CHAPTER SIXTY-EIGHT

"What do I want a rep for?" Tel Cummings asked.

He grinned, curling his lip. Zoe was grateful she was watching this on a screen in the tiny viewing room beside the interview room. If she'd been in there with him, it would have taken all her self-control not to lunge across the table and hit him.

"I really would recommend—" began Denise Gaskill.

"Listen, sweetheart, I don't need a Federation rep. Or a lawyer. Don't believe in them."

Beside DS Gaskill, Carl remained impassive.

"And look," Cummings continued, "what's a lawyer gonna tell me to do? Say nothing? I can figure that out for myself, thanks."

"That's fine," said Carl. "As long as you remember that you're currently under arrest in connection with—"

"Yeah, yeah. Save it. The bitch was dead when I found her."

Zoe saw Carl frown. Denise Gaskill managed to keep a blank face. They'd kept it vague when they'd brought

Cummings in – Zoe had seen the arrest sheet, which had mentioned misconduct in a public office, but not precisely what that misconduct was.

Cummings had spent the night in the sixth-floor custody suite. He'd have recognised Carl and Denise. He'd know they were PSD.

But he still didn't know why he'd been brought in.

Carl cleared his throat. "Just to clarify, what's your understanding of why you've been arrested, PC Cummings?"

"You tell me. You're the fuckers who decided to arrest me, aren't you?"

Carl and Denise looked at each other. Denise looked like she wanted to say something, but wasn't sure she should. Zoe saw a tiny nod from Carl, and Denise turned back to Cummings.

"Is it your understanding that you've been arrested in connection with the death of Victoria Speares?"

Cummings nodded. "Yeah. The junkie. Stupid bitch who nearly killed Roddy."

"I'm sorry to have to tell you this," Denise continued, "but although there may well be questions to answer in connection with Ms Speares' death, there are other matters we'd like to ask you about."

"Oh?" Cummings was still grinning.

"Are you familiar with a man called Josh McKenzie?" asked Carl.

Cummings frowned. "Who?"

"Josh McKenzie," repeated Carl. "Perhaps this will refresh your memory." He produced a copy of the photo from the Bothwell Inn.

"Right," said Cummings, shrugging.

"So you do know this man?"

"He's in the darts club, yeah. Forgot the name, didn't I?"

"And I'm sure you're aware that Josh McKenzie is dead, PC Cummings. I understand you were part of the uniformed presence at the crime scene."

Shit. Cummings had been there with the rest of them. Barnes and Chen, Martinez and Collins. And Cummings, on the scene, perfectly capable of hiding or destroying evidence if it suited him. Zoe found herself hoping Cummings hadn't been the one who'd killed McKenzie, because if he was, they'd struggle to prove it.

"Yeah, and that's a shame, but like I say, I hardly knew the bloke. Darts team, the odd pint. Seemed OK. What's it got to do with me?"

"I'd like to ask you about your contact with Josh McKenzie over the last year or so. In particular, shortly before a raid at the Bassenthwaite Manor Hotel."

A brief look of alarm passed over Cummings' face, but the grin was back within a second.

"Don't think so, mate. I'm done. Take me back to the cell. And then you can either charge me, or apologise and let me go."

CHAPTER SIXTY-NINE

NINA WAS BACK in the team room with the sarge. "He's a charmer, isn't he?"

He closed his eyes and rolled his neck. If she hadn't known him better, she'd have thought he'd overdone it the night before. But this was DS Keyes.

"You OK, Sarge?" she asked.

"Just tired. Anniversary dinner last night. May have gone on a bit long and drunk a bit much."

"Oh. Shit. Sorry, Sarge. Happy anniversary."

He smiled at her. It was easy to forget what he'd been through. How close he'd been to dying, just a few short months ago.

"Not part of your job to remember things like that," he said. "And you're right about Raymond. Thoroughly nasty individual."

"He doesn't do much to hide it, does he?"

"No. Which makes his protestations of innocence all the more convincing, unfortunately."

Nina nodded. She'd suspected the same thing, and had

been half hoping the sarge would disagree and point something out, which meant she had to be wrong and Raymond was the killer after all. Raymond was a sleazy piece of shit, and he'd get his comeuppance one day, but she didn't see him cutting another man up and throwing him in a lake.

He'd see that sort of thing as beneath him.

"Where's the boss?" she asked.

A look of concern passed briefly across the sarge's face.

"Not sure, Nina. Admin? The perils of promotion. That's what happens when you climb the ladder."

He turned to his screen. It wasn't like DI Finch to disappear at a time like this.

Probably something to do with Cummings, which meant PSD. Which did, indeed, mean admin, but the interesting sort of admin.

But the sarge's response had stirred something.

"Do you think I'm ready, Sarge?"

He turned and looked back up at her. "Ready for what?"

"Promotion. Exams, becoming a DS, all that. I've done most of the courses. And I think I've shown skill and application."

The sarge smiled. "I agree. It's hard work, though. You'll have to cut down on your karaoke and spend evenings in with the books. And you'll still be doing the day-to-day stuff. Think you can handle that?"

Nina pictured herself at home, eyes closed on the sofa while Elena fired questions at her and she threw back the right answers without even thinking about it.

Elena had been asleep when she'd got back from the Miner's Yard the previous night. Nina had paused outside her bedroom door, thought about knocking, maybe apologising. But in the end, she'd gone to bed.

CHAPTER SIXTY-NINE

They'd sort it all out, eventually.

"Yeah," she said. "I can."

"Good. Look up the requirements. Find out about the exams. When you're ready to mention it to DI Finch, let me know and I'll back you up. In the meantime, prove yourself."

"How?"

He raised an eyebrow. "Find out who killed Josh McKenzie."

CHAPTER SEVENTY

"It's him," Denise Gaskill said.

Carl frowned at her. "We know it's him, Denise. We've seen the footage. It's him in DI Finch's team room, and no jury in the world's going to believe whatever cock-and-bull justification he comes up with for accessing that information without authority. It's not like we need a confession."

"No, I mean, it's him that killed McKenzie."

"I don't think so," said Zoe.

The two PSD officers turned to look at her. They were sitting at the round table in the reception area on the sixth floor, and there was nothing about them, or the place, that indicated what was just down the corridor: a series of cells and interview rooms designed for one specific group of suspects.

The worst of the worst. The police who joined the other side.

"Why not?" asked Carl.

Zoe shook her head. "I'm sure he's capable of it. I just

think he'd have covered his tracks more effectively. He'd have a decent alibi, for a start."

Cummings had the beginnings of an alibi. He'd been at the Bothwell Inn on Friday evening. But he'd left at ten, and although he insisted he'd just gone home and crashed out for the night, he lived alone, and there was no one to back up his claims.

"You think he didn't do it because he *doesn't* have an alibi?" asked Denise.

"I'm not saying it definitely wasn't him," Zoe replied. "I just think he'd have come up with something a bit more convincing than 'I went home and crashed out.'"

There was a short silence. Zoe was running through what she'd seen of the interview. Cummings' arrogance. His brief moment of fear when the raid was mentioned. They had him for that, Carl was right. And they'd probably get him calling McKenzie to tell him about Zoe's upcoming visit to Carrie Wright. But that wasn't enough.

Zoe wanted whoever had killed McKenzie.

But even that wasn't enough. Because Cummings and McKenzie, between them, had the police side of things sewn up. With Huz and Carrie Wright, they'd sunk their nails so deep into Cumbria law enforcement they'd drawn blood.

But there was something missing. Someone who told McKenzie which dealers were carrying, how much they were carrying, where and when they could be found.

They had their fourth man, now. But there was someone else. A fifth. And Zoe wanted that person's name. Cummings would have plenty of time in prison to mull over his mistakes, but he wasn't talking now, and Zoe couldn't see any way of making him talk.

Except one. Carl wouldn't like it.

"We need him talking," she said.

"Agreed," said Carl. Denise nodded.

"At the moment," Zoe continued, "he's not scared. He thought he was in over Vicky Speares, and whatever he did to her, we'll probably never prove it."

Denise snorted in disgust. Vicky Speares might have been a violent drug addict, but no one deserved to die like that.

"Now he knows what we've really got him for, he'll have figured out he's screwed," Zoe said. "We need an angle."

"He's not getting a deal," Carl said.

"I wouldn't expect that. But there are other ways of putting pressure on."

Carl and Denise were watching her, expectant.

"Let's assume Cummings didn't kill McKenzie. Now, Cummings, McKenzie, all of them, they've been stealing drugs from Myron Carter's customers, agreed?"

"We don't know for sure it's Carter," Denise pointed out.

"But we can be confident it is," Carl said. "Go on."

"Carter doesn't let people like that live. Maybe that's why McKenzie's dead. Maybe it's Carter's people. Maybe it's one of the dealers themselves, like Tony Harris."

Tony Harris had killed Huz, and one of the students involved in the operation. Would have killed Aaron, too, if Aaron hadn't fought back. But Zoe knew what Carl and Denise were thinking. PSD had arrested Huz, questioned him until he broke and named Carrie Wright, and then released him, against the protestations of Zoe's team.

If they hadn't done that, he wouldn't have died.

"And then," Zoe continued, "there's the people Cummings and McKenzie blackmailed. They might be after revenge, too. The point is, whoever took out McKenzie, chances are they'd quite like to get their hands on Cummings, too."

"No," said Carl, shaking his head.

"I just think—" Zoe began.

"Absolutely not, Zoe."

Denise was looking from one of them to the other, confused. Carl turned to her. "DI Finch here thinks Cummings might be prepared to talk if we threaten him."

"No, not threaten him," Zoe protested, but if they went through with her idea, it would be as good as a threat. "Just tell him he's free to go, and remind him that there's a lot of people out there who want him dead."

"If we do that, he'll make a complaint, Zoe. Either that, or he'll just clam up completely."

"He's already clammed up completely," she pointed out. "If he makes a complaint, then what? We'll explain that we had to take an aggressive line under the circumstances, with a murderer on the loose and the possibility of a feud between organised crime gangs."

"We?" said Carl.

Zoe, who'd been about to make another point, about Kay, Huz, and everyone else who'd suffered thanks to Cummings and his corruption, fell silent.

There was no 'we.' There was only PSD, and Carl had invited her in, not because they were partners, but because she and her team were involved, and there was no way of untangling them.

And PSD couldn't screw up. Zoe didn't like to take risks, but she knew she could, if the calculations told her it was worth it. PSD had to be perfect, always, from the top down and the root up.

"OK," she said. Carl smiled at her, and she offered a weak smile back. She didn't have to like it, but he was right.

"I've got an idea," Denise said. "Just shake things up a bit."

"What?" asked Carl.

"How about I interview him with DI Finch? See if he feels more threatened by two women questioning him."

Carl pursed his lips and looked from one of them to the other. It was true, of course. Men of a certain type couldn't keep quiet, not when it was women asking the questions. They had to prove themselves.

"You OK with this?" he asked, looking at Zoe.

She shrugged. "Why not?"

He sat back and closed his eyes.

"OK," he said. "It can't hurt, can it?"

CHAPTER SEVENTY-ONE

Nina stared at Peter Raymond, her jaw clenched.

"Look," he said, "don't you think this has gone on long enough?"

Raymond sat back, his arms folded. He had the smug look of a cat who'd just caught a mouse.

She glanced at his lawyer, Stan Basham. The man was wearing his usual expression of contempt, but this time it was directed towards his client rather than the police.

Beside her, the sarge was silent. If she was going to prove she was worthy of sitting the sergeants' exam, she'd have to start now.

"What do you mean?" she asked. "You ready to confess?"

Peter Raymond spread his arms, palms facing outwards. Did the bloke think he was Jesus?

"I certainly have sins to confess, but who among us doesn't?" he replied, smiling. "But no, I don't plan on confessing to murder. More fleshly crimes, perhaps."

Nina let her lip curl.

"Not crimes," he clarified. "Vices."

"We've heard about Sophie Lambert, Mr Raymond," she said. "Do you have anything new—"

"Very much so. You see, as it so happens, I have an alibi for Friday night."

This was new. The sarge sat forward.

"An alibi?" she asked.

"Indeed."

"Why didn't you mention this alibi before?"

"Well, you see, I didn't want you to think poorly of me."

Nina bit her lip. The sarge remained silent. Basham was less successful, failing to suppress a brief snort.

"You see, Sophie isn't the only member of staff who's... Well, not to put too fine a point on it, who's seduced me."

Nina bit back a laugh. "Seduced you?"

"Indeed. On the night in question, I was enjoying the delights of Sophie's colleague, Astrid."

"Another member of the cleaning staff?"

"I'm afraid that's true, yes."

"And does Astrid have a surname?" Nina had seen the name on the various files they'd pored through, but only in passing.

"I believe so, yes. Something Danish, I expect. I do hope you don't get the wrong idea though, DC Kapoor. It's not like I..." He looked her in the eye. "I suppose it must look like I'm some awful Lothario, but really, I'm not like that at all."

"Your personal life doesn't interest me, Mr Raymond," she told him. "But we'll be checking this with Astrid, of course."

"Of course. I'm surprised the dear little creature hasn't already come forward, but she's probably frightened, poor thing. In the meantime, tell me, will you have to report all of this to my employers?"

"I don't see—"

"Because it would be a terrible shame if, even after McKenzie's threats came to nothing, my career ended up being harmed by tawdry gossip."

There were so many things Nina wanted to say in response. Instead, she terminated the interview and walked away, the sarge a step behind her.

It was a shame, really. No doubt the alibi would be good and they'd have to let the bastard go. She'd have to trust karma. If the law didn't get the likes of Peter Raymond, karma usually did in the end.

CHAPTER SEVENTY-TWO

KATE WAS behind the reception desk when Tom walked in, talking to two guests. He watched her for a moment.

She was still pale. Nervy in her movements. But then, the guests weren't exactly putting her at ease. The man stood back, tall, thin, his hands clasped behind his back, while a short middle-aged woman jabbed her finger in Kate's face. Tom caught the words 'filthy' and 'unacceptable' and decided to wait before he asked Kate to accompany him to the Hub.

He walked to the armchair and made to sit down, but stopped. There were no newspapers on the table. And the cushions hadn't been plumped. He'd lifted one, ready to do it himself, when the sound of raised voices drew his attention.

Not from the reception desk. Further away. He dropped the cushion and followed the noise.

Two men. Shouting. In the kitchens.

Tom pushed open the door. The taller man, David, had his back to a wall, while the bald head chef, Max, screamed in his face.

CHAPTER SEVENTY-TWO

At least Max wasn't holding a knife this time.

"I don't know where it is," David protested.

"It's two hundred quid's worth of fucking steak, David," said Max. "If we don't find it—"

He stopped, alerted to Tom's presence by the movement of David's eyes, and turned to face him.

"Don't mind me," said Tom.

"This isn't what it looks like. It's just..." Max turned to David, then back to Tom. "Look, a load of steak's gone missing. I don't know what the fuck's going on, but either it's not been ordered, or someone's nicked it, or—"

"This place," David said, pushing himself away from the wall, "is falling apart."

Tom nodded. He was starting to get that impression.

"Fine. We don't need anyone getting killed over it." He winced at his own words and left the room. Leo the barman passed by, muttering to himself.

Back at the reception desk, Kate was staring down at the counter in front of her, looking exhausted.

She shouldn't be working through this.

She'd just glanced up and spotted Tom when his phone rang. The sarge.

"Tom," he said. "Raymond says he's got an alibi. Another one of the maids."

"What?" Tom asked, then realised he could be overheard. He waved an apology in Kate's direction and walked away.

"I know." Tom could hear Nina in the background, saying something disparaging about Raymond while the sarge went on. "Astrid something. Raymond doesn't even know her surname. Says it's Danish. Can you find her and check it out? We'll deal with Sophie Lambert later, if we have to."

"Will do, Sarge. I'll call you back."

Kate smiled as he approached.

"Astrid Nielsen," she told him, when he explained who he was looking for. "Room five nineteen. Just down the corridor from me. Haven't seen her about for a bit, she might be in there."

"And Sophie Lambert?"

"She's just spent the night cleaning. She'll be asleep."

Sophie Lambert could wait. Astrid Nielsen, meanwhile, was a tall blonde woman who looked even younger than Sophie. She opened the door in her underwear and seemed surprised to find Tom standing there.

"Oh," she said, stepping back.

He introduced himself and waited while she pulled on a dressing gown.

"This shouldn't take long," he told her. "You were expecting someone else, yes?"

She nodded. Her initial shock had been replaced by wary interest.

"Can you tell me who that person was?"

"I mustn't," she said, her accent barely detectable. "He will get in trouble."

Tom nodded. "Loyalty is a good thing, but you do realise this is a murder investigation, don't you?"

"Oh," she said. "Of course. In that case, yes. It is Peter. Mr Raymond. He is my lover."

She said the word with a mixture of defiance and pride, and Tom found himself wondering how long it would be before she learned the truth about her 'lover.'

CHAPTER SEVENTY-TWO

"Astrid, this is important. Can you tell me if Peter Raymond was with you on Friday night?"

"Friday night? That was... Wait one moment."

She looked around for her phone, eventually finding it on a table beside her bed. Astrid's room was significantly larger than Kate's.

A perk of her specific job? Or something else?

"Here," she said, holding up her phone. "It is... This is private, you understand?"

A video was open on the screen. It was date-stamped Saturday, at one in the morning, and in the three seconds Tom saw before he looked away, he made out two figures who were quite clearly Astrid and Peter Raymond engaging in activities that were unlikely to be part of her job description.

"He likes to be filmed," she said without a trace of embarrassment.

It would have to be checked through, but Peter Raymond's alibi was looking solid. Someone had planted those knives in his room, but whoever it was, they hadn't included the one that had killed McKenzie. Sophie Lambert would have to be spoken to, but not right now. All the action would be back at the Hub.

CHAPTER SEVENTY-THREE

Denise Gaskill was leaning against the interview room wall. "You know DI Zoe Finch," she said. It was a statement rather than a question, and Cummings ignored it.

"Remember when I said charge me or let me go?" he said. "It's decision time."

"No, it isn't," Zoe told him.

Cummings turned his gaze on her. She'd never really looked at him before, not properly. She'd noticed the lack of hair, the long, mournful-looking face, the way his mouth curled into a sneer whenever he wasn't talking. And his eyes... grey and all but expressionless. He could be thinking anything behind there.

"Listen, love—" he began.

Denise stopped him. "We're coming round to the idea of letting you go."

What?

Zoe turned to her. Denise looked straight back at her, a warning on her face.

"Good," said Cummings. "Chop chop, eh?"

CHAPTER SEVENTY-THREE

"The thing is," Denise continued, leaning forward and speaking almost confidentially, "even if you didn't kill your friend Josh, we still don't know who did."

"Not my problem," replied Cummings.

"Oh, but I think it might be," said Denise.

Zoe threw a glance towards the camera. Carl would be watching them. He'd see what Denise was doing quickly enough, and come running to put a stop to it.

Zoe had been there herself. She'd heard him overrule her suggestion. She'd agreed, reluctantly, with his assessment. She outranked Denise Gaskill. She could put a stop to this herself, right now.

"Why's that?" asked Cummings.

Carl had to know what was happening here. Either that, or Zoe had to shut it down.

"Because," Zoe said, "there's every chance McKenzie was murdered by the people whose drugs you've been stealing."

Cummings folded his arms.

"Not just the small-timers, like Tony Harris, who still managed to murder two people inside your operation before we got him. But the people who supply the likes of Tony Harris. The people who wouldn't like it to get out that their operation had been compromised by insignificant figures like you, PC Cummings. The people responsible for most of the organised crime and half the murders in Cumbria, who won't think twice before adding you to their list."

Zoe heard footsteps outside. DS Gaskill took over.

"Of course, by now it'll be common knowledge that you've been picked up by PSD. Picked up and released. Won't take a genius to work out why you were picked up."

There was a bang on the door, but Zoe ignored it.

Cummings had turned white. And those eyes, those expressionless pools of grey, were wide with fear.

"No," he said.

"No?" repeated Denise.

"No. Don't release me. I'll tell you what you want to know."

"And your role?"

"Fine." The banging on the door grew more urgent. "Yes. It was me. Me and McKenzie. The tip-off. The drugs. Fine. I'll tell you."

Zoe nodded, and Denise went to open the door.

CHAPTER SEVENTY-FOUR

AARON PROCESSED THE RELEASE HIMSELF. Nina was learning to control her temper, but the combination of Raymond and Basham, in this sort of mood, might have pushed her over the edge.

He stopped by the boss's office on the way back to the team room. He'd had a message from Lynn Hedley: no news on Kevin Downes. The door was closed, and there was no answer when he knocked.

He gave the door a gentle push, and it opened. No sign of the boss.

In the team room, Nina was busy writing up the last of the Raymond interviews. Aaron sat down to add the details of the release.

A convincing alibi was confirmed by a statement from Astrid Nielsen, he wrote, then amended it. Not just a statement. Video evidence, not that he'd seen that evidence.

"What are we looking at, Nina?" he asked.

"Carter," she said. "His people. McKenzie interfered

with Carter's business. I don't know how Carter found out, but he did, and had McKenzie dealt with."

"Sounds plausible. What about this Sophie Lambert?"

"Don't think so, Sarge. We should get her in, but Tom's right. What's the connection between her and McKenzie? The fact that they worked at the same hotel? No one else has mentioned the two of them in the same sentence. Even if she's lying about finding the knives in Raymond's room, there was one missing, and I think we all know that's the one that killed McKenzie."

Aaron nodded. "We can speak to her, but she's not a priority."

"Where's the boss, Sarge?"

He looked around the room before answering.

"She's probably dealing with Cummings. For all we know they've brought him in, he's already confessed to killing McKenzie, and we're just wasting our time."

"You really think so?"

He shook his head. "No. Cummings is a lot of things, but the thing he is most is a coward. I don't think he killed his mate, and even if he had, I don't think he'd confess. And that photo of yours, him and McKenzie, it was good, but it wasn't exactly conclusive."

"Yeah," said Nina, clearly disappointed.

"Wherever DI Finch is," Aaron continued, "I'm sure she'll see fit to share it with us when it's appropriate."

"Have you seen DI Whaley in the Hub today?" asked Nina.

He shook his head. It was the obvious question. If the boss was dealing with Cummings, she'd be doing it alongside PSD, and that probably meant her partner.

"But..." He looked around the team room. The thought

CHAPTER SEVENTY-FOUR

that someone had been there, using their terminals, pretending to *be* them, it had cast a sort of shadow over the room.

"But what?"

"I don't know how," he said, "but I think Harriett Barnes is involved."

"How's Harriett Barnes involved?" asked Nina, just as the door opened and Tom walked in.

"Harriett?" he said, looking from one to the other.

"Yeah," said Nina. "Sarge thinks she's involved with whatever the boss is doing. Which we don't have a clue about and might or might not involve Cummings and PSD and who knows what else."

"Right," said Tom. He was chewing his lower lip.

"Tom?" said Aaron. "You OK?"

"Yes, Sarge. It's just..."

"Just what?"

Tom walked to his chair, spun it round to face the room, and sat down. "It's just," he said, "I think Harriett Barnes might be PSD."

CHAPTER SEVENTY-FIVE

Zoe eyed Cummings. "Your last interview, ten minutes ago, you said, and I quote, 'Yes. It was me. Me and McKenzie. The tip-off. The drugs. Fine. I'll tell you.'"

She watched his eyes as she spoke. The fear was still there. She hated to exploit a suspect's emotions like that. It could get you the answers you wanted, but that didn't mean the right ones.

"Are you still willing to talk?"

Cummings nodded.

"For the tape, please," Denise told him.

"Yes," said Cummings.

"And again, for the tape, can you confirm you're continuing to waive your right to legal representation?"

Cummings swallowed. "Yes."

To say Carl hadn't been pleased would have been putting it mildly. He'd kept his temper, but the way he'd looked at Denise, Zoe imagined he'd be having serious words with her in private. And the way he'd looked at Zoe...

"Tell me about the operation," Zoe said.

CHAPTER SEVENTY-FIVE

Cummings looked at her. "Reckon you know most of it now. The students, Carrie Wright, your mate Huz, God rest his soul." He gave a half-smile. "And then me and Josh."

"Josh McKenzie," Denise prompted.

"Yeah. The others, they didn't even know I was involved. Josh was like, a middleman. He brought them in, kept them ticking over, kept me in the shadows. He's the smart one."

"And the two of you blackmailed people, is that right?"

Cummings nodded. "Don't get me wrong, the main business was always the drugs. But the blackmail was useful. Got us the people we needed."

"How did you go about it?" asked Zoe.

"We had our ways." Cummings grinned. The fear had receded from his eyes.

"Describe them for us, these *ways*."

"Well, we both had access to sensitive information, didn't we? I could use my police credentials, and other people's police credentials, if they were stupid enough to let them slip. Josh had CCTV from the hotel, cameras he'd planted. That was how we got Carrie Wright. We never asked for money, though. We just waited till we needed something, then we asked for it."

Cummings was proud of himself. The people he'd hurt, the people who'd died, suffered, lost so much. She gritted her teeth.

"I know my stuff," Cummings continued. "But Josh, he's a genius when it comes to controlling people."

"*Was* a genius," Denise reminded him. But Zoe thought back to her trip home from Scotland, listening to Shona Murray's brother talking about Josh McKenzie. What was it he'd said?

He was a clever bastard. Pulled people's strings. Picked ones he could control.

She was building a picture of Josh McKenzie.

"Ellis Peters," she said. "Margaret Hooper. Did you blackmail them?"

"Not sure. Names are familiar."

"Margaret Hooper is a schoolteacher. Ellis Peters was a firefighter. He took his own—"

"Yeah, I remember the fireman. He was the one who copped off with Carrie."

Zoe met Denise's gaze, both of them working hard not to show surprise.

"Go on," she said.

"Firemen's night out for him, hen night for her, they ended up in his room. Josh showed me the video. He wasn't any use, but she was... Well, you know all about her."

"Ellis Peters took his own life," Zoe said.

Cummings shrugged. "Collateral damage."

Zoe found herself wondering if he actually wanted her to kick his head in.

"We'll take a break now," she announced, and paused the interview.

Outside, Carl seemed to have calmed down.

"That was impressive work," he told them both.

"Are we forgiven?" Zoe asked.

"You shouldn't have done it. But yes. Fine. It worked."

"Good. Carl, my team was looking into this blackmail. I want to go back in with Cummings. But this time, I want Aaron watching. He might pick up something we're not aware of."

Carl pursed his lips and then nodded in agreement.

CHAPTER SEVENTY-SIX

"Say that again," said Nina.

Tom's expression was odd. Usually, when he knew something Nina didn't, he couldn't resist a little victory grin. Now he just looked ashamed.

"I'm not sure," he began, then looked around the room like someone else might take over.

"Say it again," Nina told him.

"I think Harriett's PSD." The way his face was screwed up, saying it looked like a painful experience.

"Why?"

"It's just... some stuff the boss said. Ages ago. Probably nothing." He grinned, but unconvincingly.

"What did she say? When?"

Tom turned towards the sarge, and Nina could see the pleading in his eyes.

Did the sarge know something too? Was Nina the only one who'd been kept in the dark?

"Don't look at me, Tom," the sarge said. "I don't have the faintest idea what you're talking about."

No, then. That was a relief.

But really. Harriett Barnes? PSD?

"This is ridiculous," Nina said. "There's no reason..."

She thought through everything she knew about Harriett Barnes. Tom knew more; they'd dated, briefly. Harriett was a good copper. An exceptional one, for someone who was still just a PC, who'd been in the job less than two years.

Of course. If she was PSD, she'd probably been in the job a lot longer than two years. She'd have had specialist training.

"Why didn't you say anything?" Nina demanded.

Tom looked around the room again before answering. "I don't know. I wasn't sure. I'm still not sure."

"Tom, this is me. Nina. We tell each other everything, don't we?"

He looked so upset she felt guilty.

"I'm sorry," he said. "I'm sure it's nothing. And the boss said—"

"What did the boss say?" said DI Finch, standing in the doorway. All three of them turned to look at her.

From the corner of her eye, Nina could see Tom's mouth moving, but the words weren't coming out. The sarge seemed to be waiting for something to happen, like he wasn't part of it.

"Harriett Barnes is PSD," Nina said, fixing the boss with what she hoped was a steely gaze.

"Oh, good," said DI Finch, walking into the room and taking the spare seat. "Glad you know. That saves some explaining."

Nina tore her gaze away from the boss to stare at the sarge and Tom. Both of them were staring at DI Finch.

"Anyway, that's not why I'm here. Cummings is upstairs, in the sixth-floor custody suite."

CHAPTER SEVENTY-SIX

"We were right about him?" breathed Nina.

A nod. "It was him that tipped off McKenzie before the raid. He did it right here." The boss pointed in front of her, at the spare desk. Kay's desk. "We've got that on camera, and he's admitted the rest. The drugs. The blackmail ring. I've been questioning him with DS Gaskill."

"Did he kill McKenzie?" asked the sarge.

"I don't think so. But this blackmail thing. He's admitted to Carrie and Huz. Ellis Peters, too. You know more about this than anyone else, Aaron. I want you up there and watching when we go back in. See if you can think of anything we're missing."

The sarge nodded. "Let me know when you need me."

"Now, Aaron. We're interviewing him again now. Come on."

CHAPTER SEVENTY-SEVEN

By the time Zoe got back upstairs, Aaron had briefed her on the lack of progress on Kevin Downes. On the sixth floor, everything had changed. Cummings had decided he did want a lawyer, after all.

"Shit," said Zoe. She was sitting at the round table with Denise Gaskill, keyed up and ready to go in, and now they'd have to wait for the bloody lawyer to show up. She'd already sent Aaron into the little viewing room. She stood to go and get him back out again.

"It's OK," Denise told her. "She's already here."

"She is?"

"You've come across her before."

"Paula Vernon?"

Denise nodded.

Paula Vernon had sat next to Huz when they'd been questioning him a few months back. She'd been efficient but quiet, hardly there at all. Someone who whispered advice but didn't push it. Someone who allowed themselves to be led by their clients rather than leading them.

CHAPTER SEVENTY-SEVEN

If Cummings had to have a lawyer with him, Zoe was glad it was that one.

"How come Paula got here so quickly?"

Denise looked down. "I may or may not have told her this morning that we had a suspect who'd probably be calling on her services soon."

Zoe nodded. Getting things done quickly was to everyone's benefit. Her phone buzzed, and something told her she didn't need to check who it was, but she did anyway.

Ryan Tobin. Ignore.

"What's the plan, then?" she asked.

Denise frowned at her. "I was going to ask you that, DI Finch. We need to establish our goals."

That was fair. CID and PSD could be working towards very different outcomes. Best to have it out in the open.

"Right," she said. "I know you want to get as much as you can from him. Find out if anyone else involved is with the police. All that. Yes?"

Denise nodded.

"And I want to find out who murdered Josh McKenzie. Whether that's someone in McKenzie's own organisation, or someone in Carter's, or someone else entirely. That's got to be my priority."

"That's fine," agreed Denise. "We sort out the murder, the gangs, all that. If we can gather evidence for our investigation at the same time, then great. Otherwise, we'll mop up what's left of him when you've got your killer."

Zoe stared at her. She hadn't been sure about Denise the few times they'd met. Carl hadn't been sure of her himself when he'd first been introduced to her. But Zoe was starting to like her.

"It won't do any harm to remind him again that he's been

ripping off Carter's people," Zoe said. "He's got his lawyer with him now. He might have changed his mind about talking. But chances are, Carter wants Cummings dead. And if he finds out Cummings is talking to us, he's going to want him even more dead."

Denise grinned at her. "That should help focus his mind."

One of the well-muscled, smartly dressed men who seemed to act as security-cum-custody-sergeant up here approached, bent down, and whispered something in Denise's ear.

"They're ready for us," she said.

Cummings was sitting beside his lawyer, waiting for them. Zoe examined his face, searching out signs that he might have changed his mind.

The fear had leaked away, but his characteristic sneer had flattened out into something more serious.

"You've told us about your operation," she began, once the formalities had been completed. "Can you confirm again that you were running a blackmail operation with Josh McKenzie, a chef at the Bassenthwaite Manor Hotel?"

"I was," replied Cummings.

Zoe felt the tension start to dissolve inside her. Maybe this would be easy.

"You used your police access, and other police credentials you'd gathered over the years, to obtain sensitive information. Mr McKenzie did the same with footage he obtained from the hotel."

"Correct," said Cummings.

Paula Vernon still hadn't moved, much less spoken.

"You coerced your victims, including PS Carrie Wright,

into cooperating with you in the acquisition and distribution of drugs."

"We did," agreed Cummings.

Good. The background was out of the way.

It was time for the main story.

CHAPTER SEVENTY-EIGHT

AARON SHIFTED IN HIS SEAT. This wasn't the first time he'd found himself squeezed into the sixth-floor viewing room alongside DI Whaley, but this time he was capable of smiling and exchanging greetings like a normal person.

But it was still uncomfortable. A tiny space, the boss's partner, and he was expected to shed some light on what the people on the screen taking up the entire wall opposite were saying.

"Let's start with the simple things, shall we?" said the boss. She'd taken Cummings through the basics, the blackmail, the drugs: the fact that the operation existed, and that Cummings was involved.

He'd agreed. This was a very different Tel Cummings from the one Aaron had known all these years.

"OK," agreed Cummings.

"Did you kill Josh McKenzie?"

The lawyer beside Cummings leaned towards him, but he pushed her away.

"No, I didn't," he said.

CHAPTER SEVENTY-EIGHT

"Do you know who did kill Josh McKenzie?" DI Finch asked.

"Not a clue." The words were pure Cummings, but without the swagger.

"You don't think it could have been someone else in your operation?"

"Not likely." Beside the boss, DS Gaskill leaned forward, apparently eager for more, but Cummings didn't elaborate.

"What about the people whose drugs you stole? Or the people who were supplying them? Do you think they might have it in for you?"

"It's possible," agreed Cummings, then sat back.

This wasn't going as well as the boss had hoped.

"OK, let's go back a little. Establish some background. Is that OK?"

"Fine by me."

"As well as the people you had distributing drugs through Hussein Mahmoud, Josh McKenzie was selling directly from the hotel. Is that right?"

"Yes."

"And is it also correct that you heard in advance about a planned drugs raid, and used the login credentials of a retired detective sergeant to establish the timing and target of that raid?"

"It is."

"The target was the Bassenthwaite Manor Hotel, and the timing was two in the morning, on the eighteenth of February last year. Is that correct?"

"Yeah. I mean, I don't remember the date off the top of my head, but that sounds right."

"And you warned Josh McKenzie about this raid, giving him time to dispose of anything incriminating."

"I did that, yeah. You already know all this, though."

"I appreciate your patience, PC Cummings. Can you confirm that you accessed this data using a terminal that had been assigned temporarily to Kay Holinshed, and that Kay herself had nothing to do with this?"

"Yeah. Couldn't believe my luck when it turned out she was digging in where she wasn't supposed to be at the same time. Silly cow, she didn't have a clue."

Aaron exhaled loudly. Beside him, DI Whaley turned, a smile on his face.

Kay had messed up and got caught. But when it came to the worst of her alleged offences, she was in the clear.

"Thank you, PC Cummings," said the boss. DS Gaskill was sitting back now, watching, as much a bystander as Paula Vernon seemed to be. "You've told us a little about your blackmail operation. Now I'd like to focus on what you referred to in our earlier interview as your main business. The distribution of drugs."

"What about it?"

"I've got a couple of questions. First, can you confirm that one of your victims, in other words, one of the dealers you effectively stole drugs from, was Tony Harris, known as 'Topper'?"

"Yeah. He was one of Carrie's, usually."

"What does that mean?"

"It means Josh would tell her when and where to bust him, and she'd do it. One time I did, though." Cummings grinned. There it was, the old bastard, back again.

"What happened on that occasion?"

"He got mouthy, didn't he?"

"And how did you respond to that?"

"I shut the little fucker up."

CHAPTER SEVENTY-EIGHT

"You beat him up, didn't you? Beat him so badly he was left physically and psychologically scarred as a result, and went on to commit at least two murders that we know of."

"Whatever."

Aaron was breathing fast, and on the screen, he could tell the boss was going through something similar.

One of those murders had been Huz.

There was a moment's silence before DI Finch spoke again.

"My second question relates to what you just mentioned, that McKenzie was able to tell Carrie Wright when and where to make busts. I understand that she developed a reputation among local dealers for having a remarkable ability to know when they'd taken a delivery. How did you do that?"

Cummings took a deep breath, looked at his lawyer, then across the table at DI Finch.

"Wouldn't you like to know?" he said.

"We would, yes," the boss replied. "And I'd remind you that—"

"That there's a target on my back and I'm already going down for everything I've said? Yeah, yeah. Fine, then. I've got a partner at the port."

Aaron held his breath.

"The Port of Workington?" asked DS Gaskill.

Beside Aaron, DI Whaley had gone completely still.

"Yeah," said Cummings. "One of their jobs is arranging shipments to the dealers. They don't get paid that well, but they didn't want to risk taking a bit off the top."

"So you set up this whole operation to take advantage of this inside information?"

"Yeah."

"What's his name, this partner of yours?"

Aaron leaned forward. The room felt cold.

"Not his name. Hers."

Aaron swallowed.

"Her name, then. Who is she?"

"You don't know her," said Cummings. "She's called Bobby Silver."

Aaron gasped, his throat tight. DI Whaley turned to him, concerned.

"Are you OK, Aaron?" he asked. "Do I need to call a doctor?"

Aaron shook his head. "No," he gasped, and forced himself to slow down so he could speak. "No. But you need to stop this interview right now."

CHAPTER SEVENTY-NINE

ZOE TOOK A DEEP BREATH. "OK, just calm down."

They were in the team room, all six of them. Her, Aaron, Nina, Tom, and Carl and Denise. Aaron hadn't stopped talking for three minutes, jumping from one idea to another, pacing as he spoke. But the theme was the same throughout.

He knew Bobby Silver.

"I just can't believe it, boss. I know her. I actually—"

He stopped, mouth open, and shook his head.

"What is it?" Zoe asked.

"I had a drink with her and her mates. Just the other day. Wednesday. Wednesday night. I mentioned McKenzie."

"Why?"

"They work at the Port. They all do, her and Stacey and Miles. I thought if McKenzie was killed by someone on Carter's payroll, they might have heard the name."

Stacey? Miles? Who were all these people?

"They're just normal people, boss. I only got talking to them because I'd seen them with Victor."

"I've got something," said Tom, leaning over his keyboard. He tapped for a moment, then pointed at the big screen on the wall. "That's where she lives."

The image on the screen looked like an estate agent's photo. An aerial view, probably taken by drone, of a large, expensive-looking farmhouse surrounded by fields and, in one corner, the edge of a wood.

"I thought she was just a normal person," said Aaron.

"Is she on the system?" Zoe asked.

"No, boss," replied Nina, who was busy on her own keyboard. "No sign of her at all. Built up enough money to afford a place like that, but somehow she's managed to stay under the radar."

"And she'd still be there if Cummings wasn't such a..." DS Gaskill began, stopping at a look from Carl.

"OK," said Carl.

The room stilled. Even Aaron stopped and turned to look at him. Zoe watched him, wondering where he was going. Would PSD step in and take over the whole operation? Would he insist on passing it up the chain to DCI Branthwaite?

"OK," he said again.

Zoe braced herself. *We'll take it from here.* Or *Thanks for your help.*

"Bobby Silver isn't a police officer," he continued. "We've got Cummings and we'll be dealing with him, but this isn't a PSD matter. What do you want to do, Zoe?"

She resisted a smile. That was the thing about Carl. He was only territorial when he *had* to be territorial.

How could she have doubted him?

"Where is that location, Tom?" she asked.

"Middle of nowhere, boss. Outside Ireby. On the way to Caldbeck."

"You want to bring her in?" asked Carl.

She considered. "Not yet. I need to think about this some more."

CHAPTER EIGHTY

AARON WATCHED as the boss left the team room to make some calls. DI Whaley and DS Gaskill followed a minute later, heading back upstairs.

Nina and Tom were still at their desks. He could hear them talking to each other, exchanging information and ideas. How much Bobby Silver had paid for her house. The best way there. The fact that she'd squirrelled away all this money without raising a hint of suspicion.

He placed his hands on his forehead, took a step back, closed his eyes, and leaned against the wall beside the big screen.

It didn't make sense.

Cummings hadn't been much of a surprise.

Harriett Barnes he should have seen coming. Now it was out there, it seemed obvious. Someone as young and inexperienced as she was, so in control, so aware of procedure, so capable.

But Bobby Silver?

No. He couldn't process it. He couldn't process it at all.

CHAPTER EIGHTY

"Sarge?"

He shook his head.

"Sarge," said Tom again.

He opened his eyes. "What?"

"You don't think this Bobby Silver could have killed McKenzie?"

Aaron shook his head. No. Not the Bobby Silver he knew. Not Victor's friend.

It would be a year since Victor had died. There were going to be drinks. Bobby had told him all about them. She was just a normal person. Just a friend of Victor's.

He didn't really know her at all, did he?

"We're back with that taxi, aren't we?" said Nina. "I know the boss thinks it was Carter, and it probably was, but there's still someone disappearing from the hotel right when McKenzie was killed. That can't be a coincidence, can it?"

He frowned. Tom and Nina were talking to each other. *Get back. Ask questions.* Another one of those stupid bets about the stupid antimacassar, as if any of that mattered.

Nina stood, grabbing her coat, walking out of the room. Tom stood in front of him.

"Come on, Sarge."

Aaron blinked. He had to focus. "What is it?"

"The taxi, Sarge. We've narrowed it down."

"Well done," Aaron replied. *Narrowed what down?*

"It's one of these twelve."

Aaron nodded. *Twelve, what?*

"So all we need to do is call them and find out which one it was. Speak to the driver. See if they can remember who they picked up from the hotel."

Driver. Hotel. Yes. It made sense.

Someone had got in that taxi, and whoever they were,

their departure slotted perfectly into the timing of Susan Masters' late night mystery headlights.

"Yes," Aaron said. "Give me a number."

His phone rang.

"DS Keyes?" It was the front desk.

"Yes, what is it?"

"We've got someone here who wants to talk to you. Says you know her."

"Who?" Maybe they'd got everything wrong, and Bobby Silver had come in to explain it all to them.

"Theodora Harding, she says. Chef, apparently."

"Right." Aaron had all but forgotten about Theodora Harding.

She knew something. More than she'd already said.

He turned to Tom. "Sorry," he said. "Got to go."

CHAPTER EIGHTY-ONE

Zoe started with the easy call. Kay answered on the first ring.

"DI Finch. It's been a while."

It had been more than half a year since Kay had lost her job, and she'd spent most of that time waiting to find out how serious things would get. No job, no pension – she'd accepted that. She'd looked up information she shouldn't have about her daughter's new boyfriend.

She'd only wanted to protect her family. But she'd been caught and kicked out. PSD might have pushed for prosecution, but in the circumstances, they were willing to let the matter go.

Until she'd been accused of assisting organised crime by providing sensitive information to blackmailers. That was something PSD couldn't let go of, even if Zoe had assured Carl that it couldn't be Kay, that the Kay Holinshed she knew would never have done anything like that.

Zoe had tried to prove it. Until now, she'd achieved precisely nothing.

"I've got news," she said.

"What? What's happened?"

"We've got someone in. Upstairs."

Kay knew what that meant. Upstairs was where she'd been questioned herself.

"Who is it?"

"That doesn't matter. But he's admitted to setting you up, Kay."

There was a long silence. When she finally spoke again, Zoe could hear the emotion in Kay's voice.

"Does this mean..."

"It means you're in the clear, Kay. Or you will be soon enough."

"Right," said Kay. "Right. Celebration tonight, I think."

"We're in the middle of a murder investigation."

"That body in Ennerdale? If I know you lot, you'll have cracked it by this evening. Tell the team, Anchor Vaults, and the drinks are on me."

Zoe smiled. Maybe Kay was right, but she doubted it. There were too many leads, and none of them seemed to be taking them any closer to McKenzie's killer.

Before making her next call, Zoe checked the door and then locked it for good measure.

David Randle kept her waiting so long she was ready to give up when he finally answered.

"Well, if it isn't Zoe Finch," he said. "What have you got for me?"

For me. He really knew how to get her back up.

"The group who were ripping off the local dealers—"

"Carter's dealers, yes. You found a dead one, didn't you? Chef, as I recall."

CHAPTER EIGHTY-ONE

She ignored the interruption. "We've found his partner. Another cop."

"Excellent work, Zoe. But that's not why you're calling, is it? Your delightful partner DI Whaley will be taking that particular problem off your hands, I'd imagine."

"Yes. He's named someone else. Someone at the port."

"Don't tell me. Someone who works for Carter, was too sensible to rip off the big guy himself, but arranged for his underlings to rip off the big guy's customers instead. Am I warm?"

Zoe rolled her eyes. "Yes," she said. No need to correct Randle's assumption.

"Pull them in, then."

"Why?"

"Why? Because with the greatest will in the world, Zoe, if you lot have managed to ID this person, Carter's people won't be far behind you. He's at risk, whoever he is."

"My team won't leak," she said.

A snort. "You're being ridiculous. News like that always spreads. Bring him in."

"It can wait, David."

"Why did you call me, exactly? So you could listen to my advice and ignore it? Bring him in, Zoe, or you'll just be bringing in another corpse."

Why *had* she called him? 'Keep me informed,' he'd said, and she'd jumped to it, like he was still her boss.

Randle was wrong. Bobby Silver could wait. She had to trust her own instincts. Had to figure out what she could get out of Bobby, while the woman didn't know she was marked.

But first, she had to brief the super.

CHAPTER EIGHTY-TWO

Nina was sure they'd missed something, even if Tom wasn't.

She made her way downstairs, her head filled with the images she'd seen on CCTV. The taxi coming and going. All the people moving about inside the hotel.

But not everyone. Plenty of staff had been asleep at the time, or just not wandering the corridors. Raymond had avoided being seen, but that had been deliberate, and he had an alibi.

Tom had been convinced by Astrid Nielsen and her video, but people could lie, and videos could be faked, or just have their dates changed. Raymond wasn't under arrest anymore, but he wasn't in the clear. And the same could be said for Sophie Lambert.

Someone had gone out in the taxi. If they were staff, they...

"Sorry," she heard, and moved to the side just in time to avoid Harriett Barnes running up the stairs. Harriett stopped just past her, and turned.

CHAPTER EIGHTY-TWO

"Hi," she said.

"Hi," replied Nina. Not 'Why did you lie to us?' or 'Who even are you?', which was what she wanted to say. Just 'Hi.'

But Harriett was gone.

There was another interruption as she walked through the car park, still puzzling over what it was that was bothering her about the taxi.

"DC Kapoor, isn't it?"

Nina looked up and wished she hadn't.

"DI Streeting," she said. He was walking towards the building, beside another man, tall and dark, like Streeting himself, but younger. *The newer model.*

"Have you met Mulligan?"

Nina hadn't met Mulligan. She nodded a greeting, looking longingly past the two men to her Fiesta. It was parked between two shinier, more German cars, and even she had to acknowledge that it could do with a clean.

"How are you getting on with Cummings?" Streeting asked.

Nina frowned. How did Ralph Streeting know about Cummings?

"Got to grips with his little operation, I hope." Streeting seemed to be ignoring her frown.

He was a detective inspector. His remit was Specialist Crime and Intel, which meant organised crime. No doubt the boss had briefed the super, and the super had briefed Streeting. It didn't matter. He knew anyway. It was his job to know.

"Pretty much," she said. "Once we've brought in the last one, I think that'll be all of them." She paused, then remembered to add, "Sir."

"Ah." Now Streeting was nodding, a smile forming. "That'll be, what, the fifth man?"

Nina shook her head. "Woman," she said.

"Really?"

"Bobby Silver. Works at the port. She's been behind the whole thing, apparently. You can ask DI Finch for details, Sir, but if you don't mind..."

"Of course, of course," he said, and Nina hurried away to her car. As she pulled out of the car park a minute later, she noticed Mulligan standing alone by the main doors. There was no sign of Streeting, but neither Streeting nor the surprisingly good-looking Mulligan concerned her.

It wasn't until she was halfway to the Bassenthwaite Manor Hotel, and nearly through *From Elvis in Memphis*, that she put her finger on what had been bothering her.

They'd been through all the internal and external footage of the hotel for Friday night. Right up to four o'clock the following morning. And whoever it was that had left in the taxi, they hadn't come back.

So where were they?

CHAPTER EIGHTY-THREE

Zoe glanced up and down the corridor. No sign of Luke. Fiona's door was closed, as ever. She rapped on it and heard Fiona's voice.

"Come in."

Zoe pushed the door open. There was just Fiona Kendrick and her window. She always seemed to be gazing out of it.

"Sit down, Zoe. I hear you've been busy."

Zoe sat. "I take it DCI Branthwaite's been in touch?"

Fiona nodded. Carl's boss didn't have to tell Fiona everything. But he'd have done her the courtesy of informing her that someone from the Hub was in custody.

"I'd like to say it's a shock, Zoe. And I'm not going to pretend I could see it all coming. But there was always something unpleasant about PC Cummings, wasn't there?"

Zoe shrugged. It was true, of course. But there were plenty of unpleasant coppers who were utterly law-abiding and effective. And plenty of lovely ones who turned out to be nothing of the sort.

"I'm sorry, Fiona," she said.

"What are you apologising for?"

Zoe wasn't sure. "Sorry this has happened, I meant. No apologies for nailing the man."

"Good. Look, this is the same man who just happened to find Victoria Speares, isn't it?"

Zoe nodded.

"And the same man who'd left his own partner to get beaten up by her in the first place."

"Yes, but—"

Fiona held up a hand. "Who was also the same man that worked with those students distributing drugs, and tipped off his friend about a drugs raid, and helped organise a blackmail ring that led to at least one suicide, that we know of. Yes?"

"Yes, but that doesn't mean—"

"Wait," Fiona said. "It doesn't mean Tel Cummings was some criminal mastermind, because they rarely are. They rely on the fact that they're police and we're less likely to suspect them. That, and a little luck. But they're rare, thankfully. And in the case of this station, pretty much unique."

The super was smiling. Zoe could see why. The only trouble was, the super was wrong.

"I don't think—" she began, but Fiona had more to say.

"One bad apple, Zoe. It's terrible, in fact. But it's one bad apple, and we're getting rid of it before it infects the barrel."

"I'm sorry," Zoe said. "But it's not 'one bad apple.'"

Fiona raised an eyebrow.

"Carrie Wright," Zoe said.

Fiona nodded. "Fair enough. One bad apple, and it did manage to infect another one. But we got there. We got them both."

"We don't know that's all of them," Zoe pointed out.

CHAPTER EIGHTY-THREE

Fiona nodded. "No. We don't. But I gather Cummings is being talkative. Is that right?"

"It is," Zoe acknowledged.

"And if he knew of anyone else, he'd have named them by now. That's what Branthwaite reports, at least. Do you agree?"

Zoe thought about it for a moment, then nodded. "I think so, yes. He hasn't worked out what his best move is yet, but he's telling us everything we want to know."

"Two bad apples, then. It's hardly ideal, Zoe. But it's not the end of the world."

There was no point arguing. No point reminding Fiona of Huz and Kay. Not when she still had to explain that they might have got their hands on Cummings, but they'd made no more progress in finding out who'd killed Josh McKenzie.

And finding out who'd killed Josh McKenzie was Zoe's job.

CHAPTER EIGHTY-FOUR

"Cheers, Sarge," muttered Tom, as the door swung closed behind the sarge. "Thanks for all your help. Not sure I could have done it without you."

His sarcasm hung in the air, with no one to hear it.

Twelve taxi firms. Twelve phone numbers. Twelve sets of suspicious dispatchers who probably knew half their customers were crooked, and possibly some of the drivers, too. Time to make some calls.

"Acorn Cars," said the first one he called. "How can I help?"

"Hello," Tom said, trying to sound friendly. "This is DC Tom Willis from Cumbria CID."

"Yeah." Her voice was flat.

"I was wondering if you could help me track down a possible passenger of yours."

"You got a warrant?"

"We're investigating a murder, Miss—"

"Mrs. Mrs Donnelly. And I don't care if you're investigating the assassination of Arch Duke Franz Ferdinand. I won't be answering any questions without a properly authorised legal notice compelling me to."

"I'm sorry?"

"I won't be answering any questions without a properly authorised legal notice compelling me to. Capice?"

"Yeah. I was just hoping—"

"Hope away, sonny. Bye now." She hung up.

One down, still twelve to go. And Tom alone in the team room.

Where the hell was everyone?

The boss was running around with Harriett Barnes like a pair of secret agents. Nina had run off to the hotel without really explaining why. The sarge had disappeared, just when it looked like he was about to help.

"Guess I'll do the actual work then, shall I?" he muttered, and proceeded to dial the number for Charlie's Charters.

Charlie, if it was him, was less aggressive than Mrs Donnelly, without her intricate knowledge of his legal rights, but he wasn't much more use.

"Last Friday, is it?" he asked when Tom explained what he wanted.

"It is, yes."

"Wait there, lad."

Tom heard Charlie coughing, the rustling of paper, the opening and closing of drawers and doors.

"Sorry," said Charlie, eventually. "Can't help you. Chuck it all out after a week, see."

Two down. Still twelve to go, because those two weren't even out of the running.

There had to be a way of narrowing it down. Stuart Sullivan hadn't seen enough of the car to identify which company it came from. Tom flicked through the CCTV files, ignoring the internal ones. He watched the grainy footage of the vehicle itself, paused it, but couldn't see any more than he'd seen the last four times. There was another external file for the car park camera, but that didn't show the driveway. The cab wasn't on it. Just Sally Peters, turning up and...

He blinked, hit himself on the head, and opened the file. There she was, climbing out of her car, watching the hotel, then turning to the right.

Why had she turned to the right?

He checked the time stamp, compared it to the footage from the other external camera, and hit himself on the head again.

He pulled up Sally Peters' number from the team inbox.

"Look," she said, when he'd explained who he was. "I'm sorry I lied about never being at that bloody hotel. But I didn't do anything, and it's not right for you to be harassing a grieving widow."

"I understand—"

"It's not right."

"I'm sorry, Mrs Peters. And yes, we know you haven't done anything wrong, and I can assure you we don't want to cause you any further distress. It's more that we think you might be able to help us."

"Help us? Like 'helping the police with their enquiries' help us?"

"No. It's just that when you were at the hotel last Friday, it's possible you saw something that could be a piece of vital evidence."

"Doubt it. I saw the hotel. Most of the lights were off. It was late. There was a car."

Tom waited.

"A cab, actually. I remember thinking someone's changed their mind about a dirty night out, haven't they? And then I got in the car and drove home."

"This cab," he said, trying to still his excitement. "Do you remember which company it was from?"

She hummed. "Oh, yeah," she said. "Treetops Taxis. They were a—"

"You're sure of that, Mrs Peters?"

"One hundred percent."

The line at Treetop Taxis was answered by a man who introduced himself as Ahmed, listened to Tom's explanation and request, and asked him to wait for a moment. Unlike Charlie, Ahmed conducted his search in near silence, the only noise the gentle tapping of a keyboard.

"Yes," said Ahmed, after less than thirty seconds.

"Yes?" repeated Tom.

"Well, yes and no. Yes, I think it was one of ours, but that's from memory, unfortunately. The computer system is down, and it won't be up again until tomorrow. The system logs all the calls and all the trips. But I think I remember the call you're talking about."

"To Bassenthwaite Manor Hotel?"

"I can contact the driver if you want?"

"That would be wonderful."

"If it's him, I'll ask him to call you directly."

Tom sat back, smiling. He looked around and addressed the empty room.

"Thanks again, everyone," he said. "Couldn't have done it without you."

CHAPTER EIGHTY-FIVE

THAT HAD BEEN a waste of time. Zoe hadn't had much to report when it came to her main investigation, and she'd been forced to listen to the super dismissing the presence of up to four corrupt police employees as one bad apple.

Entering the stairwell, she spotted Harriett Barnes two floors down, heading away from her, and called out.

"Have you got a moment?" she asked.

"Yes, Ma'am," Harriett replied, and Zoe tried not to wince.

Inside her office, Zoe closed the door and invited Harriett to sit.

"Tell me what you know about Fiona Kendrick," she said.

Harriett's eyes widened in surprise. "I don't know if I can—"

"I'm going to assume you're not investigating her, Harriett. And if you were, you wouldn't be able to tell me anyway. But I have concerns."

CHAPTER EIGHTY-FIVE

"I'm sorry, Ma'am, but are you formally reporting a suspicion of a senior colleague?"

"No, I'm formally doing nothing at all. I'm having a chat, sharing my thoughts, that sort of thing. OK?"

There was a long pause. "OK," said Harriett, finally, looking about as uncomfortable as Zoe had ever seen her.

"I've just been to see her. She's chalking Cummings up as a win."

"She's right. We've arrested a corrupt police officer. We should be pleased."

Zoe shook her head. "If Cummings was the only problem we've got, then fine, but you and I both know that's not the case."

Harriett looked even less comfortable now. *Good.*

"Before I started here, a man named Noah Cane was murdered. While DS Keyes was investigating, along with Tom and Nina, they discovered that most of the local dealers had disappeared. Now we know why – they were being run out of business by Cummings, McKenzie, and Carrie Wright."

"Yes. Two of them are in custody, and the third one's dead."

"That's not the point. DS Keyes raised this with the super. With Fiona Kendrick. She told him it was all in hand and not to worry about it."

Harriett nodded.

Zoe leaned forward. "Doesn't that concern you? Because it concerns me. But not as much as what she then said. She said it was being handled by Ralph Streeting. You're familiar with him?"

"I know DI Streeting, yes. Specialist Crime and Intel. This would come under his remit."

"Streeting's not to be – bloody hell."

She'd just glanced out of the window to see a figure she recognised standing in the car park. She beckoned Harriett to the window.

"Do you recognise that man?"

Harriett nodded. "That's DS Mulligan. Works for DI Streeting."

"I thought so. What's he doing here? And why the hell is he standing out there in the freezing cold?"

"Ma'am, you were saying something about DI Streeting."

"Yes." Zoe turned back to Harriett. "I don't trust him. I'm convinced he's working for Myron Carter."

Harriett stared at her. "No one trusts DI Streeting, Ma'am. But no one's ever been able to get anything on him. It's possible he's just one of those officers who's merely unpleasant."

PSD, with all their resources, didn't have anything more on Streeting than Zoe did. Less, in fact. Zoe had claimed to have evidence about Victor Parlick's death, and that evidence had gone up in flames the moment Streeting found out about it. The evidence hadn't existed, not in real life. But Zoe could join the dots. And now she had the photographs too, which she was convinced showed Carter instructing Streeting to kill Victor Parlick.

"There's more than that," she said. "I'll tell you about it later. It's Fiona I'm worried about."

"You don't have to worry about Detective Superintendent Kendrick," Harriett replied, with a hint of a smile.

"Why not?"

"Because she wasn't lying. It *was* all in hand. And not with DI Streeting."

"What do you mean?"

"From what I understand, she already knew about the disappearing dealers, and suspected there might be corrupt police involvement."

"So why didn't she tell PSD?"

"She did, Ma'am. That's why I'm here."

CHAPTER EIGHTY-SIX

IT FELT GOOD, this.

Like a weight had been lifted off Harriett's shoulders.

Back when Branthwaite had approached her in training, she'd been flattered. Who wouldn't be? When the job had actually turned up and she'd been fast-tracked into the team, it had still been a sort of dream. But then she'd been dropped into the Hub.

It was easy enough, imagining a cover. Contemplating the lies she'd tell, the little twists she'd have to put on them to make sure they worked, tailoring them to the person she was talking to. It would be fun. It would be a game.

She'd spent more than a year and a half lying to almost everyone she knew. It hadn't been easy. It wasn't a game anymore.

Telling DI Finch had been the right thing to do, operationally. But it was more than that. She felt like she could breathe again. Nina seemed angry with her. The others – DS Keyes, and Tom, of course, Tom most of all... Time would tell.

CHAPTER EIGHTY-SIX

But it was worth it. And she'd done what she'd been put there to do. It had been her covert surveillance, her little hack into the CCTV system to grab files that were supposed to have been deleted. That was what had got them Cummings, finally. The man behind it all. The reason she'd been sent there in the first place.

Watching DI Finch's mouth fall open as she explained this was just a bonus.

DI Finch's mouth was still open when her phone rang on her desk. Harriett cleared her throat and looked at it.

"Nina," said DI Finch, putting it on speaker. "I'm here with Harriett Barnes. What's up?"

"Oh." Harriett could hear hesitation. "Just thought I'd tell you I'm heading out to the hotel. Nearly there, actually."

"Why?"

"I want to talk to Astrid Nielsen. Get some certainty on Raymond's alibi. I want to see Sophie Lambert. And I want to dig around this taxi a bit more. Someone left the hotel, and we've been assuming it's staff, but there's no sign of them coming back. Not on Friday night. So where are they?"

"OK," said DI Finch. "Good work. I still think it's Carter's people, but we've got to cover every angle." She glanced out of the window. DS Mulligan was still standing there, talking into his phone now, nodding. "You didn't see DI Streeting on your way out, did you?"

"Yes," said Nina.

DI Finch's expression changed from casual to serious.

"You did?" she said.

"Saw him in the car park. With his DS. Mulligan, I think. He asked about the case."

"The case?"

"Cummings."

Harriett met DI Finch's gaze. "Nina," she said.

"Yes," Nina replied. Was Harriett imagining the hostility in her voice?

"Can you be very specific, please? Can you tell me precisely what Streeting asked, and what you told him?"

"Yes. Hang on."

Hang on?

"Sorry. The roads here aren't brilliant. Still a lot of snow. He asked how we were getting on with Cummings. Asked if we'd got to grips with his operation. I said we still had to bring in the last one, and then we'd be done. That's OK, right?"

"Of course it is," said DI Finch, quickly. Harriett looked up. The DI had paled.

"Is that it?" asked Harriett, looking at the phone. "Nothing else?"

"No. There was... I'm just trying to remember."

They waited. The line was bad now, the fells interfering with the signal the further Nina got into the National Park.

"I said it was a woman. Explained she worked at the port."

A woman at the port. That would narrow it down, but not enough for Streeting to just wander around killing all the women who worked at the port. Assuming DI Finch was right about Streeting, of course.

"And that's all?" Harriett asked.

"I gave him the name," said Nina. "Bobby Silver."

Harriett felt the breath catch in her throat.

"Thanks, Nina. Call me with updates from the hotel," said DI Finch, and ended the call.

Both women were on their feet.

"I gather you're an excellent driver," said DI Finch.

CHAPTER EIGHTY-SIX

Harriett felt briefly flattered, and wondered who'd told her that.

"Yes." No point in being modest.

"Go to the team room. Grab whoever's there. And pick up Bobby Silver. We've got to get there first."

Harriett ran to the team room. When she pushed open the door, her first thought was that the room was empty. Then she saw Tom, staring at the grainy image of a taxi on the enormous screen.

There was nobody else there.

Her and Tom, then. It would have to be her and Tom.

CHAPTER EIGHTY-SEVEN

OF ALL THE shocks Aaron had been through over the last few hours, the arrival of Theodora Harding was the mildest.

He'd almost forgotten about the chef, with everything else going on. She wasn't a suspect. But still, she was here. She wanted to talk to him.

She'd have to do so under caution. He wasn't taking any risks.

Interview Room Four was occupied, so they had to make do with Room Two. Bare walls, metal chairs, plastic table. It wasn't conducive to a pleasant conversation, but it tended to focus the mind.

"Fine," said Theodora, unphased by either the room or the caution. "Oh, and call me Theo. Nice place you have here."

He raised an eyebrow. "What did you want to—"

"Enjoy your meal, last night?"

"It was excellent, thank you," he replied. It had been, but now his head was pounding. And there was something else,

CHAPTER EIGHTY-SEVEN

something he'd realised when he'd woken in the middle of the night.

He shouldn't have accepted the free meal. Theodora Harding was a potential witness in a murder investigation. He *really* shouldn't have accepted the free meal. She'd want something in exchange. People always did.

Was that why she was here now? Had she come to collect?

"Look," she said. "I'll cut to the chase."

Here it came.

"I'm sorry."

He wasn't expecting that. "What?"

"I'm sorry I've been so evasive. But you have to understand. There's a code in our industry."

"What do you mean?"

"We sort out our own problems. We don't like to get the police involved."

"Right." Aaron had suspected as much. "But you—"

"And I had more reason than usual to be wary. Because this... This thing, whatever it is. It involved drugs. On our premises."

Cautioning her was looking more and more like a smart move.

"So you didn't want to talk to the police, because of something involving drugs, even though we were conducting a murder investigation?"

She nodded. "That's why I'm here," she said. "That's why I've come to tell you everything."

"Go on, then."

"McKenzie. He was dealing. That was why I fired him."

Aaron felt a pang of disappointment. Was this all she had?

"I told him I didn't care what he got up to in his private life, but he couldn't use my restaurant for it. He said fine, and I thought he'd stopped. Oh, and I thought it was just cannabis."

"I take it you were wrong."

She screwed her face into a rueful smile. "He hadn't stopped, and it wasn't just cannabis. Coke, heroin, meth. I don't know what else."

"And he was using your restaurant?"

She nodded. "He was using the bin yard as a meeting point for his customers. But that wasn't the worst of it. He was pushing among the staff as well. He'd turned one of the young waitresses into an addict."

"Addicted to what? Meth?"

"Yes, that. But also cocaine."

Aaron sat back and looked at her. Everything she'd said so far added up. But not this.

"You must pay your waitresses very well if one of them could afford a coke habit," he said.

"We pay all our staff well, because they're very good at what they do, and I'm a very demanding boss. But as it happens, I don't think she was paying."

"What?"

"McKenzie was giving her a supply. He wanted to be in control. To have power over her."

Control, again. Cummings had said something similar. And so had Shona Murray's brother, Iain, when he'd called the boss.

"So what happened?"

Theodora shrugged. "I found out and told him to get out." She stopped and ran a finger over the scar on her cheek.

"He just stood there like an idiot, and then I grabbed his knife bag and he absolutely lost it."

"What do you mean?"

"He went berserk. Like a madman. He grabbed a knife and went for me. Gave me this." Her finger was still on the scar.

"You didn't call the police?"

She shrugged. "Maybe I should have done. But we were just glad to get rid of him. And before you ask, yes, I did tell Peter bloody Raymond that McKenzie was trouble, but he just wanted someone cheap."

"And the waitress?"

"I paid for her to go into rehab. Six months, and then she was back on the team. She was your waitress last night."

The woman with the red hair who'd smiled politely while Serge clowned around with the lobster carcass. She'd looked normal. Fine.

"Fully recovered, then?"

"Once an addict, always an addict. That's what they say. But otherwise, yes. Fully recovered."

There was something she'd said, though. Aaron shut his eyes and tried to blunt the pain in his head.

The knife bag.

"You say he didn't go for you until you grabbed his knife bag?"

"Yup."

"Grey canvas thing, folds up?"

"That's it. He was protective of it. Like, *really* protective. I don't know if it was where he kept his stash or what, but I've never seen a chef lose it like that. Took three of them to pull him off me."

"So you don't think he'd be likely to just leave that behind if he went somewhere?"

"Why?" Theodora was eyeing him. "Wasn't it with him?"

Could he tell her? He couldn't see any reason not to.

"No. It was found back at the hotel."

"That's not like him." She touched her scar, an unconscious motion triggered by the memory of the man who'd put it there. "If he didn't have it with him, either he was coming back for it, or he'd have arranged for someone to bring it to him."

CHAPTER EIGHTY-EIGHT

Harriett took the back roads, and Tom found himself gripping the door handle as the patrol car lurched around corners that were on them almost as soon as they came into view. The snow and patches of ice didn't help, but every time it looked like they were about to skid, she would let it happen, just for a moment, then bring it back under control.

He'd known Harriett was a decent driver, but this? This was terrifying. He wanted to talk to her as she drove, to discuss what had happened to them, but...

He decided to give it a few minutes. He was feeling too sick to talk about anything serious.

It wasn't until they'd passed Cockermouth, and the road straightened out a little, that he felt able to talk, but Harriett beat him to it.

"This must be weird for you," she said.

"You're not kidding."

"I'm sorry, you know." She glanced at him, and he saw that earnestness on her face, the total honesty he'd bought so completely.

Idiot.

"Was it all part of the cover?" he asked.

Her attention was back on the road, but he saw her flinch.

"Do you really believe that?" she said.

"I don't know what to believe."

She was shaking her head as she moved out to pass a slow-moving Honda that had noticed neither the lights nor the siren.

"I'm so sorry, Tom." Harriett's face was flushed. "I never meant anything like that to happen."

The road was weaving gently now between fells as they rounded the tip of Bassenthwaite Lake. The trees were bare on either side of them, and the reflections of snow-capped hills shone in the lake. Nina wouldn't be far from here, down a handful of lanes to the hotel.

"Like what?" he asked.

"I wanted to keep my distance. But... No." She pursed her lips. "It really wasn't part of the cover. I promise you that."

A handful of tractors slowed them as they passed through Uldale, and then Harriett jerked the wheel to the left and they were off the main road, the snow lying thick on the verge, and drifting onto the asphalt itself. It was coming down again, a brief, heavy flurry, then drying up. Harriett slowed slightly.

"I really didn't want to lie to you, Tom. I hope you know that."

Did he know that? Why should he believe her now, when so much of what she'd told him had been untrue?

"I do," he said. Because what was the point in her lying now?

CHAPTER EIGHTY-EIGHT

Harriett ploughed straight onto a track as the road itself veered left. The snow here was even thicker, but she forced the car through it, seeming to know where the sides of the track lay even though Tom could see nothing more than slightly different bands of white.

He still hadn't asked the question that had been nagging at him for months now, that had tormented him ever since DI Finch had suggested Harriett might be PSD. She slowed as the house came into view, smoke rising from its chimney, and he took a breath.

"Is that why you ended it?"

"What do you mean?"

"Because you're PSD. Because you had to. Is that why?" he said.

Without speaking, she braked sharply and cut the engine.

The house was even larger in the flesh than it had seemed on camera, its stone rising from the snow like part of the earth itself. A few feet away, another car was parked, a yellow Honda that looked like it hadn't been cleaned in a while. Bobby Silver's car, according to the records.

Harriett opened her door and got out, and Tom followed suit.

"Look," she said, turning to him, and then they both heard it.

A growling noise. A roar.

Tom frowned. Harriett was looking at the house, then past it.

That was where the noise was coming from.

The growl of an engine gunning into life, around the back of the house.

CHAPTER EIGHTY-NINE

NINA SPOTTED a couple of twigs skittering across the frozen lake as she got out of her car and shivered.

Stuart Sullivan was shivering, too, as he approached.

"Alright?" she asked.

He shrugged. Was it her imagination, or was he looking even more unkempt than the last time she'd seen him?

Inside, Kate Bellamy was back behind the reception desk. Pale as ever. Seven guests were lined up, waiting to speak to her. But her attention was on the tall, youngish-looking man at the front, who was talking loudly about the state of his room. Her knuckles were white as she gripped the desk and listened to his litany of complaints.

The bar hadn't been restocked. The room hadn't been cleaned. The newspaper hadn't been delivered. And when he'd tried to order room service, no one had even answered the phone.

The poor woman was shaking, and Nina couldn't blame her. But there was nothing she could do to help.

Or was there?

"Cumbria Police," she said. "I need to speak to this woman."

Kate smiled gratefully as Nina pushed her way to the front of the line. The man shook his head in disgust and stalked off. Nina turned to the people waiting behind her.

"We might be a while, I'm afraid. I'd come back later if I were you."

The line dispersed, accompanied by a low grumble.

She turned to Kate. "What the hell's going on?"

"Half the staff haven't turned up. Sophie and Astrid are both shut in their rooms, and the other maids refuse to do extra work, so nothing's getting done."

"What's Raymond doing about it?"

Kate looked around, checking she couldn't be heard, before answering.

"He's locked himself in his room and he won't come out."

"Is there a deputy manager?"

"Joanna Grey. She quit last month."

"Why?"

Kate looked towards the corridor that led to Raymond's office. "Why do you think?"

Even if he hadn't killed McKenzie, that man had a lot to answer for.

"Who's in charge now, then?" Nina asked.

Kate screwed her face up. She seemed calmer now, with a little more colour in her face, but occasionally a shiver would run through her body.

"Well, not Max," she said.

"The chef?"

A nod. "He's just walked out. Says it's not manageable with just the two of them. So poor David's having to do everything by himself. Not surprised he's not answering room service calls."

"Who can I speak to?"

Kate hesitated, then nodded. "You know Leo? The barman?"

"Yeah," replied Nina, unhappily. She hadn't liked what she'd seen of Leo. But he was definitely preferable to Peter Raymond.

"He's not management. But he probably knows more about what goes on around here than anyone else."

"Busybody, then?"

"Nosy bastard," Kate replied, with a hint of a laugh.

"Think he'll be able to get me some CCTV footage?"

Kate frowned. "Not sure," she said. "Haven't you had all that?"

"Looking for some more," Nina told her. "Thanks." She headed reluctantly for the bar.

CHAPTER NINETY

HARRIETT WAS STRUGGLING to control the car. The snow had fallen heavily and nothing had been done about it. But Bobby Silver would have the same problem.

Wouldn't she?

Harriett was gaining on her now, slowing to avoid a shape in the snow that revealed itself to be a dog moments before she was on it, then accelerating again. She could see the vehicle she was chasing. The vehicle she'd been chasing since they'd heard it roar into life around the back of the house, tearing off along a rough track that snaked out beyond the house towards a line of trees.

A Jeep.

Shit.

The sort of car she was up against didn't usually make much difference, not with response vehicle training and skills so advanced the instructor had her demonstrating the moves almost as soon as she'd learned them. But there were exceptions. And the Jeep she was chasing was one of them.

Harriett would just have to be at her best.

She threw the car sideways as it threatened to leave the path, controlled the skid, moved forward again smoothly. Ahead, the Jeep disappeared into the trees. There had to be a track through there. Either that, or at least one car was going to end up in pieces.

The engine noise rose in a whine as the tyres struggled to bite. "Come on!" she said, to herself as much as the car. Beside her, Tom was muttering quietly. If she hadn't known him better, she'd have thought he was praying.

The trees were close now, and there was still no sign of a track. There was a noise beside her, a sort of panicked grunt as she accelerated.

There had to be a track.

There. Barely visible against the snow, but there, and as she drew level with the first of the trees – pines, a recent plantation – she could see it growing clearer as it wove deeper into the woods, with the ground sheltered from the worst of the snowfall by the foliage overhead.

She was maybe thirty seconds behind the Jeep. Closing, but too slowly.

If anything happened, if visibility grew worse, she'd lose it. Tom was still muttering. Ignoring him, she yanked the wheel hard to the right, cutting around a curve in the track, heading straight for where the Jeep had been a few seconds earlier, just hoping the patchy snow wasn't hiding anything nasty.

She felt the car tilt up, on the nearside, and then ease back down, and now they were so close she could almost smell the fumes. Without warning, they broke from the trees onto a patch of open land. The sudden brightness was almost blinding, but she kept going, ignoring the protest of the engine as she followed in the wake of the Jeep towards yet another thicket of trees.

There was something there, though. She could see it, ahead, past the first line of trees.

A line. A sort of dip.

"Shit!"

Tom turned to her, still muttering.

The Jeep pushed on, Harriett racing behind it, and even as she drew within what felt like touching distance, she knew she'd lost.

She watched as the Jeep dipped, slowed, then rose again and sped away. She kept going until the last moment before slamming on the brakes and skidding to a halt.

Tom turned to her, still muttering, a question on his face.

She pointed ahead, at the two-metre drop into the narrow frozen brook beyond.

"Low Loughing Beck," she said. "We won't make it over that."

Tom shrugged, and pointed back in the direction of the house, still muttering. Not prayers. Letters and numbers.

"What are you saying?" she asked, as he pulled out his phone. She reversed, slid the car into a one-eighty turn, and headed back.

"The plates," he told her, as they were enveloped once more in the shade of the pines. "Couldn't type them into my phone. We were moving around too much."

Ah. That made sense.

"This is DC Tom Willis," he said. "We're in pursuit of a green Jeep Wrangler. Lost them crossing Low Loughing Beck heading north from Ireby."

Harriett felt her heart rate slowly returning to normal as they emerged from the wood and the house came into view. Tom was going through the registration and trying to explain what had happened, but it was useless. They'd be long gone.

Still, though. It had been fun.

CHAPTER NINETY-ONE

Zoe answered her phone. "Who is this?"

"It's Paul Wiggins. Who's this?" There was noise in the background. People talking. Someone singing, Zoe thought.

Who the hell was Paul Wiggins?

"This is DI Zoe Finch from Cumbria Police. Can I ask—"

"Oh, right, yeah. That explains it."

She'd just walked into the team room when her phone had rung. Aaron was standing there, looking around in confusion, no doubt wondering where Tom was.

She'd explain later. When she'd got rid of Paul Wiggins.

"I'm sorry," said Zoe, "I'm really not sure—"

"It's like this," said Paul Wiggins. "I was trying to get hold of... Hang on. What's the name?"

There was a rustling sound, and then the noise of liquid against glass.

Was Paul Wiggins calling her from a pub?

"Yeah," he said. "Tom Willis, that's it. Apparently he

wanted to talk to me. I tried to get hold of him on the number dispatch gave me, but no dice."

Zoe had been trying to get hold of Tom, too. Him and Harriett. No news on whether they'd managed to pick up Bobby Silver. And Aaron didn't even know...

"Hang on," she said. "Can you just wait thirty seconds?"

"Fine," said Paul Wiggins.

She muted her phone and turned to Aaron. "Tom and Harriett have gone to pick up Bobby Silver."

He frowned. "Why?"

"Because Streeting's heard about her."

Aaron sat down hard. He looked exhausted. He'd only just come back full-time, and he'd been thrown into something more intense than he'd have expected.

But there was no time to worry about that now.

"Mr Wiggins?" she said.

There was a brief sound of chewing before Paul Wiggins spoke again. "Yep. So, where's this Tom Watson, then?"

"Tom Willis. I'm his...Tom works for me, Mr Wiggins. Do you know why he wanted to talk to you?"

"Something about a fare. Last week."

She put her phone down on the spare desk and switched it to speaker. "You're a cab driver, Mr Wiggins?"

"At your service," he replied. "Hang on." There was a short pause, followed by a loud belch.

"Christ," muttered Aaron.

"Sorry about that," said Wiggins. "Yeah. He wanted to ask me about a fare."

"Right," Zoe said. "I can talk to you about that, Mr Wiggins. It's last Friday."

Another pause, with more rustling and the clear sound of drinking. "You mean yesterday?"

"No, eight days ago. Last Friday. A fare from the Bassenthwaite Manor Hotel. Midnight. Could that have been you?"

"Not sure. Where to?"

Zoe looked over at Aaron. She didn't want to lead the man.

"We're not sure. But did you pick up someone from that hotel last Friday?"

"Friday, you say? Let me have a think. Shit. Hang on."

Another pause.

"Sorry, love. It's my round. Bear with me."

"Mr Wiggins," said Zoe, but there was no one to hear her, just general laughter, conversation, and singing.

"Try Tom," she said. Aaron picked up his phone, dialled, did the same for Harriett Barnes. Nothing.

"Just been talking with Theodora Harding," Aaron said, as Zoe listened to the sound of whichever pub Paul Wiggins was in still leaking out of her phone. "She said McKenzie used to deal from her restaurant."

"No surprise there."

"He lost it after she fired him. Attacked her when she touched his knife bag. Very possessive about it, apparently."

"And yet he didn't take it with him when he fled the hotel."

Aaron nodded. "Not just that. He got some waitress hooked on coke. Gave it to her for free, apparently. Theodora said he loved the control. We've heard that about him before, haven't we?"

Zoe was opening her mouth to agree when Paul Wiggins' voice filled the room again.

"Last Friday? Listen, sounds familiar, but I'll need to refresh my memory."

"This is a murder investigation, Mr—"

"Tell you what, give me five minutes to check the satnav record on my phone, and I'll call you back," he said.

"Can you just tell me who your—" Zoe began, but he was gone.

CHAPTER NINETY-TWO

"I THOUGHT YOU'D BE BACK," said Leo. He was turned away from Nina, drying a glass, but she could hear the smirk in his voice.

Why had he thought that?

"I'm told you're the man I need to talk to if I want to find out what's going on around here."

He turned to face her, and the smirk switched to a mock grimace. "I thought the same. And then I found out Raymond's shagging most of the cleaning staff and I only knew about one of them. So maybe not."

Nina had come across Leo's type before. The ones who had to be in the know. And if they hadn't been in the know, they always found a way of telling you they'd been halfway there, and they were all the way there now.

She had to keep her temper. That was what a DS would do. And besides, there was too much at stake. The bet she'd just made with Tom. Proving herself, as the sarge had suggested.

Finding McKenzie's killer.

"I'm after some CCTV footage," she told him. "Peter Raymond was supposed to have gathered it all together for us, but he's..."

"Not exactly around," completed Leo.

"And," she went on, "I want to know if any guests or staff have been missing since last Friday. Apart from McKenzie, obviously."

"No one missing. Not that I know of, anyway. As for CCTV, yeah, I can probably help you. What do you want?"

"Let's start with external footage, the car park and outside cameras. From four o'clock last Saturday morning."

"Follow me."

There was a little break room behind the bar, with shelves, a storage unit, a single chair, and a small metal table in it. As Nina entered, she noticed Leo pulling something off a shelf into a little drawer in the storage unit, and pulling the drawer shut. Drugs, she thought at first, then changed her mind. Porn. Or something porn-adjacent. She sighed.

The room smelled of beer and sweat, but she'd been in worse. Leo opened the drawer again, keeping his body between Nina and whatever was inside it, and pulled out a small laptop. Nina sat down on the chair and waited. Within a few seconds, the laptop was on the table in front of her, with the files neatly set out and clearly labelled.

"Thanks," she said, and looked meaningfully towards the door. Leo nodded and left. Nina opened the first file.

The car park. There was no movement between four and five. Shortly after five there was a van, someone exiting, two people, opening the back and dragging out an enormous bag, then disappearing off screen with it.

They repeated the operation twice before Nina realised this was the laundry service.

At six, staff who didn't live on site started to turn up. At half past six there was someone who was probably a guest, emerging blearily from a Jaguar with the stiff gait of a man who'd been driving all night.

She turned to the other camera, the one that gave a view of the driveway and the grounds beyond it.

She'd opened the first file before she realised the smell had all but disappeared. It wasn't the room that stank of beer and sweat, then. It was Leo.

There was nothing on the driveway between four and five. The laundry van drove up shortly after five, with the same staff cars and Jaguar she'd seen in the car park between six and seven. Between the first and the second staff cars was another van, but this one she knew was the meat delivery: she'd noticed it driving past the first time they'd been to the hotel.

"Shit," she muttered, and started on the later files. The driveway first, but there was still nothing interesting, only as it got brighter, the lake gradually came into view.

A sheet of ice. She couldn't see it, but she knew it was there, and she was shivering when she heard a voice behind her say, "I know, makes me cold just looking at it."

She turned. Leo had slipped back in. She swallowed her instinctive reply and nodded.

Cold. If only it was just *cold*.

If only it was that simple.

If only it wasn't the images that flew through her mind whenever she saw that lake, whenever she saw any frozen lake, anything that looked like a frozen lake, or a frozen pond.

Any decent-sized body of water, with a thin layer of ice over it.

She felt her skin contract.

Water.

Cold water.

Nina had done everything she could to avoid it. It wasn't easy living up here, but...

She had to avoid it. The alternative was to face the memories.

That day, with her mates. Skiving off school, again. Messing around on the ice. Some pond. She didn't even know its name.

She didn't want to.

She closed her eyes. *Stop thinking about it.*

But she couldn't. This case. The lake, the bloody frozen lake... it was bringing it all back.

The noise. That awful, terrible noise. A crack behind her. A scream.

She'd turned to see where the scream had come from. Her friend, Dawn, not even a close friend, just one of the gang.

She'd been right behind Nina. But then, as Nina turned at the sound of the scream, she hadn't been.

Gone. Replaced by a hole in the ice.

Nina closed her eyes. *Stop thinking about it.*

It was still there, in her mind's eye. The hole, the patch of darkness gaping at her from the ice. The feel of the cold on her belly as she'd got down to her stomach and slithered over to it, desperate.

But it had been too late.

It had changed Nina. She'd gone from skipping school to being a swot. From constant trouble to working hard and getting good grades and making her parents look at her funny. They'd known.

CHAPTER NINETY-TWO

Now, here she was. Her hard work, those grades, they'd got her a job in the police.

She should have known there'd be a case like this one day.

She swallowed. *Focus. Push it away.* She'd got good at that.

"I know what you mean," she said, and moved on to the next file. *Stop thinking about it.* Even though the smell had followed Leo back in, she didn't ask him to leave.

Right up to nine am, played at eight times normal speed, there was nothing interesting. Nina had managed to push down the memories, intent on finding evidence.

"Definitely no one else missing?" she asked Leo.

"Definitely," he replied, and she went back to the start.

The driveway camera, first. Any vehicle would have to use the driveway, even if it didn't enter the car park. She wasn't sure why she'd bothered with the car park. She leaned forward and focused on the driveway, and the grounds beyond it, and slid from four to five, and five to six, and—

"What's that?" said Leo. He was squinting closely at the screen, at something on the driveway, no, something beyond it.

Nina leaned in. Just a difference in the shade of darkness, but it was moving around, slowly...

She rewound. There it was again, shortly after five. And continuously thereafter. A change in the darkness, right through the footage. She'd assumed it was just a glitch. She hadn't really been focusing on the grounds. Just the driveway.

"Hang on," she said, and moved forward. Past seven. The sun didn't rise until more than an hour later, but soon, features started to appear on the ground.

And there was the shape.

Not a glitch. A person. Walking. Around and around.

Around the lake. A figure walking around the lake, over and over, hour after hour.

A figure carrying something on its back. And – was there something in its hands, too?

Soon after nine, the figure finally stopped in its tracks, turned, and walked away from the lake, towards the back doors of the hotel, and out of shot.

It was grainy, of course. The face wasn't clear. But there was something in the movement that reminded Nina of someone she'd met.

She stood.

"Is that—" began Leo, but Nina turned and shook her head.

She picked up the laptop and walked out of the room, leaving him sitting there. She made her way back to reception.

The queue hadn't reformed. Perhaps word had got out that the police were in the building, and the guests had decided to keep themselves to themselves.

"Kate," said Nina. "I think we need to have a chat."

CHAPTER NINETY-THREE

Zoe looked at Aaron. "You think Theodora Harding's still hiding something?"

He shook his head. "No. I think she was hiding the fact that McKenzie had been dealing on her premises, and she hadn't called us in. That, and him slashing her face. If ever there was a murder victim who—"

Her phone rang again, with a mobile number she didn't know.

Hopefully Paul Wiggins.

"Hello?" she answered.

"It's Iain Murray. Shona's brother. I don't know if you remember—"

"I remember you, Iain. I hope you don't think I'm rude, but we're sort of in the middle of something here."

"I won't keep you, DI Finch. I just wanted to tell you something."

"OK." She put her phone back on the desk and put the speaker on. "I'm here with Detective Sergeant Keyes, from my team. What is it you wanted to say?"

"Look, I'm sorry about this, but there's something you don't know. None of the polis know it, DI Finch. The thing is, it wasn't me who attacked McKenzie."

Zoe frowned.

"I know you're thinking, well, he would say that, wouldn't he, but I wouldnae, DI Finch. I was happy to take the fall, because it were my sister, see? It were Shona, and she couldnae handle dealing with you lot after all she'd been through."

"I'm sorry," Zoe said, "are you telling me it was Shona that injured Josh McKenzie?"

She thought back to the report. *Facial injuries. Abdominal. Back. Head.*

"Aye. She'd had enough, DI Finch. She'd finally cottoned on what sort of man he was. How he'd used her."

The more she thought about it, the more likely it sounded. Certainly more likely than Iain Murray doing it.

"Why are you telling me this?" she asked. "You don't think she could have come down and killed him, do you?"

Iain Murray laughed, a low, bitter laugh.

"No chance, DI Finch. She couldnae get out of Glasgow these days, much less make it to wherever you lot are and back again without passing out and gettin' herself picked up by the emergency services. No. I just— Well, you said he was dead. And I remembered how Shona went for him. I was the one who stopped her in the end. Anything could have happened."

"I understand. But that was years ago, Mr Murray. What makes you think it could be relevant now?"

"It's the way of it, though, isn't it?" he replied. "People, DI Finch."

Aaron was staring at the phone. He didn't seem to understand what Iain Murray was trying to say any more than Zoe did. She waited.

"The thing is," Murray continued, "sometimes, when people realise they've been controlled, they can fight back with a strength you dinnae think they had."

CHAPTER NINETY-FOUR

Tom put his phone back in his pocket as Harriett parked outside the house beside the yellow Honda. Half a dozen missed calls, but they could wait a few minutes.

His breathing had finally returned to normal, although he could still feel his heart pounding.

Back when they'd been seeing each other, Harriett had mentioned that she enjoyed driving. That she was good at it, which wasn't like Harriett, usually so quick to downplay her own abilities. He'd believed her.

But he hadn't expected this.

There was a glow to her features, and the hint of a smile. She'd enjoyed it. He'd been expecting to die at any moment, and she'd enjoyed the experience.

They got out of the car. Tom first, Harriett just behind him. He'd taken no more than two steps when the dog they'd driven past rounded the corner, raced up to him, and sat there, blocking his path, looking thoroughly cold and miserable. It was a dachshund. Belly to the ground, in this weather. No wonder it wasn't happy.

CHAPTER NINETY-FOUR

"Come on, then," said Harriett, quietly. He turned to see her opening the door of the car. The dog didn't wait for a second invitation, scampering inside. Harriett closed the door gently, and Tom saw the dog's face pressed against the window, watching them. Golden-haired. It reminded him of someone, but he couldn't think who.

The front door, first. Tom knocked and waited.

No answer.

He knocked again. Still nothing.

Bobby Silver had fled in her Jeep, but there could still be someone there. And Tom wasn't taking any chances.

Harriett nodded towards the back of the house, where they'd run, when they'd first heard the engine noise. In silence, they made their way slowly around the building. Tom glanced through the windows as he passed. The edge of a living room. A conservatory. A kitchen. Some sort of boot room.

With a back door that was swinging open.

She'd heard them, then. She'd heard them coming and got out of there so fast she hadn't even had time to shut the door. The dog must have run out the same way.

He gestured at Harriett; *what should we do?*

She shrugged back at him.

He walked up to the door and looked inside. There were walking boots and wellies lined up. Some tools. Coats. Nothing obviously out of place.

"Hello?" he said.

Nothing. He moved closer, put his head through the gap, and listened, but all that greeted him was silence.

No. Not silence. A whooshing sound. A sort of beating.

"Hello?" he said, louder this time. When there was no response after a few seconds, he shouted it.

Still nothing.

He'd just raised his right foot to walk inside when he felt a hand on his shoulder and jumped in surprise, hitting his head on the frame of the door and staggering back in pain.

"Sorry," said Harriett, as he screwed his eyes shut and waited until the throbbing dulled.

"What did you want?" he said, trying not to sound annoyed.

"We should go back to the car. I've got forensic suits in there."

He nodded. She was right. Bobby Silver might be gone, but if she'd been in such a hurry she'd left the door open, she might have left valuable evidence behind as well. And besides, most of those missed calls had been from the boss.

CHAPTER NINETY-FIVE

"We've been hearing a lot of this, boss," said Aaron.

DI Finch turned to him and nodded. She'd know he was thinking about other things. Like, where the hell was Tom? Where was Harriett? Had Nina found anything new at the hotel?

But there was nothing they could do about any of that. Best to focus on the things they could influence. So Aaron wasn't thinking about Bobby Silver. Or the guilt and betrayal and downright stupidity that flooded through him whenever he did.

"Iain Murray, Theodora Harding, Tel Cummings, boss. They've all mentioned it. It can't be a coincidence."

She nodded. "I'm starting to wonder if maybe we've been barking up the wrong tree. Not that banging Cummings up is a bad result."

She grinned as her phone rang. Her eyes widened as she hit the speaker button.

"Tom? Is everything OK?"

"Fine, boss. Well, sort of. We're at Bobby Silver's house."

The boss glanced at Aaron, then back at the phone. "Is she still there?"

"Don't think so. Looks like we surprised her. At least, I assume it was her."

"What d'you mean?"

Aaron listened, standing next to the DI, as Tom explained that they'd been in a car chase, that the vehicle they'd been after had got away, over a brook the patrol car couldn't cross, and that they'd called it in, but already learned it had cloned plates.

It made sense. Someone with Bobby Silver's money would have more than just an ageing Honda.

"But she left in a hurry, boss," Tom added. "Her dog was loose outside, and the back door's open."

"No sign of anyone there?" asked Aaron.

"Not that we can see, Sarge. Harriett's got forensic suits, so we're going in. Hopefully she's left something important behind."

"OK," said DI Finch. "Be careful, both of you."

She ended the call and turned to Aaron. "You know you're going to have to talk to PSD about this, don't you?"

He nodded. His friendship, if that wasn't too strong a word, with Bobby Silver. When he'd first made contact with Victor Parlick, it had been all about the intel. Learning the secrets of Carter's empire. But when he'd stumbled across Bobby Silver, months after Victor's death, it had been different. It had been about Victor's memory. About having a drink with decent people. His job had been entirely irrelevant. Only, he now realised, it hadn't been. It hadn't been at all.

He'd sat there like an idiot and mentioned McKenzie. He'd watched as Bobby and her friends looked blankly at him. And then he'd told them McKenzie was dead, and

Bobby had spat her drink out, and carried on like nothing had happened, and he'd never suspected a thing.

He sighed. "I know, boss."

Her phone rang again, Paul Wiggins. Still in the pub, if the noises coming out of the speaker were anything to go by, but he seemed a little more focused than he had been.

"It was me," he said. "I took her."

"Her?" said the boss.

"Yeah. Some lass. Don't remember much about her, didn't get her name or anything and dispatch don't have it either. I remember how pale she was, though. I told her, you want a bit of sunshine, love, but she didn't want to talk."

"Where did you take her?"

"Ennerdale. Near enough. Dropped her on the side of the road. I told her, this weather, you'll catch your death, but she wasn't having any of it. Made me wait there for her."

"Did she say where she was going?"

"Said something about her boyfriend. I mean, I know people sometimes have to sneak about, but this was taking it a bit far. That's what I said to her, anyway."

"Did she have anything with her?" asked Aaron.

"No. Hang on, yeah. She had a backpack. And a smaller thing. Sort of bag. Grey. No idea what was in it."

DI Finch looked back at him. "What happened afterwards?" she asked.

"I was there about an hour. Had to run the engine, it were fucking freezing, 'scuse my French. Anyway, an hour later, she gets back in. Shivering, poor thing. Even paler than she had been. I said to her, you didn't fall in, did you, coz she looked wet through, but she still didn't want to talk."

"And you took her back to the Bassenthwaite Manor Hotel?" Aaron asked.

"Yeah. No, not quite. She wanted me to drop her about a mile away. Maybe two. Don't remember the spot. I said she was mad, but she insisted, and you can't do anything when they get an idea in their heads. Made sure I got full fare, though."

"Thank you, Mr Wiggins," said DI Finch.

CHAPTER NINETY-SIX

Kate smiled at Nina. "Absolutely. Is everything OK, Nina?"

There was a fixed quality to the woman's smile, a sense of the immense effort it was taking to keep it there.

"Do you want to go somewhere a bit more private?" Nina asked. There was still nobody around, but this wasn't going to be an easy conversation.

Kate glanced down. She was gripping the underside of the desk again, and Nina thought she saw movement in the corner of her mouth. A tiny tic. The smile was costing too much.

"It's fine to talk here," she replied.

Nina set the laptop down on the desk, spun it round to face Kate, leaned over, and tapped the play icon.

"Is that you?" Nina asked.

"Oh." The smile was replaced by a frown of... Was that confusion, or concentration? "It might be. When's this footage from?"

"Saturday morning."

Kate nodded. "After I'd had that call. Yes. I couldn't sleep that night." She looked at Nina. "After what Josh said to me. He blamed me. And I was so angry. If I'd known..."

She looked back down at the screen, at her own image, walking around the lake, circle after circle. Nina watched her blink. Were those tears in her eyes?

"Tell me what happened," Nina said, gently.

"What happened?"

"That night. Why did you go out? When? Why there?"

Kate looked back up. "I don't remember when, exactly. I just couldn't believe it. The way he'd spoken to me. I'd been convinced he was coming back, you see. I hadn't realised it was really over. Not till then. And I think... I really do think I loved him."

"I understand. But why there, Kate?"

"He used to take me on that lake. Take a boat out at night, when there was no one around." She smiled again, a private smile over private memories. "And it looks so lovely, all frozen over, don't you think?"

Nina gave a small shiver and shrugged.

"So I thought maybe I could get him out of my system? Or sort of understand why he'd done it? I'm not sure what I thought, really. Whatever it was, it didn't work."

Her smile was resigned now. Better than the tears, Nina supposed.

And it made sense. McKenzie had been scum, but people couldn't help who they loved, and Kate had loved him. And after what he'd said to her... Anyone would have been upset.

Not that she'd have chosen to walk around that lake herself...

But there was something playing on Nina's mind. She

CHAPTER NINETY-SIX

nudged the laptop, so the screen was facing her, and stared at it.

"You say you don't remember when you came out?"

Kate shook her head.

Nina hadn't seen Kate leaving the hotel. She might have snuck out in the dark, but Nina would have noticed if that patch of darkness was moving from somewhere else. From the hotel building towards the lake.

She'd have had to cross the driveway, wouldn't she?

Nina would have to go through and watch all the footage again, starting earlier. Finding the point at which that figure began to circle the lake. And check...

Her thoughts were interrupted by her phone ringing.

"Boss," she said, her eyes on the screen. On the figure by the lake. She shuddered.

"Are you still at the hotel?" DI Finch asked.

"Yes, why?"

"We think we've got an ID on the taxi passenger, Nina. We think it's Kate Bellamy."

Nina looked up. Kate was no longer smiling.

And in her hand was a knife.

Eight inches, Nina guessed, the lights from above reflecting in its polished steel blade.

A chef's knife.

"I think you're right," Nina said into her phone.

CHAPTER NINETY-SEVEN

THEY'D DONE this once before.

It struck Harriett as they stepped as silently as they could through the boot room. Another empty house, only that time it hadn't been empty. Maya Priest had been hiding there, in her dead neighbour's bungalow, and they'd found the girl. Tom and her, together.

But Bobby Silver was long gone. Probably halfway to Scotland by now. Or Wales. Or an airport, maybe. Someone who lived in a house like this could go anywhere. The notice had gone out, of course. But Bobby Silver would have fake documents.

Ahead of her, Tom eased himself around a corner into the kitchen. She watched his back for signs – would he tense up, take a step backwards, say something?

He took another step forward, and she followed. A big kitchen. Huge range cooker – an Aga? Whatever it was, it seemed to be warming the room. She'd left the back door open and could feel the icy wind at her back. But ahead of her, it felt almost like summer.

CHAPTER NINETY-SEVEN

She sniffed. What was that? Not just the woodsmoke. But something else, also smoky. Sweet. Coffee, maybe?

Another step, another two. They'd reached the end of the kitchen. There was that noise. A whooshing, beating sort of noise. There was a thick rug, and beyond it an open door and a short passageway with a cream carpet.

"Wipe your feet," said a voice.

Harriett stopped. Ahead, she saw Tom stiffen.

"Bugger off, Cummings," said the same voice. Tom turned to look at her, frowning, pointing onwards, then placing the finger to his lips.

Harriett didn't need telling. She tried to remember what she'd seen from outside. They were in the kitchen. Which meant the passageway opened out into the living room.

She mirrored Tom's steps ahead of her. Stopped when he stopped. She moved to the side to see what had stopped him.

A parrot. Flying around the room, watching them with what looked very much like disdain.

"Bugger off, Cummings," it said.

The carpet gave way to wooden flooring as the passageway opened into the living room. There was one long sofa, and opposite it, a fire burning. Another rug lay in front of the fire, the smell of wet dog competing with the burning wood. Harriett felt a breeze to her left and turned to see an open window. Movement in the corner of her eye had her jerking round again, but it was just the TV, silent, the screen dominated by a heavily bleeding man dragging himself up a flight of stairs with a gun in one hand.

Trying to ignore the bird, Harriett pointed to two closed doors, and they checked the other rooms in turn. A study. A small dining room. All clear.

They moved back through the living room to the hallway,

with its huge glass front door and stairs leading up. The smell here was even stronger, the one she'd noticed in the kitchen.

Slowly, they climbed the stairs, her in front this time. The bird remained downstairs, silent now, as if it knew things had turned serious.

There was a landing at the top, and more wooden floors. The smell was so strong she could taste it, and underneath it, something else. Something waxy.

Three of the four doors were closed. She pointed at the other one, half open, the pattern on its rounded handle glinting in the light that slanted in up the stairs. A book had been left on the floor, just outside the room. *Bleak House*.

An odd place to put a book.

Tom was on the landing behind her. She moved forward slowly, getting a wider view of the room, then stopped.

There was something on the floor.

"What is it?" Tom whispered.

She pointed. Was that hair? The top of someone's head?

"Hello?" she said.

No response. No movement.

She stepped forward, ready to back away, but there was no need. Nothing to back away from.

Just the face of a woman lying on her back, staring up at the ceiling. A woman with wiry hair and glasses that hung from one ear.

It hadn't been Bobby Silver in the Jeep, then. And Bobby wasn't going to be straightening her glasses. Not now. Not ever.

Because there was a neat round hole through Bobby Silver's forehead.

CHAPTER NINETY-EIGHT

"I'm sorry," said Kate.

Nina thought it was a bit late for that. "Put the knife down, Kate."

Kate looked at the knife in her hand, and frowned at it, like she hadn't realised it was there. For a moment Nina actually thought the woman was going to put it down, but then she shook her head.

"I really am sorry," she said. She looked it, too. Like she hadn't just picked up the knife at all – where had the damn thing been, anyway? – but instead someone had placed it in her hand and told her she couldn't put it down.

Like she didn't actually want to use it.

"Tell me what happened," said Nina.

"I couldn't forgive him."

"For what?"

Kate frowned at her. "For abandoning me, of course. For running off like that. Remember what I said, when he got that call from his friend?"

Nina nodded. The way she was talking, Kate should have been under caution. But this wasn't the time for something like that. Her eyes flicked down, at the knife shaking slightly in Kate's hand, and then back up to the woman's face.

It *really* wasn't the time.

"'I need to get away.' That's what he said. *I*. Not *we*. Just him. I thought it was all about us. Turns out there was no *us*."

Kate's voice was low. Bitter. And that knife was still shaking.

"What about the call? On Friday? What did he really want?"

Kate smiled. "He called me up. Said to bring things. He wanted his knife bag, but he wanted other stuff, too. And I thought he meant stuff for both of us."

"So you had his knife bag?"

"It was in his room. I got it from there. And some clothes for me, and some for him. Not a lot. I thought, we'd have to figure out a way of making money, getting things, it didn't really matter what we had now as long as we could get through the first few weeks."

There was still a smile on Kate's face. A wistful sort of look.

"I don't understand," said Nina. "What were you planning?"

"I think I thought we were going on the run together."

Nina wasn't sure what she'd expected, but it wasn't that.

"I didn't know what sort of trouble Josh was in, but I thought, me and him, together, it was kind of romantic. Do you understand?"

"Of course," Nina agreed. It *was* kind of romantic. If you

were stupid, or so blinded by the light of someone else's self-regard, you couldn't see them for what they were.

"I made sure I got picked up round the back. We met at the old Anglers. You know it?"

Nina saw the lake again, the tent with the body in it, the ice. "Yes," she said, repressing a shudder.

"We used to have picnics there sometimes. I thought that was why he'd said to meet there. Like we would take all that love, all that passion, and fire a new life with it. But then..."

Kate's face crumpled.

"Then he told me he couldn't trust me. Said he knew I'd spoken to you, to DC Willis. Said it was over. Told me to hand over what I'd brought for him, and then he'd never see me again."

She barked a short, rueful laugh.

"He wasn't wrong about that, was he?"

Nina waited.

"So, yes. I killed him. I needed him, and he wouldn't have me..." Her cheek twitched. "I pushed him into the lake. I changed my clothes out there in the snow, but it was dark and the cab driver didn't even notice. I came back here and spent half the night just walking around the hotel grounds, trying to work out what to do."

"And you decided to frame Peter Raymond?" asked Nina, regretting the question immediately.

Kate shook her head. "I had a bag full of clothes with his blood on them, a knife with his blood on it, I was going to turn myself in."

Nina said nothing, but the scepticism must have shown on her face, because Kate nodded.

"I was. But then I thought, why should I? He was the one

who did it all, wasn't he? He was the dealer. The blackmailer. I was just his little plaything, when it was convenient."

Nina resisted a glance down at the knife and held Kate's gaze. "I understand."

"I dumped the clothes, and I hid the knife in here." Kate pointed the knife at the desk. "There's a false interior. No one knows about it. The Raymond thing, that came later. And you can't say he didn't deserve it."

Nina found herself nodding before she'd even thought about it. Kate smiled at her and seemed to relax, the hand holding the knife dropping to the desk.

Nina held Kate's gaze for a moment, Elvis, as ever, her guide.

Wise.

Men.

Say.

And then she lunged.

She pushed back with her right foot to propel herself forward. She'd covered the hand holding the knife with both of her own hands before Kate knew what was happening.

She pushed down, hard. Kate tried to pull away. Nina didn't want to hurt her, but that was the only way she'd release the knife.

She leaned forward, most of her body weight on the hand beneath hers, her eyes still on Kate's face.

Kate was looking down, crying, pulling back, or at least trying to. Nina felt a change in the pressure under her palms.

Kate had released the knife.

Carefully, Nina allowed the force she was pressing down with to lessen, and a moment later, Kate's hand emerged.

Without the knife.

CHAPTER NINETY-EIGHT

"Listen," Nina said, but Kate was shaking her head, the tears still coming, a look of betrayal in her eyes.

And then Kate was around the desk and running towards the exit.

Nina looked at the knife. She couldn't just leave it there. She picked it up and raced after the fleeing woman.

CHAPTER NINETY-NINE

Zoe heard the phone go dead. She looked over at Aaron and saw her fear reflected in his eyes.

He snatched up his phone, dialled a number, and put it on the table in front of her.

"Aaron," she heard a moment later. The reassuring tones of Morris Keane.

"Inspector Keane," said Aaron. "I'm here with DI Finch. DC Kapoor's at the Bassenthwaite Manor Hotel, and we think she needs immediate assistance."

"Right. Details, Aaron," replied Keane, all business.

"She was in the process of apprehending a murder suspect when she was cut off. We believe the suspect is likely to be armed, and probably unstable."

"I'm sending units now. Do we need an armed response?"

Aaron looked at Zoe. She frowned before answering.

"Possibly. From what we know of this woman, she's liable to be highly unpredictable. It's possible we'll have to..."

"Don't worry, Zoe," said Keane. "I understand."

CHAPTER NINETY-NINE

Zoe's phone rang. Tom.

Had he found Bobby Silver? Aaron was briefing Morris Keane. Between the two of them, she wasn't needed. Not now.

"Boss," Tom said, panting.

"What's up, Tom? Are you OK?"

"Yeah. Yeah, we're fine. It's Bobby Silver."

"What about her?"

"She's dead, boss. She's been shot dead."

Zoe felt her mouth drop open. Aaron was still talking, still looking at her. She knew from the expression on his face that the blood had drained from hers.

Shit.

CHAPTER ONE HUNDRED

IT WAS LIKE KATE KNEW. Like she'd read Nina's mind and figured out the one place she could go where she wouldn't be followed.

Kate cut across the car park, and Nina chased her across the driveway onto the grounds beyond. The snow here had started to turn to slush, and Nina found herself slipping, regaining her balance, pressing on. Gaining ground.

Until she realised where Kate was heading, and stopped short.

The receptionist was standing by the frozen lake. As Nina watched, she put one foot tentatively on the ice, then stepped onto it fully, more confidently.

One step.

Two.

"Come back," Nina shouted.

Kate took another step onto the lake.

Then another.

"Come back," called Nina again.

CHAPTER ONE HUNDRED

Kate shook her head. "What's the point?" she shouted back.

"It's dangerous!"

Kate looked down at her feet, at the ice.

She nodded and took yet another step. Nina didn't know how deep the lake was, but it didn't have to be deep. Cold shock response. Hypothermia. Drowning. You didn't need much water.

"You've got to come back," Nina said. Again, she wasn't getting through. Kate took another step, and another, and now Nina reckoned she was a quarter of the way to the centre of the lake, where the fountain still shot jets of water glittering into the air.

"What's the point?" Kate repeated. "I need him."

When the sound came, it was quiet. Nina might not even have noticed it if she hadn't been waiting for it. If she hadn't heard it a thousand times in her nightmares.

Nina couldn't see the cracks in the ice, but she could see Kate registering them, realising what they meant.

"Come back!" she shouted.

When Kate looked at her, there was a sort of pleading in her eyes.

"Shit." Nina looked around for something, for someone. Anyone but her.

There was no one.

What there was, though, was the low wooden structure Stuart Sullivan had pointed out to her. The boathouse. Maybe there would be something in there she could use.

She ran for the door, found it shut, pulled at it, pushed at it.

Nothing happened.

She kicked it, and it fell in at once.

"Sorry," she said to no one in particular, and plunged inside.

It was dark, and she forced herself to stop and allow her eyes to adjust. Silent, too: she could hear herself breathing, the creak of the wooden structure itself, the door hanging loose where she'd kicked it.

And the sound, of course. The sound of the ice cracking, which she couldn't hear from inside, but which had somehow burnt itself into her brain and followed her in.

She could see. In front, boats. A dozen of them, maybe, stacked on their sides.

To her right, shelving.

On the nearest shelf was a heap of something, and Nina could smell the blood before she saw it. This was where Kate had dumped the clothes she'd been wearing. Beside them, a metal tin. Locked with a padlock, but dented where someone had tried to smash their way in.

Something more than bait in there. She picked it up and shook it, hearing something move around inside.

There was a scream from outside.

Had she imagined it? Was it the same scream she'd been hearing for years?

It came again, loud, desperate. She didn't have time to worry about the box.

On the next shelf up she found what she was looking for, grabbed it, wound it round one arm and rushed back out.

"Kate!" she shouted as she ran. "Take this!"

She reached the edge of the lake and looked across, at the woman standing, frozen in terror, looking back at her.

Nina couldn't look down. Keeping her eyes on Kate, she threw the rope out as far as she could.

It landed short.

CHAPTER ONE HUNDRED

She pulled it back, tried again.

Closer, but still short. Nina glanced down to see the lines in the ice, a network stretching from the shore to where Kate stood, almost surrounded by it now.

She tried again. This time, the end of the rope landed close enough for Kate to grab it.

Kate stood there, staring at her, unmoving.

"Take the rope!" Nina shouted.

Kate looked down at the rope, then back up at Nina.

"What's the point?"

"For Christ's sake, take the fucking rope!" Nina shouted.

"I need him," Kate said.

Nina opened her mouth to shout something else, something peppered with the sort of four-letter words she hadn't learned in police training, and then stopped.

The box.

The locked box that someone had tried to get into, and failed.

Kate, pale and shaking all the time. The shock, they'd thought. Or the grief.

Or just the fact that she'd found McKenzie's supply, but she couldn't get into it.

Control. That was what McKenzie did. He found women he could control. And he found a foolproof way of controlling them.

"You don't need him," Nina shouted.

Kate laughed mirthlessly.

"No, I mean it," she continued. "You don't need him. You just think you do. He made you an addict, didn't he?"

Kate stopped laughing.

"He made you think it was him you needed, but it wasn't him. It was just the drugs."

Kate looked back down at the ice. Nina heard that sound again, the crack. She saw Kate stumble to one knee as the sheet she was on split down the middle.

"Take the fucking rope!" Nina screamed.

Kate reached for the rope.

"Wrap it around both your arms," Nina shouted.

Silently, Kate obeyed.

"Now run!"

Kate ran. Nina pulled in the rope, keeping it taut. She watched the receptionist leap over one gap, two, three, before she stumbled again, and then the rope jerked in Nina's hands.

Kate was in the water.

Nina took a step back, the rope coiled around her arms. She looked down at her feet, planted them apart, and forced one back. She heard the cracks and the screaming as she took another step, and another, and another. Then there seemed to be more slack, and when she looked back up, Kate was on her feet again.

It felt like hours, but it couldn't have been more than a minute before Kate was back on the shore. Shivering on the ground.

She'd need a blanket. She'd need to get inside. She'd need medical help. And all that would come.

There was something Nina had to do first.

"Kate Bellamy," she said.

Kate looked up at her and gave a slight nod.

"I'm arresting you on suspicion of the murder of Josh McKenzie."

CHAPTER ONE HUNDRED ONE

Zoe could tell there was something else on the super's mind. The smiles and the congratulations were almost automatic, and Fiona forgot to ask how Nina was doing.

"Nina's fine, by the way," Zoe said. "Uninjured. Kate Bellamy's in hospital, but she'll recover from the hypothermia soon enough, apparently. The addiction's going to be a lot worse."

"She's confessed, though?" asked Fiona.

"Yes," Zoe said. "Not just on the lake but in the ambulance, after she'd been arrested, and again in hospital. Says she wants us to throw the book at her."

"So, manslaughter, out in a couple of years?"

"I suspect so," Zoe agreed.

The woman had killed McKenzie, violently and probably painfully. But it hadn't been premeditated. It was easy to see her as someone who'd been driven to the point of desperation. And in Kate's case, there had been no brother like Iain Murray or boss like Theodora Harding to pull her back from the brink.

"Look," said Fiona. "I've heard from our friends in PSD."

"About PC Cummings?"

"*Former PC* Cummings," Fiona corrected. "He's become talkative. Victoria Speares. He's admitted he was involved in her death."

"Involved?" Zoe didn't like that word.

"The way he puts it, he 'helped her along.' She was unconscious when he found her, vomiting but on her side. He says he turned her onto her back and let her choke."

"Has he said why?"

Fiona shook her head, but Zoe knew the truth. Vicky Speares had seen Cummings when she'd gone for Roddy Chen. She'd seen Cummings run away like a coward while his partner was almost killed. He couldn't risk that becoming the talk of the station.

"It's good, actually," Fiona said.

"How so?"

"Well, we've got an investigation starting here. The IOPC are on their way."

The Independent Office for Police Conduct. Zoe had been lucky over the years. She'd never been involved in an IOPC investigation. She wasn't sure she wanted to be.

"Because of this?" she asked.

"Partly because of how Hussein Mahmoud was released and then killed. Death following police contact. But that's a formality. Mainly because your mate Jake Frimpton's been stirring things up to the point where they can't be ignored any longer." Fiona frowned at Zoe. "They're going to tear this place apart, Zoe."

Zoe nodded, silent. Fiona didn't have to say any more. Cummings was hardly the sacrificial lamb, because lambs

CHAPTER ONE HUNDRED ONE

tended to be innocent. But he'd be getting offered up as the cause for all the Hub's ills, and that was...

"You know he's only the tip of the iceberg, Fiona," she said.

Fiona cocked her head.

How much was Zoe ready to tell her?

She licked her lips. "Bobby Silver's dead," she said.

"I know."

Zoe wasn't surprised. You couldn't keep something like that under wraps.

"We know she wasn't killed by Kate or Cummings or Topper. We also know she was almost certainly taken out by organised crime."

Timing was everything. Even as Fiona was reaching for her phone, Zoe had her hand on the super's arm, stopping her.

"What?" asked Fiona.

"You were about to call Ralph Streeting, yes?"

"I know you don't like him, Zoe, and frankly, neither do I, but it's his remit. Specialist Crime and Intel. Ralph Streeting has to know about this."

Zoe pulled in a breath. "And I'm sure he already does."

"You've told him?"

Zoe shook her head. "There's a lot you don't know about Ralph Streeting," she said.

"So tell me."

And Zoe did.

When she'd finished, Fiona was staring at her, not quite wide-eyed, but shaking her head with the sort of disbelief that was really just recognition.

"Does PSD know?"

"They suspect," Zoe replied. "No one has any evidence. Not yet. They're trying, though."

Something else occurred to her. The reason she'd come close to suspecting Fiona herself. And the super could have done a lot to allay that suspicion if she'd been more open.

"Why didn't you tell me about Harriett?" she asked.

"What do you mean?"

"Harriett Barnes. PC Barnes. She's really DC Barnes, and she's PSD. She tells me they sent her here at your request."

"Harriett Barnes?" Fiona's eyes were wide.

"Yes."

Fiona was shaking her head.

Shit. If Harriett's cover hadn't been blown already, it certainly was now.

"I don't understand," Zoe said. "She told me PSD had inserted her in response to your concerns."

Fiona smiled, still shaking her head. "I requested someone," she said. "But they never got back to me. I didn't realise they'd actually done it."

Shit. Never say anything if you don't have to. There was secrecy, and there was paranoia, and then there was PSD.

"Bloody Branthwaite," Fiona said. But she smiled as she said it.

CHAPTER ONE HUNDRED TWO

"Absolutely no fucking way," was Nina's response when the sarge suggested she might want to head home and have an early night after everything she'd been through at the hotel. Instead, she made it back to the Hub in time to watch Tom drape the antimacassar over the back of his chair, and then found herself in the passenger seat of the boss's Mini, heading into Whitehaven, and looking forward to a few drinks.

Looking forward to seeing Kay, too. It was good, the way things had worked out. The sarge had seemed pretty cut up about the death of Bobby Silver, but he couldn't blame himself for that. Hopefully, he'd loosen up with a few drinks in him.

The boss wouldn't be drinking, but then, she never did. Nina had wondered why that was, but had never been quite drunk enough to ask. The same way no one had ever mentioned her thing about the ice, even though someone must have noticed by now. Tom, for a start.

What a day, though. Nina closed her eyes and listened to the sound of the windscreen wipers.

What a day.

She ran through it in her head. Peter Raymond. Cummings. Harriett Barnes. *Harriett Barnes!* And then Bobby Silver, and the taxi, and her realisation that no one seemed to have come back in. Heading back to the hotel, and…

"Boss," she said, her eyes still closed.

"What's up?" replied DI Finch.

"You and Harriett Barnes were very interested in what I'd said to DI Streeting."

"Hmmm," said DI Finch.

Nina screwed her eyes shut and tried to remember what had happened. Before the knife. Before the frozen lake.

"She used the word 'precisely,' didn't she? And you…"

Nina sat up and opened her eyes. The boss was staring ahead, unblinking, her attention on the road.

"You sent Tom over to Bobby Silver's house. With Harriett."

"That's right," replied the boss, without taking her gaze off the road.

"And Harriett's PSD."

No reply.

"And by the time they got there, Bobby Silver was dead."

Was it her imagination, or had the boss's shoulders just lifted a little? Were her hands gripping the steering wheel more tightly?

"Shit," Nina muttered with feeling.

DI Finch glanced in her direction. "What is it, Nina?" she asked.

But surely she knew what Nina was about to say.

CHAPTER ONE HUNDRED TWO

"Streeting's corrupt, isn't he?" Nina said. "Streeting had Bobby Silver killed. He heard the name, sent someone over there, and she was dead before Tom and Harriett could bring her in. That's it, isn't it?"

She switched her gaze to the windscreen. The rain seemed heavier now, or was it just her imagination?

Beside her, the boss was looking ahead again, then indicating and pulling to the side of the road.

"Nina," she said.

"Christ," said Nina.

"Don't blame yourself."

Nina looked at her in disbelief. "I'm not blaming myself, boss. I'm blaming that bastard."

DI Finch nodded.

"Aren't you going to turn around?" asked Nina.

"What do you mean?"

"I mean, turn around. Back to the Hub. Organise Uniform. Bring that fucking... Bring Streeting in. Get the bastard."

There was a pause.

"I'm afraid it's not that simple," the DI said, her voice gentle.

"Why not?" asked Nina.

"Because we can't prove it, Nina. Because we've suspected Streeting for a long time, and the more we've learned, the more confident we are that we're right. But without evidence, we can't do anything about it."

"That's ridiculous," said Nina, with a sense of angry powerlessness.

Something occurred to her. "We?" she added.

"Me and the sarge," DI Finch replied.

"Is that all?"

"The super too, as of this evening. Harriett Barnes, of course."

"Which means Tom probably knows, too."

"Maybe," agreed the DI. "But like I say, there's nothing we can do about it now. So let's go out and celebrate. You've arrested a murderer, Nina. Forget Streeting. Just enjoy yourself."

It would be difficult to forget Streeting, Nina thought. Difficult to enjoy herself.

But she was always up for a challenge.

CHAPTER ONE HUNDRED THREE

Zoe felt a lump in her throat that had nothing to do with the bag of crisps she'd just eaten in place of tea.

"Love you too," she told Nicholas. "And I'll see you in two weeks."

She turned and walked back into the Anchor Vaults, unable to wipe the smile off her face. She'd have to clear it with Fiona. And she'd have to work hard to keep her phone switched off while he was down. It would be close to impossible.

But not completely impossible. Not if Nicholas was coming to stay.

Nina was standing by the bar, holding what looked suspiciously like a glass of water. She'd been up to sing twice already. But Zoe hadn't seen her throwing the customary lurid concoctions down her throat.

"Not drinking?" Zoe asked, in a rare moment of privacy by the bar.

"Nah," Nina said. "If I drink too much, I'll say the wrong thing to the wrong person."

Zoe nodded and walked away. Then she stopped and walked back.

"Thank you," she said. Nina smiled at her. "And yes."

"Yes, what?"

"Yes, you're starting to act like a DS. You think you're ready?"

Nina didn't hesitate.

"I'm ready."

Zoe smiled and walked away.

Aaron was flagging, but then, he'd started the day struggling, and then been hit by so many shocks it was a wonder he was still standing. If this had happened a few months ago, he'd have been a wreck. Instead, he was conscious, smiling, sitting down talking to a good-looking young blond man who looked vaguely familiar.

"Boss," he said, noticing her approach. "This is Davey."

"We've met," said Davey, standing to shake her hand. He was tall, towering over her by nearly half a foot. But there was something reassuring rather than menacing in his size.

"We have." Zoe remembered. "Kept yourself out of trouble since then, I hope?"

"Hope away," he replied with a wink.

She'd met Davey Grant in her first week up north. One of three local troublemakers who'd helped her nail her first Cumbrian killer. She wasn't sure she'd ever thanked him for that. It must have been a few months later that he'd started seeing Kay's daughter Abigail. And then Kay had made the mistake of looking him up, and the rest...

Well, there was no need to worry about that anymore. Not now that Cummings had confessed.

Abigail herself was deep in conversation with Nina by the bar, running her hands through her hair and trying to

CHAPTER ONE HUNDRED THREE

look both cooler and older than she was. Zoe had noticed this with the young women of Whitehaven, and a fair few of the young men, too. They might say they hated the police, but when it came to Nina, there was a sort of hero worship.

It couldn't just be because of the way she sang Elvis.

Harriett and Tom were sitting together at another table. Or at least, they had been the last time Zoe had looked.

They weren't there. Had they slipped out without anyone noticing, while Zoe had been talking to Nicholas?

Had they slipped out *together*?

Zoe breathed out, long and slow. She shouldn't have to worry about Tom. He was a DC. A grown man. It hadn't ended well last time around, but maybe things were different now.

And there wasn't much she could do about it if they weren't.

Carl had called a few minutes earlier, to congratulate her on the arrest, commiserate over Bobby Silver, and promise they'd get Streeting, eventually.

She believed him, too. They could. They were getting closer and closer. She could feel it. Streeting's luck couldn't hold out forever.

She'd been on the verge of suggesting Carl join them. There was a collaboration of sorts building between her team and his, and while she knew it was wrong, and Branthwaite would soon put an end to it, she'd been pleased to see how well they all worked together.

Not just Tom and Harriett. Carl himself. And Denise Gaskill, whose approach to interviewing suspects seemed more in tune with Zoe's own than anyone she'd worked with before, and whose spiky unapproachability had waned with familiarity.

But she hadn't invited Carl along. This was her team's celebration, not his. Harriett might be there, but she'd just been in a car chase with Tom, and they'd found a dead woman. If anyone deserved a night out, Harriett did.

Time to head home.

Outside, she stopped on the corner, shivering in the rain, and called Jake Frimpton.

"You've got what you wanted," she told him.

"What do you mean?"

"Cummings. The one who found Vicky Speares."

"What about him?"

"He's confessed. He 'helped her along.' Turned her onto her back and let her choke."

"Zoe." She could hear the tension in his voice. "He's not getting away with it, is he?"

"You don't need to worry about that, Jake."

She couldn't tell him everything Cummings had done, but she dropped a few hints. That, and the IOPC investigation, which he was pleased to hear about, would do Vicky Speares justice.

She'd just said goodbye to a happier-sounding Jake Frimpton when her phone buzzed. She checked the display, started to put it away, and then answered instead.

"Enough," she said.

"Good to finally hear your voice," replied Ryan Tobin.

"I mean it, Ryan. You've called me ten times in the last three days, and it's enough."

"I had to keep calling. You wouldn't answer."

"Because I know what you're going to say. You're going to ask me why we haven't found your friend Kevin, and I'm going to tell you we're looking into it, and you're going to say

CHAPTER ONE HUNDRED THREE

we're not looking hard enough. I've asked DS Keyes to look into things, and we'll let you know if we find anything."

"Right," said Ryan Tobin, sounding a little stung.

"Did you have anything else you wanted to say?" Zoe asked, as she turned away from the sea and began to head inland.

"Erm, no," he replied. "Just... Just keep doing what you're doing." He ended the call.

She rolled her eyes at the phone. "Certainly, Chief Constable."

CHAPTER ONE HUNDRED FOUR

A COUPLE STOOD outside the fish and chip shop, sharing their food and trying to shelter it from the drizzle. Zoe smiled as she walked past, but they were too caught up in each other to notice her. She'd just reached into her pocket for her keys when her phone rang again.

It was David Randle. She answered it and carried on past the house.

"Did you bring him in?" Randle said without preamble.

She wondered who he was talking about, before she remembered what she'd told him about Bobby Silver. And, more pertinently, what she hadn't.

"Her," she said. "And no, we didn't. She's dead. So yes, you were right. No need to go on about it."

She waited for the 'I told you so'.

"I said you had to act quickly, Zoe," he said.

Typical.

"Did you at least secure the forensic evidence?" he asked.

She smiled. Randle was as unpleasant as he was untrustworthy, but he knew what was important.

"Yes," she told him. "My people secured the scene. CSI are there now, and there are signs the killer had to leave in a hurry."

"Good work," said Randle. "Let me know what comes of it."

He'd killed the call before she could remind him he wasn't her boss anymore. First Ryan Tobin, then David Randle. What was it about these men that made them think they could order her about?

It didn't matter. The only reason she was telling these men anything at all was that she wanted something from them. It was an arrangement. *Let them think they're in charge.* As long as she got what she needed.

She had her key out when she looked up and saw the front door was already open, Carl standing framed in the light, looking quizzically at her.

"I saw you walking past," he explained, closing the door behind her.

"Fiona called," she replied. Since when had she found it so easy to lie?

He stepped aside, took her coat, and waited while she pulled off her boots. Then he pulled her in for a kiss, and pushed her gently away, looking her in the eyes.

"Ammonia."

Zoë frowned at him. "If you're telling me I smell, there are gentler ways to break the news."

"Ammonia," he repeated. "The warehouse. Where Elena was kept. Remember?"

Elena was staying at Nina's now, and couldn't remember much of her experience, of the early days of her time in England, after she'd been trafficked by Carter and his associates. One of the few things she could remember was the smell of ammonia.

"Yes," she nodded. "Why?"

Carl took her hand and led her through to the kitchen. Instead of food, the table was covered in paper.

"Look," he said. Sitting in the middle of it all, an island in a sea of paper, was Carl's laptop, open on a set of search results.

What industries smell of ammonia?

He pointed at the third result. "Here. And here." His finger moved down to the fifth. And the seventh. And the tenth.

"Pulp and paper industry," she read. "Paper mills. Paper."

"Now look at this."

He directed her attention to the sheets around the laptop. He'd printed off a series of maps.

"Is this..."

"It's Workington," he told her. "I've blown it up in detail so you can see all the major buildings nearby."

"Nearby what?" she asked, but she'd seen it already.

Right in the centre of the collection of maps was a single building, over which Carl had scrawled in red felt tip the words *WEST CUMBRIA PAPER MILLS*.

"Really?" she asked.

"Really," he said. He stepped away, and Zoe saw what surrounded the paper mills. There were factories, and retail outlets, and even the odd block of residential buildings. But there were others, too, and Carl had helpfully labelled them the same way he'd labelled the mill.

WAREHOUSE, it said, in red felt tip, on each of them.

Even though they'd lost a potential witness, and arrested

a murderer, and finally unmasked a bent cop, and more than anything she needed to sleep, Zoe felt her heart quicken.

Warehouses. Warehouses, surrounding a paper mill, with the smell of ammonia.

It might be a long shot. But they could be there. More women. More of Carter's trafficking victims.

If they were there, then she could get them out. And maybe, just maybe, they could take down Myron Carter.

We hope you enjoyed reading *The Lake*. The story continues in a free short story, *The House*, which is available at rachelmclean.com/house-book.

Happy reading! Rachel and Joel.

READ THE CUMBRIA CRIME SERIES

The Harbour

The Mine

The Cairn

The Barn

The Lake

The Wood

...and more to come

Buy from book retailers or via the Rachel McLean website.

ALSO BY RACHEL MCLEAN

The DI Zoe Finch Series – buy from book retailers or via the Rachel McLean website.

Deadly Wishes

Deadly Choices

Deadly Desires

Deadly Terror

Deadly Reprisal

Deadly Fallout

Deadly Christmas

Deadly Origins, the FREE Zoe Finch prequel

The Dorset Crime Series – buy from book retailers or via the Rachel McLean website.

The Corfe Castle Murders

The Clifftop Murders

The Island Murders

The Monument Murders

The Millionaire Murders

The Fossil Beach Murders

The Blue Pool Murders

The Lighthouse Murders

The Ghost Village Murders

The Poole Harbour Murders

...and more to com

The McBride & Tanner Series – buy from book retailers or via the Rachel McLean website.

Blood and Money

Death and Poetry

Power and Treachery

Secrets and History

The London Cosy Mystery Series by Rachel McLean and Millie Ravensworth – buy from book retailers or via the Rachel McLean website.

Death at Westminster

Death in the West End

Death at Tower Bridge

Death on the Thames

Death at St Paul's Cathedral

Death at Abbey Road

The Lyme Regis Women's Swimming Club series by Rachel McLean and Millie Ravensworth – buy from book retailers or via the Rachel McLean website.

The Lyme Regis Women's Swimming Club

...and more to come

ALSO BY JOEL HAMES

The Sam Williams Series – Buy now in ebook, paperback and audiobook

Dead North

No One Will Hear

The Cold Years

The Art of Staying Dead

Victims, a Sam Williams novella

Caged, a Sam Williams short